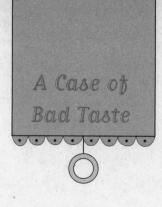

A Case of Bad Taste

P9-DWJ-926

A Morning Shade Mystery

A Case of Bad Taste

LORI * COPELAND

Tyndale House Publishers, Inc.
Wheaton, Illinois

Visit Tyndale's exciting Web site at www.tyndale.com

Copyright © 2003 by Lori Copeland. All rights reserved.

Cover illustration © 2003 by Donna Kae Nelson. All rights reserved.

Lori Copeland photograph copyright © 2002 by The Picture People. All rights reserved.

Edited by Kathryn S. Olson

Designed by Julie Chen

Scripture quotations are taken from the *Holy Bible,* New Living Translation, copyright © 1996. Used by permission of Tyndale House Publishers, Inc., Wheaton, Illinois 60189. All rights reserved.

The Scripture in the epigraph is taken from *THE MESSAGE*. Copyright © by Eugene H. Peterson, 1993, 1994, 1995, 1996. Used by permission of NavPress Publishing Group.

Published in association with the literary agency of Alive Communications, Inc., 7680 Goddard Street, Suite 200, Colorado Springs, CO 80920.

This novel is a work of fiction. Names, characters, places, and incidents are either the product of the author's imagination or are used fictitiously. Any resemblance to actual events, locales, organizations, or persons living or dead is entirely coincidental and beyond the intent of either the author or publisher.

Library of Congress Cataloging-in-Publication Data

Copeland, Lori.
A case of bad taste / Lori Copeland.
p. cm.
ISBN 0-8423-7115-X
1. Women detectives—Fiction. 2. Female friendship—Fiction. I. Title.
PS3553.06336 C37 2003
813'.54—dc21 2003001099

Printed in the United States of America

09 08 07 06 05 04 03
9 8 7 6 5 4 3 2

To
Becky Nesbitt, Anne Goldsmith, and Kathy Olson
for their experience, vision, and guidance.
Thanks, ladies!

God is a safe place to hide,
ready to help when we need him.

—Psalm 46:1, THE MESSAGE

1

I rolled to my side and punched the pillows into shape. Getting old is like sucking peanut butter through a straw. Difficult. Sleep comes in snatches, and if a body part doesn't hurt, it isn't working.

Herb, how could you leave me to face old age alone?

Not that I'd welcome the alternative. Sixty wasn't ancient, but since Herb died, I'd started to go downhill. It was only a matter of time until I turned sixty-five, then—Lord willing—seventy. There would be no way I could look in the mirror and tell myself, "Hey, Maude, you don't look so bad," when my mirror told me different. Short-cropped gray hair, wrinkles—and the sand in my hourglass figure had shifted to the south.

Sighing, I rolled onto my back and stared up at the slit of light dancing across the ceiling. Wind rattled the spruce outside the window and jangled the wind chime Herb had hung from its branches. Sounds I wouldn't have noticed in the light of day at night became as jarring as a calypso band at a church social. When Herb died a year ago, all I wanted to do was crawl into a hole and stay there. My attitude hasn't changed much since then.

My problem is acceptance. I'm having a hard time accepting my life now. I need Herb lying here beside me. I'm too conscious of the emptiness of this bed, of the loneliness. Even his snoring would be welcome.

I never wanted to live alone. Writing is the only thing that's familiar to me, and creativity has turned on me.

Ka-bang!

My eyes flew open and I sat up straight in bed.

Gunshots!

Gunshots? At—I squinted at the alarm clock, fumbling for my glasses—2 A.M.?

Street light streamed through the venetian blind, picking out the four posts of my bed, the ruffled muslin curtains, the robe I had tossed over the cane-bottomed rocker. A car, probably Hargus Conley's old truck, rattled down the street. Pansy Conley's boy, Morning Shade's Barney Fife, was up till all hours drinking Chocolate Cow soda and swapping tall tales with Finley Priest, a local stock-car driver.

I lay back, fighting annoyance. I'd taken two Advil PMs before going to bed and had just dozed off when—

Ka-bam!

Bolting upright, I tried to clear sleep from my brain.

I listened, but couldn't hear anything other than the ticking clock next to my bed. I must've dreamed the gunshot. Maybe I'd been thinking about the book I was writing: a mystery . . . with no plot. A lackluster, dull whodunit with second-rate characters even *I* didn't care about.

I was getting nowhere with my forty-second book. Zilch. Everything I wrote was bland and totally uninspiring. The characters were wooden, and the plot was as predictable as summer road construction.

What I needed was a good, uninterrupted night's sleep. Maybe if I was fresh in the morning . . .

A dog? I slowly opened my eyes when I heard a low, menacing growl.

A dog.

I sat up again, clutching the end of the sheet to my chest.

A very *big, mean* dog.

Breaking out in a cold sweat, I wondered if an animal was in the house—then I wondered who had a dog that sounds like a junkyard rottweiler? Certainly not old Mrs. Post, the ninety-year-old retired postmistress. For a deacon's wife, she talks pretty tough and drives stray animals out of her yard with a rake. Maybe the dog belongs to my next-door neighbor, Victor Johnson. He's deaf in one ear and can't hear out of the other. Could be he's bought a mastiff or one of those big breeds you have to follow around with a shovel.

I thought about my mother-in-law sleeping two doors away. *If she hears the barking she'll be upset.* Herb's mother had moved in the week before, and she was uneasy with her new surroundings. Gunshots and barking dogs were not a soothing combination. Stella wasn't the type to pull the covers over her head and ignore strange noises. I'd be lucky if she didn't come barreling out with a flashlight in one hand and a poker in the other.

Having Stella in my home wasn't anything either of us

wanted, but after Herb died, there wasn't enough money to keep her in the residential-care facility any longer. I worked myself into a blue funk over whether to bring her here to live. I finally moved Stella into the spare bedroom.

She hadn't wanted to leave the retirement home, and I hadn't wanted her to either, but finances had stripped us both of our privacy. I'd always gotten along with my mother-in-law, but getting along and living together are two different things. I knew Stella probably felt the same way. Stella was here, probably awake by now. I settled back and drew a breath of resignation.

What had happened to my sane life—the one I'd shared with Herb and a close circle of friends? I'd never realized how much death could impact the ones left behind. Losing Herb had derailed my world, and I couldn't get it back on track.

And now CeeCee had problems. Newly widowed, my thirty-one-year-old daughter had called to ask if she could come home for a while. Cee said she would only stay "until I can put my life together." But I wasn't so sure three women with such different personalities could coexist under the same roof.

No, I know we can't—not without inviting a bunch of trouble.

Still, I didn't have the heart to tell my daughter she wasn't welcome. I couldn't look the other way and ignore what was happening in Stella's and Cee's lives.

But what about my *life? Has anyone thought about* my *needs?*

Herb sure hadn't. He never thought much beyond the end of his nose. Still, he was a decent sort—and an attentive father. He wasn't as social as I am, but maybe our differences balanced each other, which accounted for why we'd stayed married for thirty-two years.

Life isn't supposed to be this way: widowed at sixty, burned out on writing, short on money, and living with my mother-in-law and my widowed daughter. Herb and I were supposed to retire together. But that's not going to happen. Not now.

According to the ambulance attendant, Herb had had a freak fall, hitting his head on the side of the bathtub. A hotel maid found him the next morning when she came to clean the room. As sudden as that, my life had taken a nosedive, followed by a landslide.

Stella was supposed to have lived out her remaining years in the company of her peers, comfortable and content at Shady Acres.

Cee's husband, Jake "Touchdown" Tamaris, wasn't supposed to die from a blood clot when he was only thirty-three, and I wasn't supposed to be responsible for everyone's welfare. How did I get elected to be the strong one?

When I got my AARP card at fifty, I thought I'd reached the time when life got easier. But three months into sixty, my solitude had been disrupted by both my mother-in-law and my daughter.

I had an October deadline for my book, and my creative juices were as dry as beef jerky. In five months, I had to send off a manuscript that was currently going nowhere. In fact, I'd hardly started on the story. With all the interruptions, I'd deleted more than I'd written. I'd have to buckle down and make headway.

I sighed and closed my eyes. *Face it, Maude, you're burned out. Fresh out of ideas.*

I thrust my fingers through my thick, gray hair. What a mess my life was. I needed regeneration and quiet, and neither was going to happen.

I scrunched my pillow beneath my cheek and willed sleep to come.

Bam!

My eyes popped open.

Another gunshot? What was going on?

This time I wasn't taking any chances. My fingers groped for the aluminum bat Herb had kept handy. Morning Shade wasn't New York, but we had a few teenagers who liked to keep Hargus Conley hopping.

After a moment, I eased out of bed, clutching the bat to my chest. Moving carefully, I crept downstairs into the living room. Avoiding the moonlight streaming through the front window, I moved stealthily to the side pane and looked out. The street was empty. None of the lights were on at the Peacocks'. Maury Peacock went to bed with the birds and got up with the chickens. What the man did with his time was a mystery to me.

Bam!

I threw myself flat on the floor—not an easy job for a woman my age. I listened for sounds of movement outside. I couldn't hear anything except that crazy Hargus roaring down the street with that silly Confederate flag waving from a pole on the bed of his truck. Maybe some transplanted Yankee was taking potshots at the flag, fighting the Civil War all over again.

I suddenly sat straight up, slapping my hand to my forehead. *What an idiot I am!*

Rolling to my knees, I pushed up with the help of the bat.

The sound of the barking, growling dog was coming from my computer. It was my new program.

The "dog" had detected a virus. A gunshot meant the program was "killing" the unwanted or virus-laden message.

"My nerves are shot," I told myself as I went to my office to shut the thing down.

Isn't technology wonderful?

* * *

The next morning, Stella was rattling the paper when I walked into the kitchen, yawning. She looked as fresh as you can look at her age, which isn't saying much. Evidently it took more than dogs and gunshots to keep her awake. Maury Peacock, my next-door neighbor, had cranked up his lawn mower at sunrise, and I couldn't hear myself think over the sound of the blade chewing up rocks and sticks.

Stella had the paper turned to the obituary page, the section she always read first. My mother-in-law would be doing well to top the scale at a hundred and ten pounds. On her bad days she looked frail, on her good days she was as belligerent as an ill-tempered rooster, and on any day she was a threat to my sanity.

I wondered if Stella read the obits because she expected to find her own name there someday.

"Do you know Mary Grace Hodson?" she asked.

"No, I don't." Morning Shade is small, but I don't know everybody.

"She died," Stella said. "She was only seventy-nine. Eight years younger than me. Says here contributions should be sent to the American Cancer Society. Must've died of cancer."

"Must have."

I dumped Raisin Bran into my bowl and poured milk over it. I had a million things to do today: run to the post office, address the last of my publicity mailings, call my agent and ask about the status of my new proposal, get bread and milk, and then come home to write at least twenty-five hundred words.

Wouldn't it be nice if I could buy words like I bought groceries? *I'll take sixty-five hundred words, a dozen catchy phrases, and, let's see, how about two best-sellers? And throw in a blockbuster. Yes, plastic sacks are fine.*

My toast popped up, charred. "Did you change the settings?" I asked Stella.

"Yes, I can't chew tough toast. Do you know Harry Beauford?"

I switched the setting on the toaster back to where I liked it. "No Stella, I don't."

I stirred creamer into my coffee. *A roast. I'll buy a roast at the store and put it in the Crock-Pot for supper.* Quick and easy. As long as Stella could chew the meat. Her dentures were bothering her. I'd found her bottom plate on the coffee table last night. When I asked her why she didn't put her teeth in the denture case, she said she'd forgotten. Forgotten? Forgotten her teeth?

Was this my future?

"Harry was only seventy-one. Sixteen years younger than

me. My, my, my." She shook her head. "We just never know, do we?"

I didn't mind her reading the obits, if only she wouldn't read them out loud. The ritual was depressing, and I had enough gloom in my life right now.

I knew she resented having to leave her friends. She had flourished under the camaraderie she'd found at Shady Acres Residential Care. She loved the weekly bridge and bingo games held every Saturday night in the rec room, and she went to the occasional funeral of an old friend to break the monotony. Maybe that's why she reads the obits, planning her social calendar.

That wasn't nice. I needed to get a grip. Stella had her life, and I had mine, and neither was anything to shout about, but that wasn't any reason to get snippy, even if I never said the thought out loud.

There was nothing, according to the eighty-seven-year-old, she didn't like about Shady Acres. But, in truth, I knew there wasn't much Stella was happy about—including the fact that the good Lord had overlooked her and she was still alive. With every breath, she made it clear she didn't expect to be around long enough to be a bother to me. Sometimes it sounded like she was looking forward to the trip.

"Well, it seems that I've outlived my usefulness, just like these folks. I'm not here for much longer, that's for certain."

"That's morbid, Stella. None of us knows from one day to the next how long we'll be here. We just have to be ready to go."

Stella looked at me, her eyes wide. "What? Has the doctor told you something he hasn't told me?"

"Of course not." For someone who made a habit of predicting her own demise, she seemed startled at the thought that it might be around the corner.

I pressed a finger to my temple. It was too early in the morning to be discussing death. I wanted to slip carefully into the day, not be slapped in the face with mortality.

Stella rattled the paper, folding it in the middle, I assumed to better read the rest of the obituaries.

"My, my, my," she said. "Richard Peaks died in a wreck on the highway. Pulled in front of a truckload of fertilizer. He was eighty-three, four years younger than me." She shook the paper again. "Humph! Look at this. They have a whole article about testing old folks more closely to make sure they have all the faculties they need to drive. The way some of these young folks tear around . . . "

I felt a headache blooming. "Did you take your pill?"

"Yes," Stella said sharply. "I took my pill, for what good it does."

Stella took half a pill a day for her blood pressure and was certain the diagnosis signaled the end of her life. She was so sure she wasn't long for this earth that she refused to buy green bananas. Evidently I had irritated her by asking about her medicine. Being irritating seems to be one of the things I do best. A brand-new talent just discovered since Stella came to live with me.

"I'm going to watch my program," Stella announced, leaving the pillaged newspaper on the table for me to sort out.

Her "program" was a morning talk show that centered around two women fighting over some poor miscreant that

I would've shot. I can't understand Stella's fascination with these kinds of programs.

Other than Herb, we had nothing in common. Stella hated crowds, and I loved to socialize. She reads the obits; I read the society pages. She hated malls, and I thrived on shopping.

Wal-Mart was my obsession. I could impulsively outspend the best of 'em. Herb had once bought me a T-shirt that read "When the going gets tough, the tough go shopping." I still had it.

Stella plunked herself in front of the television, ready to spend her morning sitting in an easy chair, getting no exercise at all.

"Why don't you take a walk," I suggested. "It's a beautiful morning, and the fresh air will do you good."

"You want me out of the house," Stella announced. "Well, if that's what you want, I'll just walk down to the Citgo and drink my coffee."

"I didn't say I wanted you out of the house."

"I can take a hint. Never let it be said that Stella Diamond is a burden to anyone."

She snapped off the television, grabbed her black vinyl purse, and moments later disappeared out the back door. I got up and went to the window over the sink to watch the five-foot-two dynamo march down the sidewalk at a fairly brisk clip, her purse clutched snugly under her right arm.

I'd hurt her feelings again. She'd probably blab to everyone in the Citgo deli that her daughter-in-law was thoughtless and mean. Some of them would probably believe it. Sighing, I sat back down at the table.

Morning Shade was a small, safe country town in Izzard County, Arkansas. There were three hundred and fifty people living here, at the most. So I didn't have to worry about Stella's safety. She could come and go as she pleased, and she enjoyed the local Citgo. Although she liked to pretend she was only going because I wanted her out of the house. I had a feeling that she was spending most of her time with the regulars at the convenience store now that she was living with me. That was okay. I was glad she had made new friends, and it kept her out of my way. Gave me time to write, not that I was making any headway there.

Twenty miles from Morning Shade sat Evening Shade. That town was once the premise of a television show starring Burt Reynolds. Nothing really noteworthy happened there either, unless you counted a building named for Reynolds and another one named for Linda Bloodworth Thomas, the show's producer.

Morning Shade had no notoriety. There was nothing here of any significance. Culver Street was the main thoroughfare and had six side streets. The Citgo Gas and Convenience Store had a small deli area with five booths, located across the aisle from the pet-food department, where locals gathered every morning for coffee and news.

In addition to the gas and convenience store was a school where CeeCee—and I—had graduated with honors. There were Methodist, Catholic, and Baptist churches. There were a mobile-home park, Shady Acres Residential Care, a one-truck fire department, two small grocery stores, a Sears appliance outlet, a car wash, a feed store, the Kut 'n' Kurl beauty shop, a small engine-repair shop, and the post office. Not exactly a metropolis.

There's a small park with two picnic tables set off to the side for those who wanted to brave the summer heat—mostly used by young couples letting their children play. The Fourth of July festivities were held there, and the VFW held their annual Labor Day Picnic under the covered pavilion every September.

Nothing noteworthy ever happened in Morning Shade.

I shook my head and picked up the newspaper, smoothed it carefully, reinserted the pages in the right place, and began reading. I was in no hurry to start the day or face a blinking cursor.

Stella got back in time for lunch. I had planned a nice salad, but in deference to her teeth, switched the menu to baked minute steaks with mashed potatoes and gravy.

"How was everything at the Citgo?"

"Did I tell you I ate breakfast there?" Stella said. "They've got quite a good breakfast."

"Good."

"For $1.39 I had biscuits and gravy with sausage. Don't matter that I eat biscuits and gravy at my age. I'm not long for this world anyway."

That afternoon, when I'd procrastinated all I could, I sat down at my workstation and stared at the computer screen. I was supposed to be writing. But instead, I had pulled up a Web site listing this month's Christian best-sellers. Hmm. My recent title hadn't made it. Again.

Figures. The publisher hadn't loaded enough books into stores.

Best-seller lists didn't use to matter to me. It used to be that just the very elation of being published was enough. I didn't need any more validation than that. But twenty-five years later, I suddenly find myself measuring my worth by twenty numbers a month. I don't want to feel like a failure, but that's what reading the best-seller list does to me.

And it isn't just fame and recognition I seek. While I once was able to write for the sheer joy of it, I now find myself desperately needing financial security too. Authors who make the best-seller list have choice positioning in the bookstores and sell even more books as a result.

I constantly prayed about my obsession to make the list. Sales were healthy, but I could never quite push over the top, never quite achieve my heart's desire.

My agent said to be patient. But I knew patience was only a small part of the writing world. Stronger marketing was the answer.

Certainly, I put out the best book I could. Why couldn't one hit the best-seller list? It seemed like a small request. Twenty authors make it every month. If the Lord loved me as much as He did those twenty, it only stood to reason that I should show up on the list some month. But I hadn't, and I was starting to resent it. Resent my house, my agent, even M.K. Diamond, my pen name. Maybe I even resented the Lord. I'd sure prayed enough over this. Why didn't He listen?

Maybe I needed to start over—take a new pen name and write a different kind of book. I could do that. I still had my mind. Although it didn't seem to be working all that well on the current book.

I switched to the Barnes & Noble Web site, then Amazon.com, and finally Parable.com, the site for an association of small, independent stores—all with the same results. I could see that M.K. Diamond wasn't a best-seller. If my newest book, *Eyes of the Night*, didn't make it in September—well . . . I'll write another one. At least hope was renewed with each new forthcoming title, enough so to keep me writing.

Was my desire to make it on the best-seller list wrong? Was it wrong to hold that up as a measure of my worth? Had I set the right goals? Maybe God didn't want me on the best-seller list. Was He teaching me to be humble? If so, it was working.

I closed my eyes and clicked off the Internet. I needed to work, but nothing was coming. I needed a new idea, a fresh plot. There was just too much upheaval in my life. Too much stress, too many things to worry about. And there was no one to worry about it but me.

I tried not to resent that. Herb had promised to get a life insurance policy, enroll in a company 401(k) retirement plan, but he never had. Now I have to watch every penny in order to make ends meet. Sometimes it hurts to think that my husband thought so little about my future, in case anything happened to him.

Now my income is limited, and royalty checks come in sporadically. I need to finish this book and have it sell well.

Concentrate, Maude. Write!

But my mind wandered to CeeCee.

Now the widow of a professional football player, Cee had her own problems. Jake was great on the long pass but had proved to be short on fidelity and commitment. Cee had found it hard to cope with his long absences and the fame his career brought. The couple never had a vacation without his career interfering or gone to dinner without fans interrupting. Pushed aside, ignored, and sometimes neglected, Cee had withdrawn into a shell. Maybe Jake hadn't intended for it to be that way in the beginning, but it had happened.

Two months ago, Jake had a blood clot to the brain and died during a workout at the gym. Cee knew Jake had been unfaithful to her—she'd read about it in the papers, yet for some reason she'd blocked out his infidelity. She'd never been blessed with overconfidence, and maybe she thought Jake's trifling would go away.

Had it been the other way around and she'd died, Jake would've brought a date to the funeral. The thought made me angry.

Jake had made big money as a football player, but he'd spent big as well. He, like Herb, hadn't seen beyond his nose, so Cee was left with only a small insurance policy and an uncertain future. What is it with men who don't provide for their families? Do they think they are going to live forever, or are they afraid to face their own mortality? Is having a life insurance policy a sure ticket to an early grave? Like me, Cee had some important decisions to make. She was coming home to regroup.

I've learned to like my time alone. I like my own schedule, my own way of doing things. It's not that I'm set in my ways like Stella; I just need some space.

Herb had traveled through the week, and I filled my time writing. But now that had changed. Stella gets up before six o'clock; I sleep until at least eight. I can see right now that will be the first obstacle to overcome.

Cee would be coming home Friday. She would have her own schedule, which wouldn't mesh with either mine or Stella's. Putting three women with three different personalities and needs under the same roof could stir up more friction than a burlap bag full of tomcats. Nothing about my life was going to be the same.

The front door slammed, then opened and closed softly.

Stella. I gritted my teeth. As if closing the door softly the second time corrected the slam.

"Maude?"

"Yes, Stella. I'm in here. Working."

I concentrated on the words on the screen, trying to pick up the thread of the story from where I'd left off yesterday. If I thought reminding her it was my work time would make her go away, I sure had misjudged her capacity for driving me to distraction.

"I won't bother you. I just wanted to let you know I'm back."

"Good. Thanks."

The paragraph I'd written was flat. No life. Cardboard characters. Stupid plot. Stupid book. I should delete the whole thing and start over.

"Nothing ever happens here," Stella said, interrupting my thoughts again. "This town has died and don't know it."

"Count your blessings. A lot of people would like to wake up in a peaceful, happy place like Morning Shade."

"Be more to the point if someone would wake up Morning Shade. Anything for dessert?"

"Baked custard."

"Same thing we've had three times already this week. I rest my case."

"Hmm." Maybe if I ignored her she'd go away.

"Guess who I met at the Citgo?"

"Can't imagine." I typed a sentence, hoping she'd take the hint.

She didn't. "You'll never guess."

"Hmm."

"Maude?"

"Yes, Stella." I blew out a sigh and saved the two sentences I'd managed to revise.

"Simon Bench. You remember him. He's at Shady Acres, but in the apartments. We played bridge every week. He's seventy-six, you know. We've made plans to play bridge with Frances and Pansy, like we always did."

"Good." Maybe I'd get some peace during Stella's outings.

"We'll alternate homes. We're playing here next week."

Good grief! Not here! I caught my tongue before I exploded. This was Stella's home too. I couldn't deny Herb's mother a social life. But the thought of senior citizens playing cards in my living room while I tried to work gave me the hives. I kept my voice level. "Sounds like fun. Maybe you could make those lemon bars Herb liked so well."

"Why, I could, couldn't I? I'll start looking for the recipe right now."

I released a mental sigh and looked at the paragraph again. Passive. I highlighted the sentences and hit Delete.

Stella's voice came from the kitchen. "Where did we put that box that had *kitchen* written on it?"

I drew a breath. *God, give me strength!* "Your boxes are in the closet under the stairs," I called out. *Open your eyes.*

My fingers curled on the keyboard and I set my mind on the story. *Okay, back up a bit. Relax, Maude. The story is in your mind; just let it flow onto the paper*. I sighed. The only thing flowing around here was the time I wasted sitting in front of the computer writing junk.

"Found it," Stella called from the kitchen.

"Good."

I scooted back in my chair and closed the door to my office with my foot. I didn't want to offend Stella, but I might have to if this kept up. I couldn't even write junk if this steady barrage of interruptions didn't stop.

Bob Barker's voice came from the living room. I sat up straighter and pushed the door tightly shut. I couldn't let Stella get on my nerves. I needed to plan for the future—but how, when I couldn't even handle the present?

* * *

Tuesday afternoon, I shut the computer off at twelve-thirty. I'd written three coherent sentences and wasn't happy with those. I was thinking a ham sandwich might jump-start my creativity.

"Humph." Stella was in front of the blaring television, grumbling under her breath, when I came out of my office. "Thought you'd hole up in there all day," she said.

"I'm working, Stella." *Correction, trying to work.*

"Saw Hargus Conley down at the Citgo this morning. Buying a cappuccino, of all things. He's an embarrassment to law enforcement. 'Course nobody would ever say that in front of Pansy. It's hard on her to have a boy that useless."

"Hargus tries." He wasn't a fireball, but he looked after our small town.

I'd hoped to cut off Stella's running commentary on Hargus, but there was no getting her off the subject. "Everybody knows he's had every odd job in town, but he can't hold any of them. Heard tell he quit his job fixing flats down at the service station 'cause it was too stressful." She snorted. "Too stressful. What could be stressful about patching an inner tube?"

"Tires no longer have inner tubes, Stel."

Stella had followed me into the kitchen. "Since when?"

I slathered mustard on two pieces of bread and then added two slices of the ham I'd baked the night before. "Hargus does a fair job of protecting the town."

"What's to do? There's no crime here. Never has been. So somebody reports a dog barking or some silly boy laying a strip of rubber on Culver Street. He's got no authority for anything."

"The sheriff authorized Hargus to keep the peace in his absence."

"Peace. Never been anything but peace in this town." Stella grunted as she opened a bag of potato chips. "I know when Herb was growing up there was a problem with someone papering the trees at Janice Brown's house. 'Course all the boys were sweet on her. Too bad she moved away. She was a nice girl."

"She went to college in Springfield, Missouri," I told

Stella. "Her mother said she's teaching in a small town outside of Springfield. She's raised two girls."

"Did Herb go to the class reunion two years ago? He should have. Johnny Moist died, you know. And Jack Hilland's as fat as a pig and going bald. Got that Dunlap disease. His belly done lapped over his belt."

I put my sandwich on a plate, grabbed a handful of chips, and thought about making a break for the office. But that would be rude.

Stella finished her lunch and sat with a glass of soda, thumbing through the mail.

"You brought in the mail?" I rather liked that chore. It gave me time to sit down and think about something other than word count.

"Uh-huh. Nothing much."

I swallowed a spurt of anger. Stella had screened the mail! She had no right! I reached for a Christian book catalog. I was determined to lay down some ground rules. The mail was to be put in the same place, every day, unopened.

I ripped open a letter from my agent and skimmed it quickly. It was a reminder that my deadline was looming and asking if I would need an extension to complete the book.

Yes, I would no doubt need an extension, probably several of them. I had too many problems to worry about deadlines, and a fresh batch of trouble was moving in Friday, along with my daughter.

I tossed the catalog on the table. "I'm going back to work."

"Well, I'll just find something to do around here. Don't mind me. I'll be quiet. I can take care of myself."

She couldn't open the childproof cap on her medication without a hammer. But that didn't matter. She was convinced she didn't need help—unless she needed help.

I heard the theme song of a talk show come on at megavolume as I closed the door to my office.

Patience, Maude. Lord, give me patience.

And while You're at it, can You throw in a plot?

2

CeeCee called the next morning.

"Mom?"

I closed my eyes and clutched the receiver in my right hand. Now what? Had she changed her mind about coming home? My heart pumped faster. "How are you, sweetheart?"

"Fine."

She didn't sound fine. My daughter sounded depressed. But then, why shouldn't she? Her life had just turned upside down. I knew all about that. "What's going on?"

"I need to move home today . . . if that's okay?"

I wanted to say no, it wasn't okay, but we had already agreed she could move in, so two days earlier wouldn't make much difference. Things were tense now, and I had a feeling we wouldn't make it any better by adding another female to the crew. Three generations, three different viewpoints, God help us. No one else could. "Do you need help with your things?"

CeeCee sniffed. "There's not much left."

I frowned. "What do you mean?"

"Mom, I had to sell everything. Jake wasn't good at handling money."

"I'm so sorry, honey. I wish—"

"He spent money like a sailor on leave." I heard a forced laugh. "Wine, women, and song. Guess who got the song?"

I knew all of this, of course, but she needed to vent. What could I say? *I wish too, Cee. I wish things were different. I wish Jake was alive.* Could I really wish she still had to put up with Jake's infidelities? *I wish I could kiss the hurt and make it well.* Unfortunately, as much as I wanted to help, there wasn't much I could do.

Of course I wanted to protect my daughter, but I knew from experience that no one can protect anyone else from life and its problems. No one had protected me, and I couldn't protect CeeCee. Life happens.

"I know, Mom. There's nothing you can do. It will help tremendously to just get back home for a while until I decide what to do next."

"You come home, honey—and be careful on the road."

"I will." CeeCee hung on the line. "Mom?"

"Yes?"

"I love you."

My heart turned over. I hated what had happened to my daughter's marriage, hated that CeeCee was only starting to experience's life's ups and downs. I prayed she would be strong enough to handle the ride. "I love you too, Cee."

I hung up slowly. I felt so bad for my daughter. If Jake hadn't died, I'd most likely have strangled the creep. The thought that he cheated on his wife and refused to start a family infuriated me. CeeCee had planned to have children, but kids hadn't been on Jake's agenda. I knew he wouldn't have made a good father. He wasn't even a good husband. But now Cee was alone, and that made me mad.

While CeeCee had never understood or liked football, she had understood the adulation sports figures receive. Jake had been drawn to the fame and money. Cee hadn't been. Her lack of interest in the parties and the demands she made for a personal life with him had caused problems between them. The party guy and the stay-at-home wife. They hadn't been able to work out their differences. Now Jake was gone and Cee was reeling.

I shook my head and turned on the computer.

* * *

Two hours later I was still sitting in front of a blank screen. Nothing would come. Absolutely nothing! I'd never faced writer's block before, but I couldn't call this anything else. No new revelations. Not an idea.

I could see the editorial remarks now: dull, unimaginative, stilted characterization. Providing this manuscript lived long enough to see an editor's desk. No more life than I had been able to pump into it, I had a feeling it might die in the computer.

How was I going to breathe life into this machine?

I sat with my chin resting on the heels of my hands. This was awful. I was writing the same old story over and over and over. Different characters, same old plot. What had caused this mental block? Age? Stress? Burnout?

Did other writers have this problem? Probably, but few admitted it. Other writers seemed prolific to the max, while I languished, agonizing over a story line, every plot, and every detail. At the last writer's conference I'd attended, one woman casually stated she wrote a minimum of ten pages a day. I wanted to slap her.

"Maude?" Stella's voice came from the other side of my office door.

I closed my eyes. "Yes, Stella."

"Are you working?"

No. "Yes."

"Well, I just wanted to tell you I'm going to play bridge with Simon, Pansy, and Frances."

"Good. Have fun." I waited to hear footsteps and the door close. Nothing.

"You'll have to come with me." Stella was still on the other side of my door. "My blood pressure's acting up today."

I drew a deep breath. *Lord, help me.*

"See for yourself," she shouted.

"You don't have to yell. Come in."

Stella entered, dragged the blood-pressure cuff out of her purse, and handed it to me.

"Sit," I directed, pointing to a chair beside the desk.

Stella sat with her purse perched on her lap as I inflated the cuff, then let it release.

"See, it's high."

"No, it's perfectly normal."

"I feel a little light-headed."

"I have to work this afternoon, Stel. I have a deadline."

Stella got up, mumbling under her breath. "Okay, but with all your other problems, I'd hate to add a dead mother-in-law."

Sighing, I shut off my computer. Obviously I wouldn't get any work done today. "Where's the game?"

Stella brightened. "In Pansy's room."

I didn't know what I was going to do about this situation, but I couldn't send Stella off to faint in the street. "All right. I'll take you."

I had figured it was going to be this way. I just didn't think it would start so soon.

* * *

That night I tried to write again. The house was quiet. Stella was sitting on the front porch reading her Bible in the glow of the porch light. I could hear the swing creaking as she pushed it back and forth. When it got quiet, I figured she was praying. Maybe she could put in a good word for me. I needed one.

I've had forty-one books published . . . and forty-one failures. At least in my opinion they were failures, because I'd never reached my goal. Okay. My *obsession*. I *had* to make the best-seller list. Especially now that I was the sole support of Stella and CeeCee. I needed to be a valuable asset to the publisher—and instead I was merely filling space.

Maybe my agent wasn't working hard enough for me. I sat up straighter. That was a possibility I hadn't considered. I like Jean Sterling, but she wasn't aggressive. Too polite, if you ask me. An agent had to believe in your work in order to sell it to a publisher, and I sometimes wondered about Jean.

That was the problem! I needed better representation, an agent who would work hard for me. A tough agent, an aggressive agent, an agent who believed in me. The right person would have to be a tough negotiator. Unlike Jean, they would keep track of print runs and sales growth with each book, and whether or not the publisher allowed sales to stagnate because of poor marketing. He or she would *demand* to know why others were given more advantages.

An agent who believed in M.K. Diamond's work would truly earn his or her 15-percent commission. A publisher who would recognize a book's potential and market it as a best-seller.

I came back to earth. Jean wasn't the problem. Neither was the publisher. I was. I could write new book proposals, shop them around, and start a bidding war because my sales were as good, or better, than some of those already on the coveted Christian best-seller list.

But, I didn't have a story left in me. Not one. And certainly not a best-seller. My shoulders drooped and I heaved another sigh. *Think, Maude. Think of something!*

* * *

"This world's going to you-know-where in a handbasket," Stella predicted as she shuffled through the living room. "Why, the things I see when I'm downtown. Girls wearing next to nothing. The music—just a bunch of annoying racket. That rap stuff gives me a headache. So loud it shakes the windows of the Citgo."

"Young people have their ways," I said, hoping she wouldn't get on her soapbox again.

"You can be sure it wasn't senior citizens who took the melody out of music and the pride out of appearance. Why, my sons would never be caught dead with girls who look like these girls do. Tattoos. Rings welded in their bellies. What makes them want to mark their bodies like that?"

"I think they're expressing their individuality."

"How? When they all look alike?"

I refused to respond to that. Anything I said would just make the situation worse.

"You can bet it wasn't us senior citizens who taught them to dress like heathens. It wasn't 'old people' who took the responsibility out of parenthood, the togetherness out of family, the service out of patriotism, the religion out of school and decided that having a nativity scene in front of a public building is a violation of somebody's religious freedom or a violation of the separation of church and state."

Stella was definitely on her soapbox this evening. I felt a headache coming on.

"And the language!" She was so upset her hair—a short, white, overprocessed mop—quivered as if electrified. "I can't understand half of what those young people say! It wasn't oldsters who took the refinement out of language, the dedication out of employment. I wonder if any of those young folks ever worked a day in their life. They've got ample time to hang around the Citgo, smoke cigarettes and drink that strange-looking blue soda pop. What do you suppose they put in that stuff? I wouldn't drink a thing that stained my tongue blue."

"The kids have to do something, I guess." Not that I condone smoking. I hate the nasty habit, and I'd have to be dying of thirst in the middle of the Sahara to drink that blue pop, but young people always push the limits, trying to shock their elders. Evidently they had pushed the right button where Stella was concerned.

"And from what I read, today's youngsters don't know the first thing about holding a job. But they surely know how to spend money. In my day, we knew how to hold on to a dollar."

Apparently Herb hadn't inherited the prudence gene Stella claimed to have. He'd spent everything I'd hoped to save.

"Hey, you guys."

Stella and I looked up to see CeeCee standing in the doorway. I hadn't even heard her come in. I jumped up from the couch. "Cee!"

"Hi, Mom. Grandma."

After a big hug, I drew back to have a good look at my daughter. "How are you, honey?" I inquired. "You look . . . good." I'd seen her looking better. Her hair needed a comb, and she looked like she hadn't seen a bath or a bed in several days. She'd always been so particular about her appearance.

"I know what I look like. Awful."

"Never to me." I drew her into my arms and held her for a few minutes. Sometimes a hug says more than words. "I'm so sorry this happened to you."

CeeCee sniffed, running a finger beneath her eye. Her attempt at a smile failed. "My life is a mess."

I sat my daughter on the couch and patted her shoulder. "I'll get some iced tea and we'll talk."

Cee sprang up. "Oh! My babies are in the car! How could I forget them?"

"Babies?" *I'm a grandmother!* I put my hand to my heart to stop the pounding. And she never let me know? I couldn't believe it.

"I'm a *great-grandmother*—well, why didn't anybody tell me? I could have passed on and never known," Stella grumbled. "Nobody tells me anything."

CeeCee grinned. "My babies are all I've got left from my marriage to the great Jake 'Touchdown' Tamaris."

I followed CeeCee out to her car. Grandchildren? Surely, Cee would've mentioned . . . I stopped short when I saw the car she was driving. "Where's the Cadillac Jake bought you for your birthday last year?"

CeeCee's eyes filled. "Had to sell it. Got a good price on this Honda."

The car looked like an eighties model, a faded blue, with a couple of rust spots. I could hear dogs yipping from inside, and my heart sank. Dogs. More than one.

"These are my babies." CeeCee grinned, cuddling two white French poodles.

I was happy to see they were miniatures. They wouldn't take up much room, and I didn't smell wet fur. "Are they housebroken?"

Quite clearly, they weren't outside animals, so that meant . . .

"Frenchie and Claire are well trained, Mom." CeeCee glanced inside the car. "Burton, well, he's not as fastidious as Frenchie and Claire."

Burton turned out to be a pug—a bulldog with a smashed-in face who eyed me warily. I eyed the dog back. *You might as well get used to it, sonny. We're stuck with each other.* And I wasn't any happier than he seemed to be.

"Burton's named for Richard Burton," CeeCee said. "Don't you adore his old movies?"

Actually, I didn't, and if I did, I wouldn't admit it. The film *Who's Afraid of Virginia Woolf?* was a disgrace. All that vulgar language.

CeeCee snapped leashes on the dogs while I took a handful of clothes from the backseat of the Honda.

"I can do that, Mom."

I shook out the rumpled garments that looked like the dogs had slept on them during the trip. I didn't know how I was going to cope with three dogs. Three? Three women, three dogs. Was three my new lucky number? What was Cee doing with *three* dogs? I'd have thought one would have been enough to fulfill the mother instinct.

CeeCee attached the leashes to the front-porch railing and then helped me unload the car. How she crammed three dogs and five bags in a Honda was nothing short of miraculous.

Frenchie and Claire explored as far as their leashes would allow while Burton sat on his haunches, snorting and drooling on my porch.

"Did you store everything else?" I asked as we entered my daughter's old bedroom.

CeeCee sank to the edge of the bed in the room she'd occupied as a teenager. "This is all there is, Mom. Jake left behind huge bills that had to be paid."

I sat down beside her. The news didn't surprise me. But then, nothing surprises me anymore.

"Bills *I'm* responsible for." CeeCee's eyes watered. "I put the house on the market. I hope it sells soon. I need the money. I sold the furniture and the cars."

"And there are still bills left?"

"Yes." She shrugged.

I wondered if she ever ate. She looked unhealthy. Her hair, which used to be one of her best features, hung in limp strands.

"Jake had several credit cards I knew nothing about. The bills were sent to him in care of the team's office, a post office box, that sort of thing. I never saw them until he died."

"How much do you owe?"

"A lot." CeeCee blew out a long breath. "Let's just say he entertained well. A lot more than he contributed toward his home life."

"Oh, honey, I had no idea."

"Neither did I, until now. Since his death, it's been one shock after another. So, I hope the house sells soon so I can finish paying off the debts. If there's anything left after paying off the mortgage, that is. Meanwhile, I need time to regroup."

"I'll help any way I can."

CeeCee paced the floor. "I know I sound like a broken record." She stopped at the window. "Mom, I'm so angry. It's not fair. I loved Jake. I believed in him, assumed that he loved me. For a long time, I didn't know he was seeing other women. Then I found some receipts for items he didn't buy me and some hotel bills in towns where the team wasn't playing. He'd told me he was on a public-relations tour. Am I a gullible fool or what?" Tears spilled over. "Why did this happen? Wasn't I pretty enough, smart enough?"

"Oh, Cee, don't blame yourself." And yes, she was pretty enough, with her clear skin and a smile that used to be full of sunshine. I hated to see her crying over a man who wasn't worthy of her tears. I never understood how such opposites attracted. Jake and CeeCee's odds of making it were roughly the same as expecting a pit bull to play fair with a kitten.

"Mom, I hated the party scene. He knew that when we married. He knew I didn't like the celebrity lifestyle. Of course, when we married he wasn't a celebrity. You know that. He was just . . . he had big dreams. Apparently those dreams didn't always include me."

"He should have known you wouldn't take part in the things he did." I had warned Cee about the dangers of marrying someone who didn't share her faith, but she hadn't listened. I wasn't going to remind her again, not now. She had enough to bear, and "I told you so" never helped a situation.

"He did drugs and alcohol and hung out with the groupies. The groupies were always around—were always available for dinner, for more than dinner. Jake liked that. Liked it too much.

"He bought into it all. Loved being in the spotlight. He was different when people recognized him. If I was with him, it was like I didn't exist. Sometimes I actually felt like I didn't exist, not for him, anyway."

"Cee, I'm so sorry." She should have never married him.

Jake Tamaris had taken my beautiful daughter and turned her into an untidy, angry mess. I wanted to put my arms around her and tell her it didn't matter, but I knew it did matter. A lot. And right now CeeCee needed to talk.

"I wanted children. Some days I've wished we had kids, Mom. Other days I'm glad we didn't. I wouldn't want them hurt this way. But I've got nothing. Nothing to show for seven years of marriage. I'm worse off than when I got married. At least before, I owned a car, worked for the post office part time, and had some savings. Now, all I have is a few clothes and three dogs who are spoiled rotten."

Spoiled rotten? Well, why not? My luck was certainly holding. Who was it that used to sing about a "little white cloud that cried"? Well, my own personal cloud had been on a yearlong crying jag. But no use taking my problems out on CeeCee.

"We'll figure something out. You settle in and then we'll think about the future."

"Thanks, Mom. You're a rock."

Oh, yeah. A real boulder.

I left CeeCee standing at the window and then turned back when I thought of the dogs. "What about Frenchie, Claire, and Burton?"

"Oh, no!" CeeCee dashed from the room. "How could I forget my babies? Mom, I need to get some dog food and a feeding bowl for each of them. And a water bowl. They won't share."

"What happened to their bowls?"

"I forgot and left them sitting in the kitchen."

"Well, I guess we can find something in the cabinet. If not, we can drive to Ash Flat and get what you need."

"I don't want to go to Wal-Mart," Stella shouted.

So, don't go, I thought. Wal-Mart was my one escape valve. Take that away and I'd blow through the ceiling. "You can stay here and watch the dogs!"

Stella crept down the stairway, purse in hand. "I could use some denture cream. Think I'll ride along."

I took a deep breath. "We're not going right now, and besides, someone has to watch the dogs, because I'm not taking them in the car."

Stella eyed me, then the dogs. "Does it have to be me?"

"I don't know the dog's preferences."

So that's how we decided Stella would stay with the dogs and I'd take my daughter to Ash Flat.

* * *

The next morning, Stella returned from her Citgo morning coffee just as I walked into the kitchen.

CeeCee entered the room right behind me. "Grandma, thanks for keeping an eye on my babies while we go to Wal-Mart for water dishes."

"Since when does a dog need a special dish for water?"

CeeCee's eyes filled with tears. "Don't be difficult, Grandma."

Asking Stella not to be difficult would be like asking a volcano to say excuse me after it belched molten lava. It wasn't going to happen.

Stella clumped out to the front porch and sat down in

the porch swing, pushing it back and forth at a rapid pace. Easy to see she was ticked.

CeeCee and I stood waiting for the explosion.

"Hurry up!" Stella demanded. "It must be a hundred degrees already."

The porch thermometer read eighty-two.

"You don't have to sit out here," I reminded Stella on our way out. "You can sit in the house."

"I can't sit in the house and watch the dogs at the same time."

"Whatever," I muttered ungraciously. Between Stella and CeeCee, my nighttime confession to the Lord had become a monotonous list of petty sins, usually preceded by, "Forgive me, Lord for losing my patience."

I backed the car out of the driveway and headed toward the closest Wal-Mart. That'd be Ash Flat, Arkansas, some twenty miles to the south.

An hour later, we had purchased dog food—a different brand for the older Burton—three food bowls, three water bowls, and three rubber mats to put under the bowls so they wouldn't scoot around the kitchen floor. CeeCee insisted that they had to eat in the kitchen or they would be confused. Heaven forbid we confuse the dogs. I was the only one allowed to be confused in this household. There were also new beds and new chew toys. I figured that would have to do for their birthdays and Christmas rolled into one. It was almost like having grandchildren. Almost, but not quite.

And the salt-and-vinegar potato chips CeeCee craved. Five bags of chips. And Stella's denture cream. I'd spent a fortune, but Cee wasn't crying now. So I made a mental adjustment in my budget.

Stella was sitting on the porch, watching the dogs, when we drove up. All three "babies" had tired of fighting their leashes and now lay on the lawn. Surely I was only imagining the look of resentment in Stella's eyes that said it was my fault the dogs had spent the morning in the hot sun. I had a strong feeling she'd spent the time plotting ways to get even.

"Oh, my poor babies," CeeCee crooned, cradling each furry face between her hands. "Just wait 'til you see what Momma has for you."

Stella's audible snort filtered through the air. She clumped into the house, letting the storm door slam behind her. I began dragging the bags out of the car while Cee took her babies inside. I guess the dogs appreciated their new bowls. They ate out of them anyway.

After everyone had been fed, CeeCee spent the afternoon in her room. I hoped she was sorting out her clothes and straightening the room, but the sounds I heard didn't suggest that. The dogs had the run of the house, though Stella and I had banned them from our bedrooms and my office. I soon learned that banning them and enforcing the ban were two different concepts. Burton left us alone, but a ban to the poodles was nothing more than an interesting challenge.

It was fortunate that Herb and I had kept the big house where CeeCee had been raised. We'd talked of selling the fifty-year-old, two-story place that we'd bought five years after we married. We'd brought CeeCee from the hospital to this house. Home was probably her only comfort now.

The house had been a stretch for us at the time. But I'd fallen in love with it. The living room was large, with the kitchen reaching across the back of the house and a small service porch behind it. My office faced the living room with its fieldstone fireplace. Upstairs there were four bedrooms and a large bathroom. Plenty of storage and a comfortable, family home. The only drawback was the detached garage that was a pain in foul weather. Now with three women and three dogs battling for space, my big house was beginning to feel crowded.

Herb and I had hoped to have more children, but that hadn't happened. And looking back, it had been a blessing. God knew Herb would take the sales job that had him traveling all week and home only on weekends. I'd have had problems raising more than one child practically alone.

But CeeCee had been an easy child. She was one of those who slept through the night from the first week. Bright, inquisitive, and a joy to love, she'd loved books as much as I did. We'd spent hours at the small library at the end of Culver Street. And when she started first grade, we'd been so proud of her eagerness to learn.

In high school, CeeCee had suffered some problems with her weight. But we'd assured her that a few extra pounds didn't matter. She was bright and beautiful, and that was enough.

Now I sat in my office remembering CeeCee as a child. She was always lovely, with an oval face, a dimple in one cheek, and crystal blue eyes that danced with humor.

When she was little, I'd put her light brown hair in

pigtails. When she started high school, we'd cut it in the bob she still wears.

Herb and I had felt empty when CeeCee went away to college. But we'd known this was a part of her growing up and our letting go.

Three months later she was back. Homesick. She took a civil-service test and got a part-time job at the post office.

CeeCee hadn't dated a lot in high school and that was fine with us. We'd hoped she'd wait awhile before she fell in love and married.

She met Jake at a friend's Christmas party and he'd swept her off her feet. He was two years older and had been scouted by the St. Louis Rams. He'd also received offers from a California and a New York team. When he accepted a contract with the Rams, Herb and I had been so glad that our daughter and new son-in-law wouldn't be that far away.

But then, life hadn't turned out exactly as expected. Jake traveled a lot. CeeCee had tried to spare us from knowing how ugly her marriage was. But now I knew, and she was home again.

CeeCee loved her grandmother, but I knew they would grate on each other's nerves. Stella was eighty-seven; Cee was only thirty-one. They were bound to have different perspectives on everything from music to three dogs having the run of the house.

We were all three widows, but there was a big difference between us. Stella had been widowed for several years, long enough to pick up the pieces and move on. I'd lost my husband after thirty-two years of a good marriage. CeeCee had been betrayed by her husband and had to deal with a lot of bitterness. She had nothing left. No house, no car. Though Herb hadn't prepared for our future, at least I had a home and dependable transportation.

I went to my office and shut the door, temporarily barricading the world from my domain.

I stared at the computer screen, but nothing came to me.

Zippo.

I couldn't think of a single thing to write. This was becoming the story of my life. Outside that door people were going about their affairs, living, loving. I spent my time staring at a blank screen. No wonder I had nothing to write about. I needed to get out of this room and meet people, get some ideas.

Deciding this was a good idea, I drove downtown and bought a bucket of original Kentucky Fried Chicken, potato salad, and watermelon for supper. It was hot and I didn't want to bother with cooking at this point. I had also reached a low point in my social life if a drive to Cart Mart could be considered "getting out."

When I got home, the dogs were happily lapping their dinner, dripping water out of their brand-new bowls all over the kitchen floor. Burton snuffed and snorted his way through his food and then went into the living room to drool.

I set out the food and made a fresh pitcher of tea.

"An indoor picnic," Stella enthused. "But paper plates get soggy, so we'll use the china."

"Fine." I'd have been happy with paper plates. Particularly since I'd be the one to wash up.

I went upstairs to find CeeCee. "Cee? Dinner's ready."

"I'm not hungry."

I knocked on her door and stepped in. "You've got to eat."

"I don't feel like it."

The remains of a bag of salt-and-vinegar chips, and an empty sour-cream container littered the floor.

"You need food, not junk. Come on. We can at least eat our meals together."

I finally persuaded CeeCee to come to the table. Stella was already seated in her chair, waiting impatiently.

"Come on, child, you've got to haul yourself up by your bootstraps," Stella said. "You're not the first woman who's lost her husband. Won't be the last."

Oh, great, Stella. A word to the bereaved.

CeeCee's eyes filled with tears, and I handed her a tissue before saying the blessing.

Stella studied the platter of chicken before asking, "Where'd you get those dogs?"

"I bought Frenchie and Claire because Jake traveled so much. A friend who was moving back East had Burton. I couldn't bear the thought of my friend putting him to sleep . . . so I took him." She glanced at me. "I know he's a bother, but I couldn't see—"

"I understand," I said. "We'll figure out something."

Stella finally chose a chicken leg. She always ate a leg, so I didn't know what the holdup was about. "Are the dogs going to be in the house all the time?" she asked.

"Sure. That's what they're used to." CeeCee glanced at me. "It's all right, isn't it, Mom?"

"Well, perhaps they could sleep on the back porch while it's warm. It's screened in now. Very comfortable."

"They stink," Stella said.

CeeCee didn't look very happy about the observation.

I ate a chicken thigh to console myself. The dogs did stink.

"Well, what are you going to do with yourself now?" Stella inquired as she plopped a spoonful of potato salad on her plate.

"Do?" CeeCee frowned.

"You'll need a job. Something to do. After all, you're young, pretty. Not old, like me. I'm wrinkled, saggy, and lumpy, and that's just my left leg. The rest of me is in even worse shape," she cackled. "You'll find something to do. What did you go to school for?"

CeeCee sent me a pleading look.

"Cee has plenty of time to think about the future," I said. Tears welled up in my daughter's eyes again, and I realized I couldn't say anything without reminding CeeCee of Jake. Although I failed to see why she would grieve for a lying, cheating, starstruck, no-account piece of nothing like Jake Tamaris. Not that I'm the least bit judgmental.

"She'll probably get married again," Stella said.

"No, I'm never getting married again." CeeCee shoved her chair back and bolted out of the kitchen, bawling.

Stella didn't miss a beat. "What's the matter with her? She's young. She's bound to find some young man and marry again."

I looked at her and wondered what planet she came from. In time CeeCee might remarry, but it was too soon for such speculation.

"It's only been a couple of months since Jake died. Give her a break." *And, Lord, give me patience,* I silently beseeched.

We were three very different personalities living under one roof.

The arrangement would never work. But it had to.

3

The weekend passed. That's about the best I can say.

Burton choked on a bone Saturday, and I had to rush him to the vet. It cost me sixty dollars! We came back to find Frenchie stretched out on my sofa. Poodles do shed.

I also came back to find Stella and her friends playing bridge. They usually played on Thursdays, but it wasn't unusual to find them seated outside my office door any day of the week. The door I was headed to so I could begin working.

How could I deny Stella this social outlet, even though their chatter was enough to disturb coherent thought? But since I didn't have a coherent thought, it really didn't matter. My office faced the living room so if my door was open—which I'm ashamed to say it was—I could hear the players.

The four seniors seemed to enjoy each other's company a lot more than the actual play. None of them were good at the game. They made amateur mistakes in bidding and laughed about them. Bridge was an excuse to get together.

"What's trump?" Pansy asked. Pansy looked like her

name, with her short, cushiony lap and eyes so deep blue they resembled the dark petals on the flower that was her namesake.

"Um, diamonds are trump," Frances, her partner, intoned.

Conversation was bantered back and forth like Ping-Pong balls. I'd known most of the participants for my lifetime. Residents tended to be born here, raise families, and die here. Not Simon, though. He was virtually a newcomer to Morning Shade; he'd come here four years ago.

The players weren't alike in any way, yet they enjoyed the companionship—even formed a close alliance. The other two women and Simon were all younger than Stella.

Simon was retired Navy. An impeccable sort, he'd been aboard a ship most of his career. He'd been in charge of supervising the loading of bombs and missiles—not something I would have wanted to do. He'd visited Arkansas, near Morning Shade, once when he was on leave, and had liked the quietness and beauty of the area so much he'd decided to retire here when the time came. The time came four years ago, and he seemed happy with his decision.

A bachelor, Simon was now bald with a fringe of graying hair above his ears. His bifocals caused him to continually nod and dip his head in order to focus on the cards. But he did take pride in himself. I had to give him credit for that. His clothes were always crisply pressed, and the crease in his trousers was razor sharp. I heard he took his laundry in twice a week for washing and pressing. Stella said he was too picky, which wasn't a bad thing. More men should be fastidious. Herb had been.

"I don't know what Lucille Stover was thinking when she put that furry-looking, animal-print furniture in her living room," Pansy complained, as if the Stovers' name had been introduced into the conversation.

"I haven't seen her new living-room suite," Frances said. "She sounded real proud of it when I talked to her this morning."

Pansy shook her head. "The fabric is just awful, and Lucille has no sense of arrangement. She just lines her furniture along the walls. She's real proud of the arrangement. I wanted to tell her to leave the house and let me arrange things. I always feel like I'm sitting in a subway car."

"Pass," Simon said.

"You know how it is," Pansy continued. "The couch on one long wall, the coffee table in front of it, two chairs on a short wall with a lamp table, another chair and table on the opposite long wall, and then a bookcase crammed with encyclopedias. Plain boring."

I thrust my fingers into my hair in frustration. Pansy had no room to talk. The last time I'd been in her room it had been, well, oversimplified. If anyone's surroundings could stand a touch of Martha Stewart, it was Pansy's. She hadn't changed a thing in thirty years.

Why was I listening to this? I was supposed to be working. I typed another sentence: "Thunder and lightning shook the house . . . yada, yada, yada." It was a dark and stormy night.

"Why do you suppose Lucille chose that horrid print with monkeys and elephants?" Pansy asked. "She says the fabric and the pattern won't show dirt, but it will."

"Her grandkids live a hundred miles away," Frances said. "It's not like they're going to be having their milk and cookies in Lucille's living room. Of course, now she'll have to change the drapes—or she should. Don't know that she will, but she should. That rose-patterned chintz doesn't go with 'jungle-cat chic.' *Tsk, tsk.*"

"One heart," Stella announced.

"I think Lucille likes order: everything in one place. I know I do," Frances said.

I rolled my eyes. Tall and reed-thin, Frances hadn't changed her hairstyle in the last sixty years. She still wore her jet-black, dyed hair coiled on top of her head like a miniature beehive.

The woman had to be nearly eighty. She still wore the print dresses with lace-trimmed collars I'd complained about in grade school. I'd thought she was an old lady even then. Some people are born old.

"I never liked those jungle patterns," Stella said.

"Lucille's kids never had any sense of color either," Frances said. "I had both children when I taught fourth grade."

Frances never forgot a single thing about any of her students. She frequently reminded them of some infraction they'd made while they were in her class, no matter how long ago it was.

Frances went on. "Carol, of course, turned out to be quite a nice woman in spite of her tendency to browbeat her brother. Wonder if she remembers that, now that she has five children of her own?"

"Pass," Pansy intoned.

I leaned back in my chair, listening. It beat staring at an empty screen and fishing for words that wouldn't come.

"Of course, I never had time to be interested in decorating," Frances continued. "All my energy went into my lesson plans. I changed the school room, the décor, for every season, every holiday. . . . "

"Well," Pansy said, "Lucille should at least change the traffic pattern so the rug doesn't wear so badly in one place. It's starting to look like a blazed trail. She'll have to buy new carpet before long, and she bought good Mohawk twenty years ago. Dull, but good. Pass."

"Brown!" Stella puffed out with disdain. "Brown. Can you imagine? Brown went out with the hula hoop. Even you know that, Simon. Martha Stewart would never condone making brown the primary color of anything! At least Lucille got brave and dumped that Early American couch."

"Um-um-um," Frances mumbled, peering at her cards. "I still have to pass."

"I saw in the paper that Jarvis Pool died," Stella said, changing the subject. "He was nearly eighty."

I groaned aloud. What was this obsession with who had died? Wasn't life spinning by fast enough without dwelling on someone else's death?

Hmm. Wait a minute. A light clicked on. Wheels turned. A character near death . . .

No. Too morbid. I need to write about hope, God's love and mercy. Acceptance.

That hit too close for comfort. It would seem that a child of God could live a life of wisdom and integrity. Know

God's will for her life, and through grace and knowledge live it. But life's recent changes threw me—tilted the scale of injustice. I was adrift on a sea of . . . what? Resentment. Despair. I resented my role of enforced caretaker and encourager: *I* needed encouragement, and what I got was more responsibility. I was walking around with my chain hanging out. And the whole world jerked it.

"Yes," Pansy sighed. "Poor Jarvis had been sick a long time."

"Well," Stella said, studying her hand, "none of us can be assured of tomorrow."

"People used to live longer," Simon said. "Certainly not like the nine hundred plus years that some in the Bible lived to be. But they worked harder, ate a better diet, and exercised more."

"You got exercise by doing the things it took to stay alive," Pansy said. "They chopped wood, plowed the fields, and hauled water."

"I wouldn't want to live longer," Frances said. "My feet hurt enough as it is. All that standing ruined my arches."

"We've got all these medicines to help us live longer, and I'm not sure it's worth it," Stella said. "Some say our years are shorter because there's so much crime and we're eating, smoking, and drinking too much."

Pansy glanced up from her cards. "Everyone's taking too much medicine these days. We didn't used to take anything unless we really needed it. Now every time we get a pain we run to the doctor and add another pill to our diet."

"I'm taking a blood-pressure pill," Stella sighed.

Half a pill, my mind mentally corrected her. I typed another sentence, then deleted it. There wasn't another book in me. I was doomed.

"Um-hum. You knew Janine Pierson's husband died."

"Stroke, I heard," Pansy said.

"Blood clot," Stella corrected. "Not good." She shook her head. "Did I mention that Cee's sold everything and moved back home? Seems Jake spent every dime he made and left her with a bunch of bills."

I got up and prepared to interrupt this conversation. Stella should know better than to talk about family problems. Cee didn't need gossip right now.

"Hmm," Frances responded along with Pansy.

Stella's tone dropped. "She brought *three* dogs with her."

I sat down again, feeling that a disaster had been averted. She could talk about the dogs all she pleased. If Frenchie didn't quit targeting everything in sight, I might have a few choice words to contribute myself.

"Three dogs?" Frances queried. "Where are they?"

"On the service porch, where they can't cause any trouble. Two poodles and a pug."

"A pug? Don't they have those mashed-in noses?"

"Uh-huh. All that animal does is snuff and snore. Snores worse than my James did and he raised the roof. Kinda hard to sleep with that dog in the house."

Frances wagged her head. "Too bad, too bad. CeeCee was such a good student."

And still is, I thought with a touch of resentment. Granted, she wasn't at her best right now. She dragged around the house, looking pitiful, and stuffed herself with chips and dip while she watched TV until three in the morning.

But I'm not much better. I hole up in my office, drink coffee, and pray for an idea for my book. In my heart, I knew this should've been a time of drawing closer to the Lord and my family, and I was trying. I set aside time every morning for prayer and Scripture, but truthfully, God seemed absent. I talked, I prayed, I begged and beseeched Him to make my life easier, but He was ignoring me. Maybe I was at fault—maybe I'd turned into a whiner. I didn't know. I just knew I hated my life lately.

And Stella.

And, God forbid, CeeCee and her mangy dogs.

"CeeCee will do fine once she gets some rest," Stella said. "Losing Jake like that was a blow. And having to take care of the mess he left behind. It's just been difficult for her."

"I guess she'll be looking for a job," Pansy suggested.

"Sometime. She's in no hurry."

Talk at the bridge table turned to life here in Morning Shade. Percy Martin cleaned out his garage and made a killing in a yard sale. Margaret Falk had gone to visit her daughter in Kansas City. She'd ridden the bus. Not one of the four players thought bus travel was the way to go. But other than driving, how was Margaret supposed to get to Kansas City? Heaven knew no one wanted her on the road. She was ninety-two. The state licensing bureau had banned her from driving twelve years earlier, after she'd been ticketed for straddling the center of Highway 63 for ten miles.

It was close to four o'clock before the bridge group left.

My shoulders relaxed. I could get back to work. *Back?* There was still nothing on my screen. The afternoon was shot, and I hadn't written a single word.

I was getting a little scared.

* * *

"The paper's thin this morning," Stella complained as she shuffled into the kitchen a week later. The paper was always like that on Saturday.

I poured a bowl of Honey Nut Cheerios and waited for the coffee to drip through. I needed the caffeine before I could confront the morning.

"Look at this!" Stella exclaimed. "There's been a break-in!" She rattled the paper to fold it over. "At *Lucille Stover's* place. Why, we were just talking about her at our bridge game. Remember? I told you about that."

I remembered. The subject of Lucille's awful couch and chair with the monkey fabric had dominated the bridge game. "Was anything taken?"

"Don't think so, but Hargus Conley is investigating."

"I'm sure he'll take care of the situation." I poured my coffee and added cream.

"Humph. He's not worth the paper it takes to print his name."

I couldn't disagree. At forty, Hargus had been the bane of Pansy's existence his entire life. But Morning Shade couldn't justify a real police force and Hargus wanted the job.

Hargus had been on a ride-along with the county sheriff several times. Then he'd just kind of slid into the job of law enforcement, without authority. Hargus called himself a deputy, and the sheriff let it go as long as Hargus informed him of any real problems that arose.

His "office" was a narrow space next to the Kut 'n' Kurl. Hargus had gathered up a desk, a chair, and a bookcase, and had his name painted on the door in bold, black letters.

He might not have been much of a law officer, but he was earnest. You had to give him that. While he might not be the most effective lawman around, he was proud of being "the law." And a man needed to take pride in his job, even a man like Hargus.

Single, Hargus spent most of his time in his office drinking coffee and eating donuts in the morning, and drinking Chocolate Cow soda in the afternoon. Twice a day he cruised up and down Culver Street in his big old, black GMC pickup with a Confederate flag mounted in the bed. You couldn't miss his truck. It made a noise similar to a runaway freight train and looked like an accident hunting for a place to happen.

On weekends, he could be found at the stock-car races. He drove fifty miles each way to go to the races every Friday and Saturday night.

"He's not really a lawman," Stella said, her eyes glued to the article about the break-in. "It says here that the back door was left open and the culprit came in that way. *Tsk, tsk.* Lucille was playing bingo and Harold was with her. They got home about eleven o'clock and found . . . well, my goodness!"

"What?" I was interested in spite of myself.

"Nothing was taken!"

"Nothing?"

"Nothing."

I sat across from Stella, waiting for the rest of the story. "Well, then, why did someone break in? Were they frightened away before they could take anything?"

Stella read on. "Nothing was taken, but . . . but the living-room furniture was moved around. Hmm . . . odd."

"The furniture was moved around?" That was bizarre, even for Morning Shade.

"That's all."

"Why would anyone do that?"

"I don't know. Why, Frances and Pansy were talking about how Lucille lines her furniture around the wall. 'No creativity at all,' Pansy said." Stella shook her head and turned the page.

"Lucille must have been very shaken."

"I'd imagine. I think I'll just go down to the Citgo and see if anyone knows anything more." Stella's gaze swept over the obituaries. "Just three names today. All of them well over seventy." She folded the paper. "I'm on my last days, Maude. You won't have to put up with me much longer. I'm eighty-seven. My feet hurt. I'm tired."

"You're in good health, Stella," I reminded her.

"I take medication. A person shouldn't have to take medication."

"You take half a blood-pressure pill. That's nothing."

"To you, maybe, but I get light-headed from all that medication. . . . "

When Stella left the house, I went to my office with my coffee and, from habit, prayed for inspiration. Even my prayer life had become routine. I needed something to shake me out of my rut. I needed something to type into the computer. I sat, staring at the screen saver. Nothing. Nothing. Nothing.

I found myself thinking about Lucille's break-in. Why on earth would someone go to the trouble to break into a house and do nothing but move furniture around? That didn't make sense, did it?

I began to type and my fingers flew over the keys. I put down the facts of the break-in as I knew them. I speculated as to why someone would do that. Move furniture? I'd heard of oddball cases, but this one . . . I let my imagination run.

At least it was something.

* * *

Stella returned from the Citgo around noon. She padded into the living room, carrying her shoes in one hand. "My bunions are *killing* me."

I had a legal pad on my lap, writing like crazy. This furniture bit had me going and I didn't want to be interrupted.

Stella didn't appear to notice. "That Jenny is quite a nice girl. Can't imagine why she's not married."

Jenny Moore, a thirty-one-year-old single mother, had worked at Citgo for three years. She was pretty and popular with the regulars. If she hadn't married, it was probably from choice.

Stella sat down on the sofa with a sigh.

"Are you feeling okay?" She looked a bit dragged out.

"Oh, you know how the old song goes, 'It Is Well with My Soul.' But my back aches."

I had to smile. Stella could be a cross to bear sometimes, but she had her moments.

My curiosity—and admittedly my need for a story line—overrode my determination to steer clear of Stella's penchant for nosing into other people's lives and problems. "Anything new regarding Lucille's break-in?"

I kept my tone casual as I scribbled on the pad. I didn't want to encourage her, but I didn't want to discourage her either. The book was finally beginning to roll.

"Maybe," Stella said, propping her feet on a brocade footstool.

I hated it when Stella took that tone: like we were playing parlor games. Games were the furthest thing from my mind. I needed facts. "Okay, give," I said. "I don't know any more than you do. Does Hargus have a suspect?"

"Hargus," Stella snorted. "Pansy's like a sister to me, but that boy of hers . . . "

"He's not a boy any longer." Good grief. Hargus was going bald.

"And as useless as a shovel without a handle," Stella said. "He might think he's the law around here. But in my opinion, we'd be better off without him getting in everybody's face. The sheriff himself should be taking care of these things."

"Surely Hargus notified the sheriff about the break-in."

Pansy's son wasn't the brightest bulb in the package, but he had a servant's heart. He was humble about his assistance too. Reminded me of Saul and David. When Saul called for David to come play the harp for him, David could have become sullen and refused. He could have planted his hands on his hips and said, "Hey, you're looking at a *giant killer*. There's plenty of other harpists who'd be glad to play for you. Let's show some respect here."

But David didn't. He joyfully played for the king.

Stella shouldn't bug Hargus so much—though admittedly, most people thought Hargus should slay more giants and get out of police business.

Stella shrugged. "Think I might give him a hand with this one—if he asks."

"He won't ask."

"I *know* he won't, but if he does, I'm willing to help."

Okay by me. If she got interested in the mystery, she'd be Hargus's problem. I grinned. *That's the brightest thought I've had in days.*

* * *

Mid-May found me still in my cave sitting before the computer. Spring in the Ozarks is a special time, with pink wild roses growing along the roadside.

I'd rather be outside, but the thing about writing is this: authors write whether the muse strikes or not. In fact, more times than I like to admit, the muse misses my office completely. I think he—she—whatever—has lost my address. But in the meantime, deadlines have to be met. So I am sitting here in front of this computer, working up a mental sweat. What if I never got this book written? Writing was my only source of income, so I had to get it written. I think this was called being between a rock and cinder block—or some such thing.

CeeCee was in the kitchen. She'd slept until ten. I could

hear her rummaging around for another bag of potato chips. No one mentioned her weight lately because poor Cee was trying to eat the pain out of her body.

I was concerned about her. My daughter managed to get up and feed her dogs, but that's about the only effort she made. Except for turning on the TV. She was as bad as Stella, watching soaps and talk shows.

"Oh, my," I breathed, wishing again that I could regain a shred of the solitude I needed for my writing. The dogs were yapping in the kitchen, the television was blaring, and Stella was slamming through the front door. I could practically hear CeeCee crunch her way through another bag of potato chips.

Today I'd stuck a rug under the door's crack for noise control, hoping if I barricaded myself in my office, everyone would leave me alone. To prove how wrong I could be, a mere second later there was a knock on the door.

"Yes?"

Stella knocked again, then pushed on the door and kicked the rug aside. "I just talked to Lucille."

"What did she have to say?"

Finally. Now I could proceed with a new chapter. This might work out better than I thought. The old creative juices started to bubble.

Stella came in and perched herself on the edge of a chair. Her eyes danced. Good ole Stel never felt better than when she had information to impart—God bless her inquisitive hide.

"Seems whoever broke into Lucille's house just moved furniture, like the newspaper said. But—" Stella breathed dramatically—"she *likes* the new arrangement!"

"She *likes* it?"

"*Loves* it. You know—well, you don't know, but Pansy was saying the other week how boring Lucille's furniture arrangement was. I'd be surprised if Lucille moved anything to sweep under it. Whoever broke in even *added* a couple of lamps."

"They did *what?*" This was better than anything I could come up with!

"They put new lamps in Lucille's front room. Real nice ones with blue shades. They put her old ones in the closet, along with a ton of knickknacks, and Lucille's leaving them there. Even Harold likes the new arrangement. He can see the TV better from his recliner."

"That's amazing." I frowned. "Why would anyone do something like that?" New lamps—good ones—were costly. "What thief spends money to vandalize?"

"I don't know," Stella said, "but they sure did Lucille a favor."

My mind ran a hundred miles an hour as I speculated aloud. "Someone went into the house. But can it be called a break-in when the back door was unlocked? Can it be called a crime when all the perpetrator did was move furniture? And if Lucille likes the new arrangement so well, can it be a crime? So if Hargus managed to catch anyone . . . "

Stella snorted.

". . . can he arrest anyone? And if he did, can they be charged with anything other than a misdemeanor?"

"He can make a citizen's arrest, but Hargus won't catch whoever did it."

Now I snorted. Hargus has a hard time catching a cold, but he might collar the perpetrator. Odder things happened in Morning Shade.

"Interesting, huh?" Stella grinned. "We got ourselves a full-blown mystery."

"Very," I murmured. My thoughts were already on how to use this turn of events in my book. The mystery just might be the key ingredient to a best-seller. "I think maybe you should step in, Stella. Help Hargus—if he has no objections."

Stella brightened. "You do?"

"I do."

I did—and for purely selfish reasons. If Stella was in the fray, she could keep my story going. Besides, the adventure would keep her out of the house a few hours a day, and I could concentrate.

Now if I could think of a way to get CeeCee out of the potato chips.

4

The phone rang at seven the next morning. I rolled over and glared at the alarm. Who would call at this hour? I fumbled for the receiver and brought it to my ear. "Hello?" My agent's voice was on the line.

"Oh, I woke you," she said. "It's eight o'clock here!"

In New York, maybe, but not in Morning Shade. I cleared my throat to make it sound like I'd been up an hour.

"No, I'm up," I chirped. I threw a hand over my eye to shield it from the morning sun that peeked through my shade. "What's going on?" Maybe Jean had called with a new contract. *Please, no.* I'd grab it because I needed the money, but then I would have *two* contracts that I couldn't fulfill.

"I have an idea I want to run by you."

"Okay," I said, praying it included money.

"Would you consider ghostwriting a book for Jack Hamel?"

Whew. Jack Hamel. One of the biggest evangelists around. But why couldn't he write his own book? I've never been a ghostwriter, and I never intended to be one. Doing all the work without any name exposure? I don't think so. Not even if the money is good. Really good. And I need the money, believe me.

Are money and name recognition really the right priorities? The thought slid through my mind. I blinked. What was this? A message from God? At this hour of the morning?

"Seems you two met at a CBA function?" Jean continued.

I'd forgotten. A publisher's breakfast. Tall, steel gray hair. Nice man—seemed sincere about the gospel. I liked him; I just didn't want to write his book.

"It would be a good experience," Jean said. "And other than the book you're working on, we've had no other bites on your proposals."

She didn't have to point that out. "I don't think so, Jean. Right now I have my hands full trying to write the book I'm working on."

"I know, but Jack is willing to wait until you're available. And he needs someone with your compassion and experience to help him write the book."

"Help him, or write it for him?"

"Does it matter, as long as it glorifies the Lord?"

I considered that comment as hitting below the belt. Dragging in the Lord in order to get her own way? Surely God meant for me to write my own stories. After all, He had given them to me.

I thought about what Jean had said after I hung up the phone. Did it matter? Maybe not, but I'd never stopped to analyze my true feelings about ghostwriting because it had never come up before. I knew that many celebrities were paid a huge advance for their story, and readers assumed they'd written the book themselves. Something about that didn't set right with me.

But I'm not out to change the world. I returned to worrying about my own problems. *Lord, just give me something. Anything. A story that shows Your love, mercy, and concern for people's problems. A story that gives people hope, and maybe a laugh or two. A story that will glorify You. I need You, Lord. Where are You?*

I heard CeeCee crooning to her dogs. They sounded like they were all piled on the couch in the living room. Since she arrived, my daughter has spent all day doing three activities: crying, eating, and crooning. It breaks my heart, but there doesn't seem to be a way for me to make her understand that life isn't all traveling down a smooth road. Never was meant to be. But even my kindest suggestion is met with a look of pain, a look that says "you don't understand," piling on guilt with another burst of tears.

If Cee isn't crying, she's eating. Even her knees are getting plump. She has to stop feeding her grief.

CeeCee had been plump as a child. As a teenager she'd been aware of her weight, knowing she had a tendency toward gaining a pound if she walked past a McDonald's or a Braum's ice cream shop. As an adult, her weight problem had lessened and she'd become nicely rounded.

But now she's regressing. Packing on the pounds. She has to stop eating, but if I suggest salads, she says she deserves comfort food. Apparently she deserves it in copious amounts!

At the rate she's going she's going to be "comforted" into an early grave.

When I go to the grocery store now, I automatically put seven bags of chips and five large cartons of dip on the checkout counter. It's a sad state of affairs.

But more than being concerned for Cee's health, I'm worried about my daughter getting her life together. When Herb died, I had happy memories to fall back on. CeeCee doesn't have that. All she has is eleven years of pain, disappointment, betrayal, and resentment. Which makes me wonder if she is grieving for Jake or for those wasted years? What does the future hold for my daughter? A lifetime of disappointments? *Please, God, I hope not.*

My heart ached for her, but what was I going to do when CeeCee wouldn't let me help, wouldn't listen? I didn't have the money to help pay off her debts. I was barely keeping my chin above water as it was. I wasn't sure yet what impact CeeCee's moving in would have on my already shaky budget, but I knew this: Even though at the moment I was mad at God, I still knew that He was there and that He would keep His promises.

Promises like Lamentations 3:22: "The unfailing love of the Lord never ends! By His mercies we have been kept from complete destruction." Funny how I knew that, but yet I grieved and worried and wished at times He'd taken me instead of Herb. Herb could handle life better than I.

Okay, one crisis at a time. What could I do to help Cee get on her feet . . . besides cut off the potato chips? Not much. There is no way to help someone who won't—can't—help herself. Only CeeCee can make up her mind to change. And only God can bring about those changes.

This only added to my depression. My daughter's heart was broken, and everything in me wanted to fix it. But I couldn't. She had to do it herself.

I blew out a long sigh of exasperation and stretched back in my chair. I pushed my fingers through my hair and massaged my scalp. Who was I to think I could fix anything? I couldn't even fix my own career. Here I had been writing for twenty-five years, had all these books to my credit, and what had it gotten me? Certainly no recognition, not among my peers. When I went to book conventions I might as well not exist. No matter what my agent or publisher said, I was not in the place I wanted to be. Not at this stage of the game. Not at the end of my career.

Rubbing my forehead, I prayed that my blooming headache would go away. *I've got no new manuscript; my husband is dead; I'm struggling to pay bills. Now my mother-in-law and daughter are living with me, and I can't even feel sorry for myself outside of this office because Stella and CeeCee have problems too.*

I rotated my tired shoulders. *I'm tired. That's it. Just plain tired.* Disillusioned with everything: publishers, promises that never materialized, family crises.

Why had I ever been convinced God wanted me to write Christian mystery novels? What made me think I could be of service to Him as a writer? Hadn't that been utterly presumptuous, considering the strength of other writers who were already doing the same thing? Those with a faith apparently much greater than my own.

Grow up, Maude. He knows the plans He has for you, and it's not to pick on you—I stared at the blinking cursor—*I don't think.*

I paced to the window. The backyard needed work. A neighbor boy mows it for me, but I didn't plant any flowers this year. The beds along the back fence are empty except for the few perennials that managed to make it through the winter. Only the lilac tree added color to the yard this spring, and now it's gone.

I sighed. I didn't have time to take care of the yard, especially with CeeCee here now. There wasn't time or energy to do everything. My first priority was to write. Unfortunately, priority or not, I wasn't getting much accomplished. For all the good I was doing here, I might as well join Stella in her daily trek to the Citgo. At least I might hear some interesting gossip.

Stella knocked at my office door just then and poked her head inside. Frenchie and Claire squeezed in past her, sniffing around the room. Suddenly, Frenchie lifted his leg.

"Cee!" I screeched.

"I'll get paper towels," Stella said. "We need them by the case these days."

"You want me, Mom?" CeeCee appeared in the doorway, her eyes puffy from her most recent crying jag.

"Your poodle made a puddle on my floor."

CeeCee immediately looked contrite. "Oh, Frenchie, shame. Shame." She gathered up the dog and kissed his black button nose.

Well, that should teach him, I thought. *That kind of chastisement is about as effective as giving an errant child a chocolate bar.*

I followed CeeCee out of the office as Stella shuffled in to blot up Frenchie's contribution to the décor. Fortunately, the house has wood floors so there are no carpets to clean. Still, Frenchie's penchant for marking every corner of the house is really getting to me.

"I'm going to Citgo," Stella said, toting a handful of used paper towels to the wastebasket in the kitchen.

"How's Lucille doing?" Maybe I could glean something, a clue to the moved-furniture mystery.

"Oh, she's enjoying her new living room. Hargus can't come up with one suspect as to who broke into the house. He said a four-year-old could've walked in that back door. Lucille said she pushed the lock button on the back storm door, but—" Stella shrugged—"Hargus shook the door a bit and the lock popped open. He said the doorframe is so old that the wood has shrunk and that any idiot could jimmy it open." She looked at me. "You should check our back door. Make sure nobody can get in."

"I'll do that." My house looked bad enough with three dogs and all their dishes and toys, Cee's personal belongings strung everywhere, and Stella's messes (like her habit of leaving her teeth wherever she took them out). Maybe a visit from the burglar would lift my spirits. I toyed with the idea of leaving the door open—then backed off. This person could be more than a fastidious nut. He could be dangerous. "Too bad there are no clues. Lucille might never know who was in her house."

"Uh-huh, and let me tell you it's unnerved her something awful. To think somebody, some stranger, was in the house.

Well, they're getting a new door this week and changing the lock on the front one. She doesn't feel safe."

"But nothing was stolen," I clarified.

"No." Stella's bright eyes peered at me. "Are you thinking of using Lucille's troubles in your new book?"

I silently took the Fifth. Stella constantly offered a "what if" from something she read in the newspaper as if she knew what writing a book was about. But I couldn't be rude. I usually just listened and then forgot, but I had to admit that I *was* fishing for information that would help me with my book. Was I that desperate? Yes.

"What could they be looking for in Lucille's house?" I asked Stella. The burglar had picked the dullest residence in town.

"Oh, I don't know. You're the writer," Stella acknowledged. "What if somebody wanted to keep Hargus busy investigating the break-in so they could do something else? Like break in to the bank or something."

That wasn't likely. Our bank was more broke than I was.

Stella was on a roll now. "Wouldn't it be funny if the person who broke into the house hid something there? Hid something he didn't want anyone to know about, like jewelry or money?"

"Why would they do that?"

"Why, I don't know. You figure that out. But it would be funny if some criminal from out of town came in and hid something in . . . well, Lucille's new couch or in the closet with all those knickknacks, or even somewhere else. Maybe he's hanging around until he can get it back. Until the law goes on to something else." She shrugged. "I don't know. But Hargus would be so busy investigating the break-in, and whoever might've moved the furniture around—maybe they did that to confuse folks—that he'd never look inside the furniture or search the house."

Good grief. I hate to admit it, but this is the most plausible scenario Stella has come up with yet. It's a stretch, but promising.

"It could happen," Stella said as she shuffled toward the stairs. "I'm going to change my shoes and then go to the Citgo. Maybe Lucille will be there. I think I'll interrogate her myself."

Interrogate? Yep, Stel would do that. Try to keep a secret, and she would interrogate the life out of you until she found out. I followed her into the living room, thinking about what she'd said.

Cee came in from letting the dogs run in the yard. Burton has little energy or interest in anything. Mostly he sleeps. At least he isn't watering everything in sight.

"Sorry about Frenchie's little . . . gift," Cee said.

"It's okay." It wasn't, but what else was I going to say? Move? And take those dogs with you? Hardly. My daughter and my mother-in-law are more important than my need for solitude. I have to keep reminding myself of that. Frequently.

Nothing was the same anymore. I had to accept that. I had two other people to consider now, not just myself. Stella still had a little resentment about having to live with me, but my daughter was the greater problem at the moment. I had to find some way to help CeeCee deal with her pain.

At the moment CeeCee was in denial. Her shiny brown hair was limp and dull, her pretty oval face puffy. She hadn't bothered with makeup and had worn the same three terry-cloth lounge outfits ever since she arrived. She'd tried to bury her grief with potato chips. If I wasn't mistaken, those terry-cloth things were able to stretch just so far, and they'd just about reached their limit. The more she ate, the more weight she gained, and the less she wanted to change what was happening.

She needed a job.

Don't get me wrong. I love my daughter. I poured out my love on my only child all her life, felt blessed to have her. When she chose to marry Jake, I wasn't happy about the idea but knew it was CeeCee's choice to make. To learn that Jake destroyed everything that my daughter hoped and dreamed for hurt me deeply, and made me so angry with him that if he weren't already dead, I'd hang him.

But now I'm a little mad at Cee for letting him do that to her. I thought she had more backbone than that. She hadn't been raised to be a doormat. How had Jake Tamaris turned her into one? She had no self-esteem left. Even Stella had more confidence. Just the idea of climbing out of her rut sent CeeCee out of the room bawling. How could she face the world when she had no fight left?

"Mom?"

"Yes, darling?"

"I wish . . . " Tears welled up in her eyes as she cuddled Frenchie close to her chest.

"I know, sweetheart. We all wish for a lot of things, but we make the best of what we're given." How easy it was to say those words, how hard for me to accept them. *Who am I to try to help Cee? I can't even help myself.*

The tears spilled from CeeCee's eyes as she curled into a corner of the couch.

I sat at the other end, hoping that if she was finally willing to talk she might be willing to listen to some advice. "Life sometimes hands us a whole plate full of problems," I reminded her.

"This is a barrelful, Mom. And I don't know what to do with it."

"Does anyone know what to do with problems? I hand them over to God every morning—and take them back by noon. I want to do different. I guess giving our problems to God never comes easy for anyone."

CeeCee sniffed. "Yeah, I know. God let this happen to me. How can I give it back? I can't."

"My mom used to say that bad things happen so we'll grow stronger. Whether they're the result of our own choices—or someone else's."

CeeCee looked at me from beneath the hand that covered her eyes. "That's so cliché, Mom."

I released a long sigh. "I know, but I'm trying hard to believe there's a reason for everything, Cee." I *had* to believe that, hold on to that conviction like a life preserver. Deep down I know it will all be explained to me someday, but holding on right now is hard. So terribly hard.

CeeCee sniffed again and then drew a deep breath. "I know you do. You've got your own problems. You're still trying to get over Dad's death. You've got Grandma here, and now me. It can't be easy."

"I love having you here." Or I would if Cee would decide to live again. Seeing her mope around like this was so depressing. Something I don't need. I need to be lifted up too. I can't remember the last time I enjoyed a good spontaneous laugh.

CeeCee made a face. "I know I'm a mess."

I grinned. "That's all right. You're my mess, and I love you."

Burton sniffed his way into the living room, waddling from side to side. Frenchie and Claire settled themselves in a chair as if they were the king and queen of the house. Then Burton plopped himself on the rug in front of the chair and rolled back and forth in what was, for him, a full aerobic workout.

"I wish—"

"Don't," I interrupted. "We can wish all we want, but until we begin to *do* something, all the wishes in the world won't make a bit of difference. Pastor Healy talked about hope this past Sunday, about being grounded in the faith. Which reminds me, you really ought to come back to church. How about going with me to the Wednesday night service tonight?"

"My hope is pretty dim right now, Mom. And I'm sorry, but I really don't think going to church is the answer."

"I know, honey. But the point of that sermon was that if we expect to be blessed, to survive, we have to continue in the faith—be grounded and settled in and not be moved from hope. Know there's a better day ahead."

CeeCee sniffed again, and I handed her a tissue. "I never should've married a jock."

"Sorry to tell you this, but everyone makes mistakes. Doozies. Making a mistake isn't the end of the world."

"Well, Jake's mistakes meant the end of my world."

I leaned toward my daughter. "Hey, life goes on. What Jake did isn't important anymore."

"Yes, it is. I have to clean up his messes."

"But you can get through this. You *will* get through this. We've both got to believe that. And when you do, I know you'll find the pain less, the memories bittersweet, and you'll move on, stronger than you are today."

"I don't know, Mom. I don't know if I can do that."

"Sure you can. You're stronger than you think."

CeeCee closed her eyes. "I'm not myself. I don't even know myself anymore. I—I have to find a new me and it's hard. Really hard."

I rested my hand on her knee. "We'll make it through this. Have a little faith in yourself."

CeeCee rested her head against the back of the couch, looking frayed. "You're not getting much writing done with everyone here."

I was surprised—and touched—that she had noticed. "Not as much as I'd like," I admitted. "I'm having a little trouble coming up with a plot."

"You always come through, Mom."

"Well, I'm not too sure I will this time. I'm stuck. I don't even like my characters, so how can I expect my readers to identify with them?"

"Mom, you've written too many books to not be able to do this one. You can do it."

Hmm. Sounds easy when someone else says it. But they aren't sitting in front of a blank computer screen watching that blinking cursor. I've noticed that nonwriters seem to think all there is to writing is just dashing off a few golden words in your spare time. I'm always running into people who are "going to write a book someday." If someday ever gets here, they'll be in for a shock.

I needed a personal victory. All the turmoil in the house was eroding my confidence, sapping my strength, making me bitter when I should have been grateful for what I had. *Who am I to hand out advice? I need an attitude adjustment as badly as Cee.* "Well, the book won't write itself." I hugged CeeCee. "Fix yourself something nutritious for lunch . . . maybe a nice salad."

"I thought maybe a ham sandwich and chips. Do you want one?"

"No, thanks." My appetite lately was as weak as my writing. Was my creativity affecting my calorie intake? Another week of writing and I might fit into that slinky black number hanging in the rear of my closet. I could wear it to the wake when I bury this going-nowhere manuscript.

CeeCee went off to make herself a sandwich.

I went into my office, closed the door, and leaned against it with my eyes closed. *What's wrong with this picture? I'm preaching to Cee about having faith and hope while my own are flagging. I'm worried about my story when Stella's life has turned upside down and Cee thinks hers is over. My own problems look a bit petty in comparison. But they are my problems, Lord. I live with them. Surely I'm allowed to think about them too.*

* * *

Monday morning Jean called again. At least this time she waited until nine o'clock my time. Frenchie had scratched on my bedroom door about six, wanting out. CeeCee slept through the urgent call, so I had piled out of bed and staggered through the kitchen to let the dog out the back door to do his business.

"Have you given any further thought to the ghostwriting project?" Jean asked.

"Why, no, Jean, I haven't. I thought I'd made it perfectly clear that I wanted to write my own books."

"It's such a good opportunity, Maude. I think you'd lend needed experience to the book."

"But it would take time away from the book I'm working on," I responded. I couldn't tell my agent that in a month I was going to be desperate for income. I had to finish this book before I took on anything else, and even though I greatly respected Jack, I didn't want to write his book. If I wrote something, I wanted my name on it. Call it self-pride, call it professional survival, call it whatever you please. Right or wrong, that was the way I felt. Let Jack write his own book.

After telling Jean again that I just couldn't consider the project, I returned to trying to make something out of the little bit I'd done on my own book. The old proverb about not being able to make a silk purse out of a sow's ear came to mind. I must say, it did seem appropriate.

* * *

Stella shuffled back home that afternoon. "I'm bleeding latte through my pores," she said.

Latte?

I'd never have thought Stella would be drinking something as froufrou as latte. Why, her James would have had a fit. Good ole coffee—black, strong enough to walk out of the kitchen had been his drink of choice. But since Stella had moved in with me and started going to Citgo, she'd found she liked the taste of the pseudolatte that comes from the coffee machine. "It's not the real stuff," she'd told me the first day she tried the drink, "but getting it out of the machine is fun, and it's not much higher than regular coffee. A dime a cup. I can afford a dime a cup, can't I?"

Stella had her Social Security, a bit of retirement, and a little something left from the sale of her house—not enough to pay for Shady Acres without my help, and I couldn't help. But yes, she could definitely afford a dime more a cup for latte.

"You can have all the latte you want," I told her, and I meant it.

If, as she predicted nearly every day, she wasn't long for this world, a dime a cup extra expense wouldn't have a great impact on the budget. Good. I still had my sense of humor. I'd thought it was gone, along with everything else.

"Guess who I saw at the Citgo?"

I couldn't possibly guess. Half the town stopped there every morning.

"Hargus. He must have run out of coffee in his office. He

said he caught Simon stealing avocados down at the Cart Mart."

Words failed me. That nice, retired seaman? Was the world going *nuts?* If you're going to steal something, why bother with avocados?

Stella knew when she had an audience. She stood in the doorway, probably letting flies into the house. "Can you believe it? Hargus does his shopping in the middle of the day because it's not as busy then."

"Stel, what was Simon thinking?"

"Well, Hargus got his cart and went to the produce aisle. Simon was there squeezing the avocados. Anyway, Simon stuck an avocado in his jacket and then headed for the carrots."

"And?"

"Well, Hargus said he started wondering why Simon would put an avocado in his jacket. Hargus kept watching him a little while longer. Simon got a half pound of shaved ham and roast beef at the deli, and ten minutes later, he wheeled his cart to the checkout—not noticing that Hargus was following him."

Stella shrugged, probably wondering how anyone could miss Hargus. "Anyway, Simon had unloaded his groceries at the checkout and started to write a check for his purchases. Hargus left his cart and walked up right next to Simon. Then he said, 'How are things going?' and Simon asked him, 'How're you doing? Any break in the Stover case?' 'Not yet,' Hargus said. Then he moved closer to Simon and said, 'You planning to put those avocados out there to be weighed?' "

Stella paused for effect. "Hargus said Simon blanched white as paste and looked like he would pass out right there in the checkout lane."

Well, I'd reckon so.

But why would a nice man like Simon steal avocados?

5

"**Why on earth** was Simon stealing avocados?" I blurted. The very idea was absurd.

Stella stepped out of the house, letting the screen slam shut. "Well, as it turns out, he wasn't. Hargus saw Simon put the avocados inside his jacket and jumped to conclusions. There ought to be a lesson there. Too many folks jump to conclusions—"

"Who wouldn't?" I interrupted. "If I saw someone sticking an avocado in his jacket, I'd give it a second thought."

"Well, seems Simon didn't want the avocados bruised. He didn't want them rattling around in the cart or squashed by the watermelon he bought."

"Makes perfectly illogical sense."

"So Hargus caused a scene, and Simon was embarrassed."

I could see where he would be, but I didn't have time for this sort of nonsense and the information didn't benefit me. I had been hoping for something to advance my manuscript. I stopped short, distracted by a robin singing in a nearby bush.

Is this what it had come to? Me allowing Stella to drive my story? The idea shook me. I didn't want to believe I was that shallow. I *did* care about my neighbors' and Lucille's invasion of privacy. I did. My job just made me crazy some days.

Stella blinked. "Couldn't you use that in your story? Somewhere? It's too funny to not use. Besides, Hargus collaring Simon at the Cart Mart gave me time to talk to Harold."

Was she reading my mind? Surely I wasn't that transparent. I had to admit it was funny, though. "Harold Stover?"

"Thought he might know something about the Moved Furniture Caper. That's what I'm calling it in my mind."

"Did he?"

"No, but I was thinking he might know someone who had a grudge or wanted to play a joke on Lucille."

"Harold has no sense of humor."

"Oh yes *he* does."

I was astounded. I'd struck a nerve. I'd never seen Stella so bent out of shape. She stiffened like a wounded porcupine, her eyes narrowing in on me like pistols.

"He'd have to have a sense of humor to survive forty-seven years with Lucille. Now, *she's* the one without a sense of humor."

Okay, I had no intention of going there. True, Lucille was a tad serious. It had been said she wouldn't recognize a joke if it crossed the street to greet her, but was that a reason for Stel to indulge in a snit fit?

"I suppose Harold had no clue what happened."

"Couldn't think of a single person who would do something like that. He's like you. Thinks it must have been some kids. Maybe they were scared away before they stole anything." She shrugged. "I don't know. I was just thinking. I think I'll talk to Hargus."

"Can you think a little more quietly? I need to work." I didn't want to hurt her feelings, but this wasn't helping me accomplish anything.

"Sure. I'm not getting involved, you understand. Just trying to be helpful—thought you might use the mystery in your book."

I looked up. Did she know how I was struggling? She'd never seemed particularly perceptive, but the idea that she might be sensitive to my struggle touched me, made me feel a little weepy. "What happens next?" I asked.

"Nothing. There's nothing Hargus can do. Not until it happens again."

I hadn't considered that. *Two* furniture rearrangements? Not a chance. Not in Morning Shade. "Does Hargus think the culprit will strike again?"

"He can't think beyond lunch," Stella sniffed. "This is the first exciting thing that's happened in this town in thirty years, and he's about as useless as a concrete parachute."

"But—"

"He doesn't *know* if it will happen again. Will Lucille be the single victim? Who knows? I want Hargus to keep me informed, and he doesn't. I have to pull information out of him, and it's not easy. Solving this mystery is moving way too slow for my taste."

"Stella, Hargus is in charge of official police business here in Morning Shade—"

She held up one hand to stop me. "I'm not overstepping my bounds. These people are my friends. I can ask questions and maybe get some answers that Hargus can't. Nobody wants to tell *him* anything. You know that."

I did know that, but Hargus was still the law around Morning Shade. Not Stella. "You be careful. Whoever did this at Lucille's might not be so innocuous next time. This could get seriously dangerous."

"Yada, yada, yada. I doubt that, but I'd sure like to know who pulled it off." Her dark eyes twinkled. "Wouldn't you?"

I had to admit I would. More than she'd ever know. But mostly I just wanted Stella to be careful.

Still, she was showing more spark than I'd seen since she came to live here. If trying to solve the mystery gave her pep, what could it hurt? I doubted if there would ever be another break-in. Morning Shade wasn't exactly a hotbed of crime, but maybe I could keep the mystery going. Strictly for Stella's benefit, of course. The effect on my writing didn't enter into it.

Stella stood, using her hands on her knees to push up. "I'd better get these shoes off. My bunions—"

"Okay. Chicken for dinner." I didn't want to talk about bunions either.

Stella left me to wrestle with my characters that were stubbornly taking on the personas of the people in Morning Shade's honest-to-goodness mystery. Well, why not? I at least had words on paper. There was no real harm using the story unfolding right under my nose. Nothing too involved, not all that complicated. Just *something* to work from, and boy, did I need that at this point.

* * *

The baked chicken came out of the oven around six. Fortunately, I'd come to a stopping point in my work (that's what I'm laughingly calling it) in time to hear the buzzer on the oven. CeeCee couldn't hear the timer over the snap of potato chips.

That was a nasty crack. Cee didn't deserve that. She was trying. She was eating three bags of chips a day. Down from five. If that girl doesn't stop eating she's going to be borrowing my clothes.

"Cee, dinner's ready!"

"Coming."

Well, that was a step in the right direction. She was actually getting off the couch. Maybe she would sample meat and vegetables tonight.

Stella shuffled in, her quilted slippers soft on the kitchen floor. "Does that candy in the front room look funny to you?"

"No."

"Hmm. Must be me." She moseyed to the table. "I don't know what Frances is going to do."

"Frances?" I stirred cheese for the broccoli sauce. "What's wrong with Frances?" She'd seemed cheerful enough at the weekly bridge game. Or as cheerful as she got. Frances had never been a barrel of sunshine.

"She's getting old."

"Frances is, what, ten years younger than you?"

"Eight. But her hair is totally white. Have you noticed?"

"It's been white for some time." Over thirty years, I recalled. Had Stella just noticed?

"She calls it blonde."

I bit back a laugh. "Blonde?"

"Says the sun and chlorine bleached her hair when she was swimming a lot so it's turned albino white. But she doesn't say *white;* she says *blonde,"* Stel sniffed.

I laughed out loud, and it felt good. I haven't had a good laugh in a long time. It's been a while since I had something to laugh about. I've read somewhere that laughing releases endorphins that make a person feel better. I'm relieved to find at least my endorphins are intact.

Stella was still on Frances. "Her face looks like a road map . . . even worse than Pansy's. Am I wrinkled? You can tell me the truth; I can take it."

I wouldn't touch that with a ten-foot pole.

"Character lines, she calls them. Citgo's thinking about giving free senior coffee, like McDonald's does. Frances acted like it was an insult, but I say, 'Hey! About time we seniors got something for free.' The government isn't giving us anything but that bogus Social Security check. Three hundred twenty-seven dollars a month. That buys zero-nothing. Generic zero-nothing."

I wasn't about to get Stella onto politics. She had a thing about the government and, at times, rightly so.

"Pansy says we're *mature,* not old."

I poured cheese sauce over the broccoli. "*Mature.* I like that. I remember the first time a bag boy called me ma'am. I was floored. Didn't think I was anywhere near being old enough to be called ma'am. I came home and cried."

Stella cackled. "I was thirty when it happened to me. Had

three-year-old Herb trailing after me. I'd gone to the garage to get the brakes on the car fixed because James was too busy and it had to be done. The mechanic there talked to me like I was a bona fide idiot."

I nodded, remembering similar incidents myself. Like the time I had the oil changed, and the mechanic tried to convince me I needed a new fuel pump. Even I knew the difference between a fuel pump and an oil filter.

"He called me ma'am like I was the grandmother to my boy. I was so mad I refused to go back there again," Stella said.

I laughed again. I couldn't help it. Stella had never been taller than five-foot-two at best. I could picture her dark eyes flashing with anger, see her drawing herself up to her tallest, and telling her six-foot James he'd either fix the brakes next time or she'd sell the car. She'd have done it too. Dynamite wasn't the only explosive that came in small packages.

"Good for you."

CeeCee waddled through the kitchen to the back porch, where her "babies" had languished the afternoon away.

"Come on, sit down, Cee. Dinner's on the table."

To my surprise, she did, and while she picked at her food, a couple bites of chicken and broccoli found their way down her throat.

"When are you going to get a job?"

CeeCee glanced at her grandmother with a stricken look on her face, and my heart sank. The meal had been going so well.

"Job? Why . . . I can't." She couldn't have looked more dumbfounded if Stella had suggested she take part in the Boston Marathon.

"Why not? You're not sick, are you?"

"I–I've never worked full time. I can't do anything." CeeCee wiped a strand of hair out of her face.

Stella kept on. "Who said you can't do anything?"

"I've never done anything." CeeCee sounded hurt that her grandmother would persecute her like this. I wanted to take her part, but I knew Stella was on the right track.

CeeCee's cheeks pinked with either embarrassment or anger. Maybe both. That wasn't all bad. Maybe a little anger would shake her out of her perpetual pity party.

"Doesn't mean you can't. What would you like to do?"

"I don't know—nothing."

She had a head start on that one, I thought, then silently asked for forgiveness. I was getting plain mean-spirited lately.

"Can't sit around the rest of your life and eat vinegar and salt. You need to be productive, do something. Look at me. I had no skills. In my day, girls didn't know anything, didn't expect to work. But I took a job with the power company as a receptionist. Worked for more than forty years and loved it. Made the day long sometimes, but I liked seeing people."

I reached for the chicken. Nothing wrong with my appetite, I noted. It had returned big time. Unfortunately my creativeness was still missing. Stella liked people. No doubt about it. She liked being in the center of things and particularly enjoyed other folks' business. She wasn't all that fond of social activities or shopping, but she certainly enjoyed her daily gossip session at the Citgo.

"I don't want to be—"

"How do you know you don't?" Stella interrupted. "You won't until you try."

"Mom," CeeCee pleaded.

"I agree with Stella."

My mother-in-law looked almost as surprised as I felt agreeing with her. But someone had to bring Cee out of her lethargy. If Stella could pull it off, more power to her. I decided to lend a hand.

"You've got to start living again, do something. Try on a dress and see whether it fits. Get out of the house and meet people. Get back into school . . . put your application in at the post office. You worked there right after college."

"But I didn't finish college."

"Doesn't mean you can't now," Stella said. "Take a few correspondence courses or go to night school."

"You could do that while you're working," I encouraged. "Take a few night classes over in Ash Flat."

CeeCee clammed up, and I knew the conversation had run its course. Rome wasn't built in a day, and Cee's grief wouldn't disappear over a chicken leg.

"Honey," I said, "your dad always said we have two choices in a bad situation: either change the situation, or change ourself."

"You're saying I have to change myself."

"I'm not saying it's going to be easy. But that's usually where we need to start."

She didn't want to hear that, but truth wasn't always pleasant. CeeCee couldn't prevent Jake's death, she couldn't change events. But she could change her attitude.

But then, who couldn't? I know that as I grow older in Christ I need to grow up, stop being so judgmental. I need to find strengths in others and fewer weaknesses. Stella gets on my nerves, but I'm sure I've gotten on hers as well. CeeCee is a cesspool of despair, but I'm a bit like a city sewer myself. I've been so immersed in my own problems I couldn't see the forest for the trees.

Where will the money come from to support this family? When will I hit the best-seller list? Why don't my books sell millions? Did I have my own pity party going here?

At times—most of the time—I don't understand the Lord. I write because I love Him and want to serve Him, don't I? I want to minister to others through my writing, and yet it seems I'm ministering to no one.

On the other hand, what about me? When do I get ministered to? When does something come my way? I know the Bible says to "Give generously, for your gifts will return to you later." Or as I learned it when I was a little girl, "Cast thy bread upon the waters. . . ." I feel like I'm pitching out full slices and getting crumbs in return.

* * *

I had my doubts that CeeCee would suddenly rally and look for work, but the next morning I was surprised to see her up and dressed by ten. Evidently Stella's pep talk had borne fruit. I just hoped it wasn't lemons. She kissed me good-bye before leaving the house, saying she was going to see what the town offered. Ha. Pitiful few jobs, I'm sure, but it was a start.

While she was gone, I rounded up all the sad movies she'd

been watching and returned them to Cart Mart. *Steel Magnolias, The Beach, Love Story*. I had to admit I'd watched *Love Story* with her and shed a few tears myself. But I'd had it up to here with all her bawling about her situation. Something had to change and change now.

Christmas Vacation; now there was a spirit lifter. Cee needed more Clark Griswolds in her life. Any more tears and I'd have to shampoo the carpet to remove the mildew. I hoped she realized the need to change and that her job-hunting efforts would be fruitful.

* * *

Taking advantage of the quiet house, I hurried to my office. I turned on my computer and skimmed what I'd written the day before to get my mind back into my story. *My* story? Morning Shade's story, as it was turning out. I was using some of the characteristics of people I knew, a plot loosely based on the events of the past week and a half, and I was finally seeing progress.

Stella came in just before lunch. I heard her slam the front door, then open and close it more softly. I didn't understand her thinking, but after her prodding CeeCee to get a job, I could hardly find fault with door slamming. I figured I owed her one.

"Hey, Maude?"

"What?"

"There's been another break-in!" Stella's eyes were as wide as saucers. "Minnie Draper's house this time." She sat down. "My word! I never would have thought it would be Minnie!"

"What happened?"

"The same thing as before. Things moved around, draperies removed, pictures taken down. Nothing was stolen."

I racked my brain. "I don't think I know Minnie Draper."

"Minnie Draper? She's that woman who moved here from Egypt a couple of weeks ago. You saw her in church. My, but she's a quiet woman. Her husband had a heart attack and died. He was seventy-nine—younger than me."

"She moved to Morning Shade from *Egypt?"* That beat all I'd ever heard. Of course, the Middle East was full of terrorists now, but . . . moving to Arkansas?

"Egypt, Arkansas."

"Oh," I said. "Egypt, *Arkansas."* A small burg close to Rogers, Arkansas. She'd thrown me there for a minute.

Stella wagged her head. "Poor Minnie. Never got past the hat-and-gloves-for-church way she was raised."

I hid a grin. Stella had just recently begun to feel comfortable not wearing a hat and gloves to church, and women wearing pants or short skirts to Sunday morning worship service were enough to give her spiritual heartburn. I'd heard her mutter the word *Jezebel* a couple of times.

"I suppose there are no clues."

"Not a one."

"How did they get into her house?"

"Through the front door." Stella shook her head. "Seems Minnie didn't lock the house before she went to dinner at the Elks Club. *Tsk, tsk.* Doesn't she know how to throw a bolt? Someone just walked up and tried the door, then went in. That doesn't make sense. Seems to me it must be someone who knew Minnie and knows she would be at the Elks'."

I thought the same, but I let the gumshoe continue.

Stella pursed her lips. "That raises a lot of questions."

"Wonder what Hargus is thinking . . ." I prompted.

"Trust me, Hargus is confused."

Stella's opinion of Hargus was steadfastly negative. Had to give it to her. Once Stel made up her mind about something or someone, she didn't waffle; but she was probably right this time.

Two break-ins in Morning Shade? The wheels began to turn, and I could hardly wait to get back to work. Hot dog! A crime spree in Morning Shade!

* * *

By midafternoon I had written six pages, so I decided to get myself a celebratory soda from the kitchen. I found an opened bag of chips on the cabinet, and in a fit of pique at CeeCee for wasting her life eating junk food, I tossed the bag in the trash. Then, before I could stop myself, I ferreted out four more bags and dumped them as well, along with two packages of Ding Dongs, a quart of Rocky Road ice cream I'd love to have eaten myself, and two cartons of French onion dip. If Cee was going to eat herself into a dress two sizes larger than she currently wore, she wasn't going to do it on my dime. She'd have to support her own habit.

Stella went to her room to rest around three o'clock. CeeCee hadn't returned yet, which gave me hope that she had found a job. Something that would help her get back on track with her life. It didn't matter at this point if she had a "career." Right now she just needed a reason to get up and out of the house every morning.

I went back to the computer and tinkered with my pages. The characters I'd loathed had begun to have a reason for being in the story. Conversation and narrative started to make sense. It was a miracle and I reveled in it.

So would my creditors when the bills were paid on time . . . if I ever got this book finished.

CeeCee returned around four with a quivering lip. She'd put an application in at "every store in town" but had gotten no hopeful responses. Some said outright that they weren't hiring. Others said they'd keep her resume, such as it was, on file for six months.

"Nobody has a job for me," CeeCee lamented over tuna casserole that evening.

"Something will turn up," I encouraged, though I had my doubts. There weren't a lot of job offers in Morning Shade. She might have to venture farther out.

Burton wandered into the kitchen, slurped a quart of water, and turned those soft, reflective eyes in my direction. I wasn't fond of Burton, but he did tend to mind his own business, which consisted of eating, sleeping, and scratching. He was nicely housebroken, too, which was more than could be said of Frenchie, the poodle, or the Rainmaker, as I preferred to call him. He may have been housebroken when he came here, as Cee claimed, but he had forgotten all he knew. Which, considering his mental process, wasn't difficult to believe.

CeeCee had only worked briefly for the postal service—

maybe six months, when she was nineteen. Then she'd met and married Jake and lived in luxury. She'd never lived in the real world and I didn't want her to. The real world hurt too much sometimes, and yet I knew she couldn't be protected forever. We must live in the real world. There really is no other, and I want my daughter to learn to cope with real life because that's the way we grow.

We gain spiritual confidence when we have to trust God for the strength to face whatever life throws our way. I wasn't enjoying learning this lesson myself, but I was slowly coming around. CeeCee had been raised to go to church, but somewhere in her life with Jake church had fallen by the wayside. While I had my faith to hold on to, Cee had nothing. I had tried to talk to her about trusting God to help her, but she wouldn't listen.

"You may have to go out of town," Stella said.

As in the great metropolis of Ash Flat? I thought. There might be a few more openings there, but not all that many, and we weren't close to any large town where job opportunities would be more plentiful.

"I'm going to my room," CeeCee said.

I was glad I'd tossed the chips and dips. She would have foundered tonight otherwise. Fortunately, she didn't have the energy to go to Cart Mart for more junk food.

Even despair has an upside.

* * *

"Those tomatoes are not garden grown. I don't care what the sign says," Pansy muttered Friday morning, pushing her cart through the produce section with Simon and Frances following.

I grabbed a cart and followed Stella. The old friends had met at the front door and grouped together. I had discovered I was out of sugar, and Stella wanted to see whether there were any peaches in the store yet, though I sensed she really wanted to check out the latest gossip on the two mysterious break-ins.

"What's new on the cases?" Stella asked, going right for the throat of the issue.

"Nothing," Pansy said. "My boy Hargus says there's nothing to do now but wait to see if another incident happens."

"I hope the intruder will strike again soon if he's going to." Stella poked at the strawberries.

"Maybe it will be Vivian Parson's living room next." Frances sniffed a melon. "Vivian's taste is all in her mouth."

I held my breath, hoping someone would start a guessing game. Good old Pansy came to the rescue.

"I'd vote for Connie Fortis," Pansy said. "If she puts another thing in that yard of hers she can sell her lawn mower. Hargus says it's the town eyesore. A few flamingos, a gazing ball, one or two birdbaths is okay, but you can overdo that kind of stuff real easy."

"I agree," Stella seconded, popping a grape into her mouth. "She was doing okay until last summer then she went on a rampage. But I'd go with Margaret Post. I'm surprised that house doesn't have a fungus. Now, I like plants, but Margaret ought to get a greenhouse. She's got some sort of fern, spider plant, fichus or something stuck in every corner or hung from hooks in front of every window.

"I think the drapes probably have aphids. They haven't been changed since 1954. If someone went in there and hung new draperies it would be a blessing."

I smothered a snort as I followed the troop to the checkout lane. Margaret has not only a green thumb but a green hand. The problem is she keeps all the plants she starts. She has a beautiful perennial garden behind her house, but houseplants are her passion. Margaret loves them, croons to them like they were the babies she never had, and shares cuttings with friends and neighbors.

"I'd vote for Shirley Shupbach," Simon contributed. "I was helping Sam install a new garbage disposal and noticed their furniture was covered with plastic. I saw an old sitcom once, *Happy Days* or something, where Annette Funicello appeared as a clean-freak housewife and had the furniture all covered with plastic, with plastic runners on the floor. It was funny then, but Shirley's carried the phobia too far. I like order, but . . ."

Stella's inquiry had brought up all sorts of eccentric personalities to consider in the context of who might be next, if and when the break-in artist struck again. I considered taking notes, but I didn't want to be too obvious.

"Shirley is a corker," Frances agreed. "Visiting her is an experience. In the summer you stick to the couch; in the winter you could get frostbite, if you know what I mean. And that plastic runner trips me every time. Dangerous. It's like walking on that bubble-packing stuff."

"So, you think any one of those could be a target for the burglar?" Stella began digging in her purse for money.

"In Morning Shade there's a whole list of candidates," Pansy said.

Stella's fumbling search halted. "I just wonder where the burglar got the things he added to Lucille's and Minnie's houses? Those drapes, for instance."

"Catalog shopping?" Pansy ventured. "eBay?"

"Well, he didn't get those drapes in Morning Shade. They had to come from Jonesboro or maybe Little Rock," Stella speculated. "What if the burglar vandalized your room, Frances?"

"It would depend on what he did," Frances said. "I have my priceless treasures from my students, and I wouldn't want those thrown in a box and stuffed in a closet."

Personally—and I wasn't being catty—I thought it would be a blessing if someone cleaned up that living room, but then, that was just me. I couldn't work up much passion for tattered handwritten notes or figurines bearing a sign saying Number One Teacher. I guess Frances had earned every one of those "priceless treasures," so who was I to criticize?

It's just that I've never liked clutter. I had some of CeeCee's school mementoes, but they were packed away in a trunk for her to share with her children at some future time. I was sure she would marry again, start a family. She was too young to stop living, and I prayed she wouldn't let this experience with Jake taint her whole life. Job hunting hadn't gone well and she was depressed again. I hoped something would come along for her—and soon.

"I wish the burglar would pick my room," Pansy said. "I like change."

"Well, I don't," Frances returned. "I have enough change in my life."

"What change?" Pansy queried. "Our lives are the same day after day after day. Oh, I do get to water the Prescotts' plants while they're off to visit their daughter. They left the key to their house with me."

She sounded rather proud about the opportunity to serve.

"Not my life. There're things going on in this town that would curl your hair. I wish I knew what I've done with my check," Stella complained, half to herself.

"We're rich, you know," Frances stated.

Pansy bit. "Rich?"

"Silver in our hair, gold in our teeth." She giggled.

"Lead in our pants," Stella droned.

"I live in the hereafter," Simon said dryly. "Every time I go somewhere I have to stop and think, *Now what am I here after?* And I've stopped lying about my age. Now I'm bragging about it."

I hoped when I was their age I would have their attitude. They were a hoot. The group moved through the line with their purchases of denture cream, aspirin, and whole-grain, fibrous foods.

"Some might try to turn back their odometers but not me," Stella said. "I want people to know why I look like this. I earned every one of these wrinkles. Now if I could only remember how."

"I'm over the hill and proud of it," Frances conceded.

And I moaned about reaching sixty. Maybe I needed a reality check.

On the way home Stella and I decided an ice-cream cone sounded good. A double dip of chocolate custard would put the starch back in our day . . . and our diets.

We licked and slurped happily as we got into the car and pointed the old Buick toward home. We'd just turned the corner when Stella hit the automatic window button. I knew she was about to propel her gum out the window with a big *blip*. She chewed denture gum in the hopes it would use up some energy.

I heard the *blip*, then—

"Uh-oh."

I glanced over to see Stella, front lip sucked in, staring at me.

"What's wrong?" I wiped at sticky chocolate running down my wrist while keeping the car on the road.

"I spit out my upper plate."

"You . . . you spit out your upper plate?"

The car veered off to the shoulder, and I yanked it back before realizing we had to stop and hunt for Stella's teeth.

It took fifteen minutes to find the plate and get Stella calmed down. Unfortunately, the plate had broken in half. We spent another hour and a half at Doc Price's office, getting the plate glued together . . . not to mention we lost two perfectly good ice-cream cones.

What a morning! Who said Morning Shade was boring?

By the time we got home, Stella had moved past the episode with the teeth and was once again occupied with the mysteries.

"You think the burglar will strike a third time?" I asked her. It would be a pretty daring, in-your-face confrontation.

"Why not?"

I was ashamed of myself for hoping she was right. My burst of inspiration had a lot in common with lightning. A couple of brilliant flashes and it was all over. I needed more.

I checked the temperature on the thermostat, lowered it a notch, and then went upstairs to see about Cee. I tapped on her door. "Cee? Are you all right?"

"I'm fine." Her nasal response carried through the door. She'd been crying again.

"I thought sloppy joes for lunch."

"Whatever."

"Why don't you come out and visit while I fry hamburger? The dogs need walking."

"I'll be out soon."

I didn't believe her, but what was I going to do? I couldn't physically drag her from the depression she was mired in, though I surely wished I could.

"Do you have those whole-wheat buns?" Stella asked as she padded behind me into the kitchen. "I have to watch my cholesterol, you know."

"Bought some yesterday." I tossed a pound of lean hamburger into the skillet and salted it. "Who do you think went into Minnie's house?" Stella might be in her eighties, but she has a mind like a steel trap. If anyone could figure this out, she could.

"Beats me." She sat at the table and toyed with the salt-and-pepper shakers. "Seems real odd . . . there's a lot of people in Morning Shade."

Well, yes. You couldn't argue with that. But why that

particular house and why just rearrange the furniture? For that matter, why the new lamps? Most burglars hoped to make a profit. This one operated at a loss.

"I think the more relevant question is why would anyone pick such a bizarre act?" My observations were self-serving—to prime the pump, but the story demanded the facts, and at this point all I had was speculation. I needed something solid. I adjusted the heat under the skillet of hamburger. "I've never seen Minnie's house. Have you?"

"Once. It could stand some attention."

"I find it odd, extremely odd, that someone suddenly decides to move furniture around and hang new drapes in a stranger's house. What kind of a compulsion is that?"

"The drive to color-coordinate?" Stella offered.

The woman did have a sense of humor. I had to give her that.

6

"The Crier's late." Stella groused about the paperboy as she came in from her trek down the front walk. "How difficult can it be to deliver a newspaper?"

"Carl might have had trouble printing it," I reminded her. Carl Summit and his wife operated the small weekly edition, and their grandson, Jacob, delivered. The Summits' grandson was sweet. A little careless with his aim, but throwing papers from a rolling bicycle couldn't be easy. I didn't want Stella down on the thirteen-year-old.

I poured my first cup of coffee of the day and dumped Shredded Wheat into a bowl. Since it was Saturday I planned to try to do something in the yard, something to salvage the mess CeeCee's "babies" had made. What few flowers had bravely stuck their arms through the sod had been savaged by my canine guests.

CeeCee yawned as she wandered into the kitchen. I nearly fainted from shock and glanced at the clock to confirm that it wasn't much past seven: 7 A.M. With Cee sleeping until noon every day I momentarily thought I had my days and nights confused.

Clearly my daughter wasn't accustomed to the change either. She padded on bare feet to the back porch to let the babies out for their morning run. When she came back through the kitchen, I handed her a mug of black coffee. I didn't want to squelch the amazing feat of her early rising. Still wearing a much-washed nightshirt, she sat at the end of the table, cradling her mug.

"What are your plans for the day?" I asked. Nicely. No pressure in my tone.

"Job hunting. I guess I need to widen my circle. There doesn't seem to be anything in town. I'll go to Evening Shade first. I might have to go as far north as Love, though I doubt there's anything there not already taken by high school kids." She sipped her coffee. "Do you know how embarrassing it is to apply for jobs that sixteen-year-olds can do better than I can?"

"Something will come along," I tried to assure her, though I wasn't certain it would. Not in this town. Probably not in Evening Shade or Love, either.

"You applied at the electric company?"

"Yes, Grandma. I filled out an application and left a resume. I don't think there's anything there."

"Don't give up. Keep calling back."

"I know, Grandma."

I met CeeCee's pleading glance, but all I could do was smile my encouragement. Just making the effort to find a job was an improvement, and I didn't want to do anything to stop the momentum.

"Forty-five years I spent there. Really liked that job. Saw everyone coming in, everyone leaving. Did you tell them I'm your grandma?"

"I did. . . . There's a lot of new faces since you worked there." CeeCee brightened. "Grace Smith remembered you."

"Never did like Grace. She's a busybody if there ever was one. Well, don't give up. That's the definition of success. Not giving up."

I coaxed a piece of toast with apple butter down Cee, then sent her off to get dressed.

Stella remained at the table, drinking her second cup of coffee. "Cee shouldn't feel so down about herself," she observed. "I'm eighty-seven. My life is over. My days are numbered. She's just beginning her life. She should be happy, looking forward to every day. She's young, healthy—"

"She just lost her husband. Her life has been turned upside down, and she has a lot to deal with right now. Don't make it harder for her."

"God will take care of her problems."

"You and I know that, Stel, and somewhere deep inside her Cee knows that too. But at the moment it might be easier to say than to do." And we all said it far too glibly. God did take care of our problems, but it wasn't always that easy. Sometimes we had to go through a storm to reach the sunshine. That storm could be a strong head wind or a full-scale hurricane. CeeCee's problem fell somewhere in between.

"Horsefeathers! You know that all you've got to do is trust."

Trust. Perhaps Stella had reached the age where faith was as simple as breathing, but I was sixty and still having problems with it. I believed God wanted me to write Christian books or I wouldn't be doing it. Or I did at one time. Lately I've been wondering if I called myself into the ministry because I love Him and want to serve Him.

Is there a difference?

I believe there is. It only stands to reason that if He called me, the words would be there. He never calls anyone into His service without providing the grace and ability needed to get the job done. And right now, if it wasn't for Lucille Stover's problem (which she doesn't consider a problem) I would be wordless. Never without grace, but certainly without a story.

Now what does that tell me? Surely there is a lesson here. But I'm blind. Blinded by the need to put food on the table, take care of my family, and meet deadlines. Always deadlines.

"I agree Cee needs to trust, Stel, but sometimes there's a huge gap between believing in God and believing God."

"I suppose there's an advantage to having lived as long as I have. Believing God is a necessity, not a choice." She pushed herself to her feet. "I'm going to the Citgo."

"You don't have to. After I work, maybe we can go for a walk." I have neglected her. She's lonely.

"Aw, Maude, getting old stinks. I'm too old to work anymore. My eyes aren't good enough to quilt or knit or crochet, even if I was interested in that sort of thing. I'm pretty useless to anyone—"

"Stella, you can't feel that way. As long as there is breath there should be life. Joyful life. God isn't through with you yet, young lady."

"Tell me that when your bones are aching, when your feet hurt, when your friends are all passing on before you."

"But you have Pansy and Frances and Simon."

"Uh-huh, and I'm under your feet, a burden you don't need—"

"You're not a burden."

I get irritated with her from time to time, but she's Herb's mother, and I can't honestly say I don't like her. I do like Stella, when she isn't feeling sorry for herself. My only problem with the current situation is the three of us under one roof when we have such different interests, and worrying about paying the bills with only my income. That's natural, isn't it? I know God will provide my needs, but being the sole support of anything raises my red flag.

"I'm old; that's what I am," Stella said. "CeeCee is just starting her life, no matter what's happened. She has a future, once she begins to realize that things will be different for her. You've got a career, one that won't make you retire when you're sixty-five. My life is finished."

I sat across from her, noticing anew how rounded her shoulders were, how frail her hands were. But there was still a lot of life left in Stella Diamond, if she'd just quit feeling sorry for herself.

The slap of the newspaper against the front door must have reminded Stella that she hadn't checked the obituaries yet today. I finished my coffee while she read the deaths.

"Joseph Bennett died; did you know that?"

"No, Stel, I didn't know Mr. Bennett."

"He was only eighty-one."

"Then he lived a full life."

"I'm eighty-seven. Not too many days left for me."

"You've got more life in you than half the people in town."

Her response was to rattle the pages of the paper. I hoped they weren't too wrinkled for me to read once she was finished.

* * *

"Hey, Maude?"

I cringed and bit down hard on my lower lip. No matter that it was Monday morning, that my door was closed, that I'd posted a big DO NOT DISTURB UNLESS YOU'RE ON FIRE sign. Stella didn't get it. I *am* working. Why couldn't she respect my work hours? For the first time in quite a while I was feeling good about my work. *Thank You, God.* But I was also a little anxious to hear what Stella had learned about Lucille's and Minnie's break-ins. Maybe I had another piece to the puzzle.

"Come in."

Stella tiptoed in, as if that was going to make a difference, and perched on the edge of the chair she habitually took. "Guess what?"

I turned from my computer after saving the material I'd been working on. "What?"

"Minnie is *not* happy about what the burglar did to her house last week."

My eyebrows lifted in surprise. "What did she do?" *She? I've decided the burglar is a woman?* Not really, but I couldn't see a man rearranging furniture. The only time Herb noticed

I'd moved furniture was one night when he went to a union meeting and I rearranged the bedroom. He came in without turning on the lights and sat down on a bed that wasn't there. I don't think he ever fully trusted me after that.

"Well . . ." Stella seemed totally in her element now. Nothing thrilled her more than a good story. "I didn't get to talk to Minnie yet—she's still too upset—but everything we heard seems to be true. Her drapes were taken down. Folded very nicely, mind you, but put on a shelf in the closet. And the pictures were taken down . . . the ones her husband liked so much. Mostly fish and wildlife. Minnie believed in hanging the pictures in a straight line along the wall. Looked like a gallery of some sort, if you ask me, which no one did. Still, it was boring. And she kept every picture of everyone. Didn't take any down, just kept adding to the line."

"So the burglar took those down?"

She nodded. "All but the designer prints Minnie's daughter bought her for Christmas. Don't know how he knew that, but apparently he did. Stored the others in Minnie's attic. Isn't that odd?"

"Minnie's furious," I guessed.

"She had a full-blown conniption fit."

"Is that all that was done?" My curiosity was thoroughly aroused now. Furniture moved. Drapes taken down. Pictures rearranged. That'd give most folks the willies.

"No. Minnie had throw rugs covering the carpet in front of every chair, every entrance, even in front of the TV. Those were taken up and put in the attic. The culprit must not like throw rugs. I don't know why Minnie does that. She's got lovely carpet. And it's not as if she's had time to wear it any. Anyway, that—added to the picture thing—got her incensed. And then—" Stella hesitated dramatically—"there was a nice crystal vase and candles put on the mantel. And the candy in a dish on the coffee table was changed from jelly beans to sugar-free hard candy." Stella cackled delightedly. "Can you believe it?"

"No—" I shook my head—"I can't." Actually, I found it a trifle insulting. I wouldn't want any phantom burglar dropping hints about my weight. Some things were sacred. Evidently Minnie felt the same.

"Minnie's a few pounds overweight, you know. Since her husband died she's quit cooking and become addicted to fast food, whether it's something cooked in the microwave or bought at McDonald's. It doesn't matter. Minnie always says she spent forty years cooking and she isn't doing it anymore."

I knew the evils of fast food. Before Herb died we were junkies. My doctor had warned me rather sternly about watching my cholesterol, eating a low-fat diet, no sugars, the last time I'd gone for my annual physical.

If I remembered Minnie, she was a square little woman who habitually wore large-patterned dresses, not at all becoming. Strange the mystery burglar had not been in sync with Minnie's decorating faux pas. He'd been right on target at Lucille's house.

"So, Minnie's very upset?" That seemed a reasonable guess, under the circumstances.

"From what I was told, she's furious."

"Well, I'm sure she's insulted by what the burglar did."

"Maybe . . . Minnie is another who could stand some help in the decorating area. You know, Maude, I love my children and I love my grandchildren, but when I get a new picture, the old one goes in an album and the new one goes in the frame. That way I see how they've grown over the years."

"What about the rugs on the carpet? Herb never liked 'layering,' as he called it."

"Got that from me. I bought good carpet. I changed the furniture around to avoid a wear pattern. I did put a rug at the back door so James would wipe his feet before he tracked something in on the carpet, but that was the only place."

"I still wonder where the burglar gets these vases and candles and such." Why would a burglar spend his or her own money to buy items for someone else's house? Why would he care about that person's decorating problems? What we had here was a burglar with a sense of humor. Which definitely left out Lucille, since according to Stella, Lucille was humorously challenged. I thought about it. That didn't sound right. I'd never been able to master politically correct.

"Has to be catalog shopping, or else he goes to a larger town. Lucille's house and now Minnie's place. Someone who knows both women; I'd bet on it."

"Maybe you could make a list of people who know both ladies," I suggested.

"That would be a long list," Stella said.

Well, she had a point there. Lucille Stover was a real gadfly.

Stella pushed to her feet. "I'm going to chew Hargus out—

I don't care if it does upset Pansy. That twerp's got to get up off his chair and do something! This is getting serious."

"He doesn't want you butting in on this case," I warned.

Hargus could only be pushed so far, and Stella was nearing the limit. He didn't like butt-in-skis.

And he did have that chain saw.

Stella's chin shot up. "He'll talk to me. After all, these women are my friends and I'm concerned about them."

I figured that was as good a reason as any. Stella took off for the Citgo, and I returned to my computer, where I added this new information to my manuscript, and began to work with it. I was building the story one burglary at a time.

A couple of hours later I heard CeeCee come downstairs and putter around in the kitchen.

"Mom?"

"Come in, honey."

CeeCee was already dressed in nice slacks (slacks that fit a little more snugly today than they did last week) and a cotton sweater.

"I'm going to hang out with Iva Hinkle this afternoon."

"Iva? From the post office?"

"Yeah."

Iva had been Morning Shade's postmistress for four years. The new brick post office had been built two years ago, and Iva was so proud of it. A big American flag flew in front of the building. Every time I passed that patriotic symbol I had an urge to stand up and say the Pledge of Allegiance.

CeeCee and Iva were three years apart in age so I guess the friendship made sense. Iva was a plain sort . . . not a boy magnet, but she was good as gold. Took care of her invalid mother and never complained. Other than church on Wednesdays and Sundays, Iva stayed pretty close to home, so I imagine Cee is sort of like a celebrity to her. That's good. Iva needed a little spice in her life, though I don't know how she puts up with Cee's behavior lately.

"Have a nice time, honey, and call me if you need anything."

"I will." She hesitated. "I know I'm a drag, Mom."

"You're going to be all right. Give yourself a little time." I pray she will be. So far she's made only a baby step forward by job hunting, but hey, it's a step in the right direction.

"I don't know if I will or not." Her eyes teared. "I'll ask at the Cart Mart again to see if they need anybody."

"Attitude is a choice, honey. Remember that. Make the choice to be happy."

She nodded and closed the door softly. I worry about her, but there's little I can do except give her a soft place to land. I don't think it's healthy to let her nestle for too long before she begins to move on with her life.

But then, that's me. One thing in my favor is that I didn't have the chance to nestle. By the time I'd got my financial mess straightened out, Stella had moved in and the nest had started to fill.

* * *

The phone interrupted my train of thought about three that afternoon.

"Miz Diamond?"

"Yes." *If this is a telemarketer, I'm going to rip the phone out of the wall.*

"Hargus Conley."

Now I recognized his voice. I don't think I'd ever heard him on the phone before. "What can I do for you, Hargus?"

"Stella's in my office—"

Of course she was. Stella was questioning Hargus about Minnie's break-in.

"—because she was found sneaking around the Draper house, peering in the windows."

"What?"

"Minnie called me and—"

"You found Stella peering in windows?"

"Yes, ma'am. Minnie doesn't want to press charges—"

"I'd think not! She knows Stella doesn't mean any harm. It's these stupid mysteries, Hargus." Though who knew what the real reason was for Stella's impropriety. I stood up, knocking the thesaurus to the floor.

"Yes, ma'am. Can you come get your mother-in-law?"

"Give me ten minutes."

I didn't know what was going on, but one thing was for sure—Stella was going to hear about this from me. This time she had gone too far.

When I arrived, breathless and with my shirttail hanging out, Stella was sitting primly in a wooden chair across from Hargus's desk in the narrow office next to the Kut 'n' Kurl. Her thin mouth was drawn in a firm line that said Hargus had definitely overstepped.

"Stella, what's going on?"

She turned her palms up innocently. "I went to see Minnie. Nobody answered the door, so I peeked in the living-room window to see what the room looked like without drapes . . . and Minnie came home and saw me and—" her mouth firmed again—"the *idiot* called Hargus!"

Hargus pushed back in his chair, stood up, and jacked up his trousers. "Miz Diamond, can't you do something with her? She's gettin' in my hair."

"What hair?" Stella crossed her arms.

I stepped in. "Stella isn't going to be charged with anything, is she?"

"No, Minnie doesn't want to press charges, but she doesn't want Stella looking in her windows anymore."

"She won't," I assured him. "Can we leave now?"

"Yes, ma'am." He turned to face Stella. "Don't you be messin' around Minnie's house, or anybody else's house. You let me do the investigatin' here."

Stella stood with her purse in front of her like a shield. For someone who had been caught acting like a Peeping Tom, she was awfully spunky. I hoped she didn't talk her way into a jail cell.

"Then you'd better get on the stick," she said, "because people aren't happy about someone breaking into their houses and moving their things around. Makes people feel unsafe." She pointed a slightly crooked forefinger. "If you want to keep this job—"

Hargus hitched his trousers again, for what little good it did. "You just let me do my job, Miz Diamond."

"You don't have a job, Hargus."

"Stella," I warned, sensing war was about to break out.

"Do so! What'd you call my chain-saw art!"

"Chain-saw art," Stella said.

"And sheriffin'," Hargus claimed.

"Horsefeathers."

Hargus looked at me as if to say, "Get this woman out of here," which I did.

"I was right," Stella announced in the car. "Everybody is upset about these burglaries now. Everybody."

"You peeked in Minnie's window and still had time to talk to others about this?" She was one busy woman.

"Everybody who came in Citgo was upset about Minnie's break-in. They don't think Hargus has a clue about who's doing this. Something's got to be done."

"Is that why you were peering in Minnie's window? You can't do that, you know."

"Oh, come on. Minnie was just upset about what happened to her and didn't recognize me or she'd never have called Hargus. She told me she doesn't think he knows anything either.

"She's hot as a two-dollar pistol that someone came into her house, mad that they took down her pictures, mad that they took down her draperies. She's put every bit of it back, including the throw rugs."

"I don't blame her. A man's home is his castle." *And a woman's living room is off-limits.*

"Every bit of it," Stella repeated. "Took down the candles, put the vase away, put the rugs back in place, and hung her pictures back where they belonged. If you ask me, I think she's being a little thin-skinned about it. Knowing Minnie, I'm sure whoever did this improved the look of her living room."

"Well, it is her living room. She has a right to arrange it the way she wants. The question is, who is doing this?"

"That's the problem. I don't think Hargus will find out."

"But *you* will," I guessed. Or she was going to bust her bustle trying.

She shrugged. "Don't hurt to ask around, pry a little. You know that I'm curious by nature."

"I know." I'd have to give her that. Age hadn't slowed her curiosity bump. I couldn't fault her for wanting to help her friends, either, especially when I needed material so badly. But she couldn't invade others' privacy.

"You must be careful, Stella. Whoever is doing this doesn't seem dangerous, but if you confront him—"

"I'm just going to ask some questions."

Of course. She's just going to ask questions. As usual, it would take an act of God to stop her. She takes her orders from the top and nowhere else.

CeeCee's car was at the curb when we got home. Her bedroom door was closed. Obviously her inquiry at Cart Mart had not gone well.

* * *

I expected CeeCee to spend the next day in her room. As a matter of fact, I had expected her to spend the next week in her room, watching sad movies and drowning her sorrow in vinegar and salt. But she surprised me. Instead, she came down for breakfast and even helped with the cleanup. Later we went out to the backyard and tried to repair the damage done by her babies.

The dogs had dug three fresh holes in the lawn. One each. Although I suspected the poodles had helped Burton with his burrowing project. I doubted if he could have summoned the energy. Besides, he seemed to operate on the principle of doing as little as possible and getting someone else to bear the brunt of the work. Reminded me of Hargus.

My backyard looked like a crime scene. I wondered if I could work that into my novel. CeeCee pitched in and helped fill the holes. We pulled weeds out of the flower beds, which made them look better. I wished I had bought new plants, but it would have been money and time wasted as long as the dogs had the use of the yard.

The poodles, apparently excited by the change in their routine, ran circles around us, yapping until I wanted to swat them. I didn't, though, because I was so happy to see my daughter doing something besides crying and eating. The fresh air brought color to her cheeks and brightened her eyes. She laughed a few times, the way she used to before Jake Tamaris walked into her life. I wanted to cry.

Burton waddled over to inspect our work, shoving his face close to mine, tongue lolling out and his rear end wagging. I scrambled backward, fighting for air.

His breath would gag a goat.

That afternoon CeeCee met Iva after work, planning to drive to Ash Flat for dinner and a movie. Stella wandered back to the Citgo for a second helping of gossip, and I headed to my office.

I zeroed in on my manuscript, testing several scenarios. The plot's moving . . . barely, but it is moving. I feel better than I have in a long time. Maybe there's a ray of light at the end of the tunnel. Just a flicker, but enough to give me hope. I wrote three pages and felt good about it.

* * *

Sunday morning Stella and I went to church. CeeCee joined us for breakfast, still wearing her sleep shirt, but her hair was combed and she didn't look so moody. She refused to go to church with us, and I didn't insist. When she decided to go, it had to be her decision, not mine.

Living Truth sanctuary was full when we got there. After saying hello to several friends, we found our seats and settled down minutes before the service began.

The church of ninety members was a simple structure originally built a hundred years ago. The kitchen had burned in the early 1900s and been restored to the original design. The sanctuary was one long room with a pine-paneled ceiling supported by carved arched beams—workmanship that you don't see much anymore. The windows are tall and narrow with arched tops. Pews are padded and rather comfortable.

The congregation was fairly conservative. So far Stella hadn't jumped up to shout "amen" at the wrong time, but I kept waiting for it.

The sermon that morning made me squirm. Pastor Healy preached on God's plan for success. According to him, God wants us to succeed. A concept I hadn't considered before. God charts our lives before we are born, and He puts us where He wants us until our time for success has come. Our job is to be obedient. That's success on God's terms. Probably not the same as success on mine.

Like Moses, who was abandoned on the river in a flimsy homemade boat, grew up living away from his family, was a fugitive because of a little case of murder, kept sheep for forty years, and then when God needed him, he was right there, ready to take on the task with a little prodding from the great I AM. Now, I'll grant you that's a success story, but how does it apply to my life?

Was I where God wanted me to be, trying to tell people about Him through my stories? Did that mean God was biding His time before having me burst on the scene with a book so dazzling, so well crafted, it would hit the best-seller list at the speed of a New York minute?

Probably not, but it sure made for one pulse-racing daydream.

Because I felt so good about my work at the moment, I spent Sunday afternoon working in the backyard and fighting off CeeCee's babies.

I think I'll abandon the project as long as the dogs are here.

* * *

By Monday morning I'd taken a stance. I'm not heartless, but I'm giving CeeCee a couple more days and then we're having a come-to-Jesus meeting about her attitude. If I'd heard Elvis sing "Heartbreak Hotel" once this past weekend, I'd heard him sing it a hundred times.

At midmorning the phone interrupted my train of thought. When Cee didn't answer it, I picked up the receiver.

"Maude?"

My agent. "Jean! Hello."

"Just wanted to check your deadline. It's October 1, isn't it?"

I didn't want to look, but that sounded right. I was dreadfully behind.

"Everything going smoothly?"

"Fine, Jean. The book is coming right along." *Liar, liar!*

"Maude, Jack's still looking for a ghostwriter. He's holding out for you. Will you at least consider the opportunity?"

I was about to refuse for a third time when she mentioned the amount of the advance royalties the publisher was offering. "You're kidding." I hadn't made that much money in my whole career. Well, I had—but never in one lump sum.

"That's why I think you should consider it," Jean said. "Think really hard, Maude."

Actually, I couldn't think of anything else the rest of the day. At one the phone rang again. I prayed it wasn't Jean. The offer sounded tempting and I hadn't written a paragraph today. "Hello?"

"May I speak to CeeCee Tamaris?"

"Yes, just a moment."

I knocked on CeeCee's door. "Phone call for you."

"Who is it?"

"I don't know, Cee." I don't ask for identification when someone calls.

"Be there in a sec."

She shuffled past me to go pick up the phone in the kitchen.

A few minutes later she burst into my office, her face alight. "Mom! That was the post office! They want me to take a test."

"A test! For what?" I immediately thought of terrorists and anthrax. Had Cee opened any unusual package? I didn't think so—

"There's a rural route open, and Iva pulled strings to get me an interview."

Well, praise the Lord and Iva Hinkle! I hugged her close. "Maybe this is the break you're looking for."

"I hope so." She hugged me back. "I've got to get dressed."

"Let the dogs out before you leave," I called.

She waved as she headed upstairs to shower and change clothes. I left my office and went to the kitchen for a Coke. This called for a celebration.

Stella poked her head in not long after CeeCee left in a whirlwind. I was still sitting at the table. "Anything new?"

"The postal service wants Cee to take a test." I supposed Iva would have a lot to do with Cee getting on full time. The main office would send the postmistress three or four qualified candidates' names, and she'd be obligated to offer each one the opportunity to apply for the position. But most folks wouldn't want to move to Morning Shade even if it meant a promotion. I figured Cee had a great chance of getting the job.

"I mean anything new on Minnie's break-in."

Of course. First things first. "Not that I know about."

"Well, Cee should be happy." Stella poured a glass of apple juice and dribbled it across the clean linoleum. I got a rag and wiped up the spill.

Stel didn't notice. "Minnie's on a tear. Real peeved that Hargus took me in."

I had to wonder about Hargus's power of reasoning. Short of blatant armed robbery, there'd be no way I'd cast suspicion on an eighty-seven-year-old woman, even if I did catch her window peeping. I'd settle the confusion on the spot.

"She's really rattled by the break-in. So's Lucille. Both are rattled." She took a swallow of juice. "Rattled as you can get."

Okay, already. The women are rattled! Could we give it a rest?

"We talked about Lucille's break-in," Stella said. "Minnie agrees that Lucille's living room looks better, but can't see that the burglar improved hers at all." She shrugged. "What's that old saying? There's none so blind as those who will not see?"

"Well, the break-ins are certainly strange for a town this size. You'd think someone would have seen something." We don't have a lot of traffic, but people are out there, working, walking their dogs, keeping track of their neighbors. I mean, sneeze on Saturday and by Sunday everyone in town knows you have a cold. There are no secrets in Morning Shade. Until now.

"Sheriff can't make sense of any of it. It's a real mystery, Maude. A real brainteaser."

The front door slammed, and I whirled.

"Mom!"

"Back here, Cee."

My daughter's face was utterly glowing. "I have a shot at the job!"

The job. The rural route! Stella and I bolted out of the kitchen, and I passed my mother-in-law in my exuberance to give CeeCee a congratulatory hug.

"What job?" Stella asked as if we hadn't spoke of the job five minutes earlier.

"A postal route! I passed the test with flying colors. Now all they have to do is run a background check, but I don't even have a traffic ticket." She squealed.

"You're going to deliver mail?" Stella asked, sitting down on the sofa. "Better buy those dog biscuits."

CeeCee was too excited to sit. I was thrilled to see her happy again. It's been a long time—too long.

"I'll be a postman, or whatever they call a woman who delivers the mail. They'll assign me a route." She grinned. "I might even be delivering your mail, Grandma."

"Well, get it here on time. Ain't much to live on."

"*Isn't,* Stel."

"I'll say." Stella shook her head. "Pitiful."

CeeCee danced from the room and took the stairs two at a time.

"Quite a change in that girl," Stella said.

"Praise the Lord," was all I could say. Tears pricked my eyes. "Now maybe she can get on with her life."

I knew CeeCee needed the money, but just then, the greatest benefit was seeing her smile again.

* * *

I had coffee brewing Tuesday morning when Stella carried in the *Crier*, a special edition, apparently. She settled down at the table to peruse the obituaries while I tried to read the headlines upside down.

"Stella, look at the front page!"

"What?" She nearly dropped the paper.

"Look at the front page!"

She turned the paper around. "Another break-in! A third! Can you believe that?"

"Whose house?"

In spite of myself I had to know if it was indeed the Gainers' house.

"Prescotts' cottage. Oh, my. Leroy and Genevieve are in Arizona. She's going to be so upset. I wonder if anyone has called them."

"Read the article. Does it say?"

My fingers itched to read the commentary myself, but Stella wouldn't relinquish it until she'd read the obituaries, and that would be after reading about the break-in.

"No, it doesn't say. Lula Wilson died. She was old though. Older than me."

"Does it *say* what the burglar did? How he got in?" *Anything?* Stel was gonna drive me nuts yet!

"Nothing taken. Just like before. Got in through a basement window. Poor Lula—I knew she wasn't long for this world. Had high triglycerides, you know. Ate a lot of sweets and starches. Ate those Little Debbies like they were going out of style."

"How old was she?"

"Ninety-six."

Yep. Triglycerides got her. I steered the conversation back to the newest break-in. "Sounds to me like this is getting out of hand."

Stella leveled a stern look at me. "Whoever it was has good taste. Took down Leroy's watercolors. Of course, everyone knows Leroy paints those pictures himself and hasn't a smidgen of talent. CeeCee could do better when she was four."

She was right. Leroy had watched one of those television shows for weeks, copying every stroke, and still had created atrocities of crooked trees, blobs of leaves, mountains that looked like cones.

"Ha!" Stella crowed. "Listen to this. The culprit took down the pictures all right, but then he—or she—painted a grapevine in one corner of the living room, trailing the vine over the double entry. Then they added a floral arrangement near a framed mirror." She looked up. "You remember that gilt mirror Genevieve inherited from her mother? It would fetch quite a price on the *Antiques Roadshow*."

I remembered it. And envied Genevieve for having it. "Is that all they did?"

"Looks like it. Of course, when Leroy and Genevieve get back they may discover more missing."

"No moved furniture."

"It doesn't say. I may go check, though. Any good neighbor would do that, wouldn't they?"

"Of course." I grinned. "Any good neighbor would. So can we guess that our burglar has a talent for painting? That would narrow the field."

Stella lowered the paper. "Oh, I don't know. When I lived at Shady Acres, they had one of those decorative-painting classes. Everyone took the lessons. Some of us were pretty good."

"I didn't know that. Do you paint?"

"Oh, not me. I did better than Leroy's work, but I'll never be a Rigoletto."

"I think that's Rembrandt," I said absently, thinking about this glut of artistic talent.

"Whatever. Too bad Leroy and Genevieve are gone or I could go over right now." The Prescotts' cottage was three blocks away, but wasn't everyone in Morning Shade a neighbor?

"Well, if you find out when they will return, we can make sure they have a hot meal their first night. I know they cleaned out the refrigerator and pantry since they planned to be gone all summer."

"Done!" Stella said, turning back to the obits. "Charlotte MacIntyre died. She was only sixty-nine. I wonder what was wrong."

"Doesn't it say?"

"No. Just says she died at the home of her daughter in Ft. Smith. Didn't they used to live out toward the highway?"

"They did, but didn't Charlotte sell that house when she moved in with Sharon?"

"You're right. Didn't Josephine and Arnie Costanza buy her place?"

I nodded. "They put in that truck garden last year. Then we had that drought." There was nothing like living in a small town for keeping up with everyone's activities. Of course, there was a downside to it as well. Everyone could keep up with my doings too.

"I'm gonna go check on when Leroy and Genevieve plan to be home. I'd bet Hargus knows."

"Okay. Be careful."

Stella shot me a look of consternation. "Lived to be eighty-seven, haven't I? You don't live that long by taking many chances."

"Well, you know how your bunions are. Rest your feet at the Citgo," I advised.

Stella would go there to have her latte and catch up on the latest information about the break-in. I didn't think Hargus would be very forthcoming, since he was mad at her anyway for poking her nose into what he considered police business.

After Stella left, I carried my second cup of coffee into my office and turned on the computer. I looked out the window to watch Stel make her way up the street. Though I'd offered many times to drive her to the Citgo, she insisted she needed the walk. "Her morning constitutional" she called it, when she was in a good mood about it. She hadn't been in such a good mood when her doctor told her that walking was good for her. But right now she was trucking along rather sprightly for all her complaints.

There was nothing like a mystery to make a body forget her miseries.

7

"Tell Stella to mind her own cotton-pickin' business."

Hargus Conley blocked the cereal aisle in Cart Mart Wednesday morning, beefy hands on his hips. I glanced at the overload and prayed his trousers would hold up to the assault.

"You tell her. I'm afraid of her."

"She's pokin' her nose into official business."

"I think she's only trying to help, Hargus. After all, three break-ins without a suspect is disturbing."

I didn't want to continue this conversation, since I feared my frozen vegetables wouldn't make it to my freezer before thawing. Besides, I wasn't sure I wanted Stella to stop investigating the mysteries. I even had some plans of my own for getting her more involved.

Hargus blockaded the aisle. "You know she was skulkin' around Minnie Draper's house after it was broken into. Scared Minnie half to death. She called me and I had to give Stella a talkin'-to."

A talking-to? Whoo-hoo.

"And she was over to Lucille's, lookin' around, askin' questions. Why, she's talked to half the town. Makin' me look like I'm not doin' my job."

"Hargus Conley, you ought to be ashamed of yourself. Didn't Stella tell you she was going to help with the investigation—ask a few simple questions?"

"She's in my office every day, and I've told her to quit causin' trouble. I don't need her help."

"You'll have to take that up with her."

His head bobbed, his jowls trembled. "You tell her to stop askin' questions. She won't listen to me, and I can't do my job when she's pokin' around."

I mentally sighed. I didn't need this. How could Hargus conduct an investigation when he couldn't even control Stella? Come to think of it, *I* couldn't control Stella. "I'll tell her, Hargus, but don't count on her listening. I'm not her mother, and she's not a teenager. Not that I'd even consider putting a stop to Stella's harmless inquiries."

I wasn't nuts.

Hargus nodded, a gloomy expression on his face, and shuffled off down the aisle, his pants cuffs scraping the floor.

If that boy would only jack those pants up!

I finished my grocery shopping and drove home. I wished it would rain. A few more weeks of this and Morning Shade would dry up and blow away. The lawns I passed looked like they had been torched. Tree leaves rustled like paper in a drying wind. Even the flower beds that had been watered looked droopy. And not a cloud in the sky.

Stella was engrossed in a talk show about overweight women. I couldn't understand why she would be interested. Excess weight certainly wasn't anything she needed to worry about. The place looked like a Ding Dong factory blew up when I carried the groceries in and set them on the kitchen table.

"Has Cee been watching TV with you?" They could have cleaned up their mess. I'd probably be the one to pick up the papers and throw them in the trash. One of these days *I* was going to sit down and let someone else do the work. About time someone waited on me.

Stella nodded, eyes glued to the set.

"I ran into Hargus at Cart Mart."

"Whoopee."

"He wants you to stop asking questions about the break-ins. Says you're undermining his investigation."

I stuck a package of frozen peas and corn in the refrigerator freezer and tried to make room for the rest of the frozen vegetables. A package of sliced peaches fell out and hit me on the foot. I shoved it back inside with unnecessary force. I never used to get so irritated at little things. Maybe I needed a break. Yeah, a break from life.

"Investigation," Stella scoffed. "Hargus doesn't know the meaning of the word. He's just sitting over there eating donuts and shooting the breeze with that stock-driver fella. He's not working on the cases."

"True, but he's as near the law as we've got around here, and he could tell the sheriff about what you're doing."

That would put me in a fine fix. I needed material for my plot. I didn't even feel a twinge of guilt at the thought.

"Fine. Maybe he should. At least the sheriff might do some investigating of his own and find out who's doing this." Stella was red-faced now, puffed up like the proverbial banty hen, feathers all ruffled. In a few minutes she'd be on her soapbox.

I wasn't in a mood to listen. I backed off. "I'm just telling you what Hargus said."

"I've heard it before. He's afraid I'll solve the crimes and make him look like a fool, which he is. Him and that silly old chain saw . . . would you want one of those ugly totem poles in your front yard?"

I would not—but that wasn't the issue. The issue was Stella's interference, which I both encouraged and warned against. Talk about being a fence-sitter. If I thought there was the slightest chance she'd get hurt, I wouldn't dream of letting her get involved. I wasn't that far gone. But the information she fed me was the only thing keeping my creative juices flowing.

I put the rest of the groceries away, then went to my office to work. The bridge group would be here in an hour, but entertaining them was Stella's responsibility. At least that was one thing I didn't have to do.

I left the door open so I could listen and turned on the computer. I could at least pretend to be working.

But instead of working on my writing, I idly surfed the best-seller lists. The name M.K. Diamond was nowhere to be found. Well, the new book probably wasn't in stores yet—it was too early for a fall release to ship. But my agent ought to be on top of this. I picked up the phone and punched in Jean's number.

"Hi, Maude. How's the new book coming?"

"Coming right along," I chirped.

For once I could say that without experiencing a prick of guilt. I'd fleshed out my characters and justified their role in the plot, developed the theme, and I was well into the first draft.

"Jack called this morning. I was about to call you." Jean paused.

Uneasiness crept over me. I'd thought by now the evangelist had found a ghostwriter. This was turning out to be the opportunity that wouldn't go away. As well known as Jack Hamel was, you'd think he'd have a dozen ghostwriters standing in line to write his book for him. Why was he so determined to have me do it?

"You promised you'd think about it. Seriously. We've all been given different gifts, Maude. Jack is a pastor; he isn't a writer. You'd be putting his notes together for him, fleshing them out, organizing them. It shouldn't be a large project—probably no more than six weeks of your time."

"Sounds like a lot of work with no benefit to me." Other than financial. Granted, the money was fabulous and could pay my bills for the next two years if I was frugal.

"But the money's good, and someone's got to help Jack. He's not gifted with writing skills."

I wasn't buying this. Call it ego; call it pride. But if I was going to do the work, I wanted my name on the finished product. Even an "as told to" book would be easier to swallow, but that wasn't what they were offering me.

"Maude," Jean's voice softened. "I think this would be

a solution to your immediate financial problems, even if it's short-term. I think this project is right down your alley. Jack has a powerful story to share."

She was right, though I hated to admit it. I needed the money and it was a project I could easily write, but it had me asking, who am I looking at? Me or God? I didn't like the feeling the question generated, and it was nothing I wanted to discuss. So I quickly moved to a safer topic. "I just know I'm not going to be on the September best-seller list and, guess what, it's your fault."

"*My* fault?"

"Well, what's an agent for? There's still time for you to talk to marketing and try to get more books out there."

"You will get there, Maude," Jean assured me. "You have to have patience."

Patience, my foot. I'd been in the business twenty-five years and published forty-one books. Didn't Jean realize that asking me to write someone else's book was a professional insult? Especially since I couldn't crack a best-seller list with a ball peen hammer?

I barely held my tongue. Blowing up at my agent wasn't going to solve anything, but I was tired of hearing the same answers: The publisher doesn't know how the best-seller list works; it's all a mystery. Fiction is so new in the Christian market. They weren't even good answers, just excuses. Excuses masquerading as reasons, and I wasn't buying.

"I'm not an author, Maude, but I'd think the joy in ghostwriting would be the knowledge that I was doing something of significance."

Something of significance. The observation stopped me cold. She was right, of course. My books are fluff. They sell, but they are fiction. Jack's story would hold considerable more that readers could take away with them. A hundred years from now what difference would a name make on a cover? When you got right down to it, the only difference mine or anyone else's name was going to make was a listing in the Lamb's Book of Life. Yet pride reared its unsightly head. I wanted recognition for my writing, and I wanted it now. I had some ideas about how to get it too.

"I want better marketing for my books. My sales figures will support the request. I want you to keep on the publisher until we see concrete results from marketing." I didn't like the brash tone in my voice—had despised it for months now. I wasn't sure I liked myself anymore. This wasn't Jean's fault. Well, maybe it was, partly, but even so, losing my temper wouldn't help the situation.

"Maude—"

A headache bloomed in the back of my head. "I have work to do, Jean. I'll talk to you later."

I hung up, torn between thinking I should have been tougher and thinking I was too demanding. Where my career was concerned, I was frayed. I wanted—I needed—the perks that would go along with getting on the best-seller list: more visibility in bookstores, special displays, recognition among peers—and on and on. I was embarrassed to say I'd been writing for twenty-five years and had few awards, so little recognition, that the ultimate validation—the best-seller list—had eluded me.

But then I thought, *Just writing should be enough.* Using my God-given gift of storytelling should be enough. If that was all God had in store for me, it should be sufficient.

I heaved a sigh and stared at the last couple of paragraphs I wrote yesterday. My need was so petty. With all the problems in this world—AIDS, terminal illness, terrorism, divorces at an all-time high—I'm concerned about a best-seller list? What I had was a good case of desire, not need.

I bit my lip, suffering from an attack of conscience. *I'm sorry, God. Forgive me for acting this way. I'll try to do better, really I will.*

I heard Stella greeting her bridge friends, who all arrived at the same time. Simon, Pansy, and Frances exchanged friendly banter. Then they sat down at the table, and I heard the slap of cards against the leather top. After the bidding, the conversation turned to the furniture mover, and my ears pricked up.

"I've been doing a little snooping about the Pratt boy," Stella said. "He knows Lucille real well, and he carried Minnie's groceries to her car last week."

"That nice lad that works at the Cart Mart?"

"He may not be so nice, Pansy. I hear he got a speeding ticket last month."

"Couldn't the burglar be someone who's watching them? Takes a chance on getting in when he thinks they're gone?" Simon contributed.

"No," Pansy returned calmly. "He has to buy things like lamps and such ahead of time. Seems pretty calculated to me . . . almost brilliant."

"Could be someone in the family," Stella mused. "Maybe a daughter-in-law trying to help."

My attention was seriously caught. Stella had obviously ignored Hargus's message about butting out of his investigation. Clearly she was testing theories on her bridge buddies. I reached for a pen, ready to take notes if they came up with anything of real interest.

"None of the three people who've been hit have children here in town. Besides, a grown child would be sick to pull this kind of trick. Lucille's living room has looked the same for fifty years."

"Then it has to be someone who knows all three families," Stella concluded.

"And I think it's a woman," Pansy offered.

"Men have personal preferences too," Simon pointed out.

I grinned. A lone man among three women didn't have a chance. Particularly those three.

Stella chuckled. "Sorry, Simon. It *could* be a man, but I've already discarded that theory. Men wouldn't bother with furniture and drapes. They'd go straight for the food supply, money, or jewelry."

"Men have more to do than rearrange somebody else's furniture," Simon agreed.

"True. So do women—but it's got to be an adult. A child couldn't do this."

I could hear the edge of frustration in Stella's voice.

"There have to be clues, fingerprints, DNA—"

DNA? In Morning Shade? I shook my head and got up from the computer with the sudden urge to get away.

Get away before I came apart.

Ignoring the bridge players, I traipsed through the living room and let myself out the front door, hoping that a walk would clear my head.

Heat shimmered off the sidewalk, and I wondered why I'd picked late afternoon to leave the cool house. Summer had settled over Arkansas like a wet blanket. You could stand still and sweat. Days like this made you want to make a national hero out of the man who invented air-conditioning. Humidity was at the dripping stage, and I wondered if cooler weather would ever get here.

No wonder Hargus didn't want to leave the comfort of his office to investigate a burglary. You'd think he'd be glad to have Stella do his work for him.

Leaves rustled overhead in a hot wind that shriveled everything it touched. Even the birds had stopped singing, preferring to sleep through the afternoon or splash in neighborhood birdbaths. A couple of clouds, obviously empty of rain, floated in a burning blue sky.

So many thoughts filled my mind. The book. Jack's offer. Jean's prodding to take the job. It would solve my money problems, but it wouldn't do a thing for my resentment . . . and I had plenty of that.

I walked up the steps of the small chapel and entered. A rush of cool, musty smelling air enveloped me. I stood for a moment drinking in the dim, reverent interior. Then I entered a red-padded pew and sat down. I stared at a huge crucifix in the front of the sanctuary and wondered what I was doing there. This wasn't even my church.

But I needed time alone with God, and I could feel His spirit the moment I sat down. In all the confusion of my life, I hadn't heard His voice lately. Here I sat and listened. I was alone in the chapel. Just me and God. I liked the feeling.

"I need Your wisdom, Lord," I said.

Was He still speaking to me? I hadn't treated Him right lately and now I realized my neglect. I thought about the times Jesus had "come away" to seek time alone with His Father. My burdens couldn't compare with the weight He had carried, yet I knew that He understood I had a lot on my plate.

"About the ghostwriting, Lord . . ." I took a deep breath, ready to recite my litany of objections. But then, in the serenity and shadow of the cross, that still, small voice asked me, *Why must anyone be credited with serving Me?*

A Scripture passage flashed to mind: *"Don't do your good deeds publicly, to be admired, because then you will lose the reward from your Father in heaven. . . . Give your gifts in secret, and your Father, who knows all secrets, will reward you."*

As I really considered the ghostwriting, my mind started to clear. Each of us was given specific gifts; I believed that. Some, the gift of prophesy; others speaking, hospitality . . . on and on.

I can write; others can't. I don't have much of a story. There are no earthshaking revelations, no skeletons in my closet. I've known the Lord since I was a small child. But others have stories that will change lives. And those stories need to be told.

That thought really got to me.

If a man worked for a metal fabricator, used plant space

and materials, and fashioned the product from someone else's design, should his name be on the manufacturer's product?

"Encourage each other and build each other up." Isn't that what God asks? We are to be sensitive to others' needs—business or not. Encourage and support one another. Maybe I ought to spend more energy on developing those traits than worrying about a silly list of books.

I stared at the cross and thought what a mess I'd made of things. What difference does it make who writes the material as long as God's Word is uplifted? If the evangelist's story touched a million hearts, that would be nine hundred and ninety-nine thousand, nine hundred ninety-nine more than I would ever reach.

Pride works both ways.

When I left the church I felt better. I'd grown in those precious quiet moments. I'd reached no conclusions, but I knew I was on the right path.

As I walked home from that little, unfamiliar chapel, I thought about the fact that a church is only a building. God's Spirit lives in the heart. Too bad we Christians can't remember that more often. If we did, maybe we'd have a lot less of the we're-number-one bit.

* * *

I was in the midst of frying potatoes and onions for supper that night when I heard the doorbell ring. Muttering under my breath, I wiped my hands on my apron. "Can somebody get that?"

Not a soul answered.

I toyed with the idea of letting the summons go unanswered. It was probably a salesman, or some kid wanting to sell something.

The bell pealed insistently.

"Cee!" I shouted. "Stella! Somebody get the door!"

I'd heard Cee rummaging around earlier. She'd come in, hot and tired, and headed upstairs for a nap. When I invited her to come to prayer meeting with me and Stella, she'd turned up her nose.

When the bell rang a third time, I turned the flame down on the skillet and went to answer it myself. *I have to do everything around here.*

When I opened the door I found someone the likes of whom I'd never seen in Morning Shade: a woman on the wrong side of thirty, stick-thin, brash, bold. Her dark red hair, the color obviously from a bottle, was a curly mop hanging past her shoulders and bushed out like a brush fire.

Her red leather skirt, which seemed to be pasted on, clashed with her high, white-leather boots with stiletto heels. She had on more makeup than Ronald McDonald, and fake diamonds flashed on her fingers. They had to be fake. Real ones don't come that big. Do they?

She stuck out one hip and jutted her chest forward as if posing for a centerfold. "Hi. CeeCee home?"

I blinked. What planet had she dropped from? Her thin, scarlet lips moved in what I took to be a smile, but judging from the gleam in her heavily mascara-fringed, blue eyes, I didn't think she was here on an errand of mercy.

"CeeCee?" I repeated, like an echo. "Yes, hold on. I'll get her." I left her standing in the doorway and took the stairs with forced determination. Was everybody in this house stone-deaf? No one other than me can hear a doorbell?

Pausing before CeeCee's closed door, I rapped sharply. "Someone's at the door to see you."

"Tell them I'm not home," she said, her voice muted by the heavy wood. "I'm tired. I don't want to see anyone."

"I'm not in the habit of lying, and I've already said you were home. Hiding in here won't solve anything. Go see what that woman wants; then please reconsider about church. You haven't been once since you got home."

I turned the door handle, surprised to find it wasn't locked. I had no business invading my daughter's privacy, but I hated to shout through a closed door.

CeeCee stood at the window in her pink cotton gown. "I don't want company, and I don't want to deal with God right now." She heaved a resigned sigh. "Who wants to see me?"

"A woman. Were you expecting someone?"

CeeCee frowned. "No. What's her name?"

"I didn't ask. Go see what she wants."

CeeCee trailed me downstairs. I went to turn off the potatoes, and CeeCee waited. We walked to the front door together.

When she spotted us, the woman smiled. I'd seen that expression before. It said *sucker*.

"CeeCee Tamaris?"

"Yes?" CeeCee flushed, caught off guard. She seemed to be stunned by her unexpected guest.

For once Stella was quiet, but she kept sneaking glances in our direction that boded ill for someone.

I saw Stella's teeth on the coffee table and discreetly draped the newspaper over the revolting sight.

CeeCee sat in a side chair and I took the other, leaving the woman the couch. Stella moved to the kitchen, giving an impression of holding her skirts aside so as not to be contaminated, but I knew she was all ears.

Our visitor crossed her legs, exposing more bare flesh than I was accustomed to seeing. Even Hargus didn't go that far.

"You don't know me," she began. "But I know . . . knew . . . Jake, your husband."

CeeCee shot a glance at me.

"My name is Violet."

CeeCee and I stared at each other, perplexed.

Violet simpered. "Jake called me his 'sweet Violet.' "

Somehow, I had figured it wouldn't be *shrinking Violet.*

She smirked. "I worked at his favorite club." Her expression said she had been one of his favorite things.

CeeCee's eyes widened. "Jake?"

"Yeah, Jake. Your husband." Her tone of voice said, *Remember him?*

CeeCee flushed, and I saw a flash of that anger she'd been talking about.

Violet waited. "You didn't know about me?"

CeeCee shook her head.

Violet smiled, triumph shining in her eyes. "Well, now you do."

CeeCee's eyes were as lidless as a snake's. "And?"

My stomach took a swan dive, and I could see that my daughter was experiencing the same sinking sensation. I braced for what was coming.

"Let's get down to it," I suggested. "Are you saying you and Jake—?"

Violet grinned. "Yes, we surely did."

You could have heard a pin drop in the room. Cee had gone pale. Violet practically licked her chops.

"All right. Go on." I said, only because someone had to say something. I figured she'd come to dump on us. Might as well get it over and be done with it.

"There's no good way to say this, I guess," Violet began.

CeeCee's voice gritted like gravel. "Say what you came to say and get out."

"Jake left me a little . . . present."

"Go on." My voice cracked. I wanted to say I didn't hear her, but I did. I knew I'd heard correctly when CeeCee's face blanched the color of parchment.

"Like what?" Her words sounded forced. I watched disbelief turn to knowledge in my daughter's face. CeeCee sat with a stricken look.

Violet kept smiling, her eyes watchful. Was this woman saying what I thought she was saying?

"Jake never wanted children," CeeCee managed.

"Well, sometimes we get what we don't want." Violet twisted the ring on her hand, and suddenly I wondered if it was a fake after all. Had Jake bought this woman—this floozy—expensive jewelry? Would we find the receipt among the bills CeeCee had yet to pay?

CeeCee brought her hands up to cover her face. I felt so sorry for her, felt torn between wanting to ask the woman to leave and needing to help Cee through this.

"What—what do you want?" CeeCee asked.

Violet smiled again. "I really hate to give him up, but I can't keep him." She spread her hands in a helpless gesture. "So I've brought him to you."

The air went out of the room. For a moment we sat in stunned disbelief.

"I'm sorry," I said, wishing I could think of anything more meaningful. Like what I really thought of her. Being a lady and a Christian sure puts limits on your vocabulary. "You really can't expect Cee to take on your responsibilities."

"Not even for Jake?" She put on a sickly sweet, phony expression. "You know he'd want you to do what's right."

CeeCee exploded. "Do what's *right?* You have the nerve to sit there and tell me you had an affair with my husband and now you want to drop the result of that alliance on me while you just walk away? Guess again!"

Violet laughed, a mocking, jeering laugh that made me want to slap her. Frenchie and Claire, who had been asleep behind the couch, crept out to stare, bewildered, from Violet to Cee. Burton growled, obviously ready to come to someone's aid—if he could just figure out whom to bite.

I never said he was smart.

"Oh, you'll take him," Violet said. "You don't have a choice. I'll leave him on your doorstep."

Dear me. She'd leave her own son with strangers? What kind of woman was she? Why would Jake take up with someone like this? But then, Jake hadn't amounted to much either. I guess it's true that water finds its own level.

Violet got up off the couch and wiggled to the door. "I'll be right back. Don't go away, now." She let the screen door slam behind her.

CeeCee stared at me, panic in her eyes. "Mom?"

I stared back. This was a problem I couldn't fix. Stella peered around the edge of the kitchen door, her eyes as big as saucers and her upper lip sucked in. I remembered her teeth were on the coffee table.

Violet's stiletto heels tap-tapped up the porch steps. She pushed open the screen door and pranced in. Her eyes gleamed with a wicked light.

My mouth dropped open when I got a look at what she carried. A crate with a handle. A wire crate. A cat carrier? She put her baby in a cat carrier?

A howl straight from the heart of hades ripped the air. Frenchie and Claire yelped in unison and headed for the kitchen, colliding with Stella in the doorway. A tawny, brown streak flashed up the stairs. Burton. I stared after him, amazed. Who would have believed he could move like that?

Violet set the carrier down on the floor. "There you are. Jake's little gift to me, and now he's all yours. His name's Captain. You got the money. Now you've got this too."

She walked out.

I guess.

No one could remember later when she actually left. When we looked up, she was gone. She could have turned handsprings all the way down the walk and we wouldn't have noticed.

Our attention riveted on what was in that carrier. A yellow, battle-scarred, malevolent-looking, ill-tempered tomcat with a wicked gleam in his eye.

Burton was a lot smarter than I suspected. At least, he knew when to run.

CeeCee peered down the walk. "She's gone."

Of course she was gone. She'd done what she came to do—play a dirty, rotten trick on us. My blood boiled. Evidently she thought Jake had left CeeCee a lot of money, and she was angry because she didn't get any. She'd set us up, and we fell for it—hook, line, sinker, boat, and motor. Probably I wouldn't be so mad if I didn't feel like such a fool.

Stella crept out of the kitchen and stared at the cat. "Don't look like much, does he?"

"Not your regular mouser," I agreed.

CeeCee walked around the carrier, eyeing the cat with a curious look on her face. The cat's eyes, glow-in-the-dark green, were unblinking and hard. While I watched, CeeCee's expression crumpled.

Then she laughed.

I couldn't believe my ears.

She laughed so hard she had to hold her sides. Stella snickered. Then the humor of it all struck me. I exploded in a guffaw. We laughed until we collapsed, and even then we took turns bursting out with uncontrollable snorts.

I wondered how much of our reaction was caused by relief.

Stella approached the carrier and unlatched the door. I noticed she stepped back out of harm's way as if she expected some sort of explosion.

Captain emerged, stretched, yawned, and strolled across the room to Frenchie's favorite chair. He jumped into the seat; kneaded the cushion with his claws a couple of times, pulling threads in the upholstery; then settled down, paws tucked under him and tail wrapped close. His green eyes gleamed arrogantly.

The king had arrived.

* * *

After supper, I approached CeeCee again about going to church with us.

"Mom, I don't want any sermons, okay? You and Grandma go without me. Please. I need some privacy."

"Cee—I really want you to go with us."

"Just go, Mom. Okay? I don't want to talk about it. Maybe I'll be ready for church someday, but not right now. Give me time."

Though I knew she was making the wrong choice, I also knew she meant what she said. Time spent alone never hurt anyone, but oh, how I wanted to convince her that God had the answers if only she'd listen.

I went back to the kitchen and found Stella wiping down the table. She glanced at me. "CeeCee not going to the service this evening?"

"No, she's not feeling well." I squirted soap in the dishwasher and turned it on, forgetting that it was half full.

"Nothing more you can do except pray about it," Stella agreed. "You know what they say: Some women get all excited over nothing, then marry him. What are we going to do about that cat?"

"I have no idea."

I had a hunch it would depend on what Captain decided to do about us.

* * *

When Pastor Healy strode to the podium I settled down, ready to be spiritually fed. Wednesday night was the best for me. Absolute best. Sunday morning's messages paled in light of Wednesday's meat.

Pastor Healy opened the Bible and read the story of the farmer scattering seed, stopping with Mark 4:18-19: " 'The thorny ground represents those who hear and accept the Good News, but all too quickly the message is crowded out by the cares of this life, the lure of wealth, and the desire for nice things, so no crop is produced.' "

Oh, boy. We're talking about money tonight!

"Now, before you think this is a sermon on money, on tithing, or against having wealth of any kind, hold on." Pastor Healy chuckled, and we all tittered a bit uncomfortably. " 'Killer Pride' is the title of this evening's study. Pride, and how it kills your relationship with God."

He paced to the edge of the platform, his gaze sweeping over the congregation. Something in me suddenly wanted to duck.

"When you woke this morning, what was the first thing you thought about? Was it breakfast? Or what you were going to wear to church tonight? Or was it *How can I be useful to You today, God?*"

For me, things went downhill from there. Pride. Not a subject I liked to think about.

"Pride wears many masks," Pastor Healy said. "It wears 'self,' it wears 'ambition,' and it wears 'self-centeredness.' "

I sank lower in my pew. Now he had stopped preaching and started meddling. I felt my cheeks burn. What I'd been feeling lately about my work, the ghostwriting opportunity, was business. What I felt wasn't the pride he was talking about. *I've worked hard to get where I am. Pride has nothing to do with it. Give me one good reason why I should write someone else's book.*

"Lucifer's pride got him expelled from heaven, and from then on pride has been Satan's most useful tool to separate Christians from God."

My heart sank and I shifted in the pew, grabbing a song sheet to fan myself. The air-conditioning must not have been working properly.

"Humility is a friend," Pastor Healy reminded us. "It is not a weakness. Humility is not humiliation. It is being teachable. It is not thinking less of me, but thinking of me less. God gives grace to the humble. God respects the humble Christian.

"So, where does God dwell? Not with the prideful, but with the humble, the teachable person."

I bowed my head. *You're not going to let me off the hook with Jack, are You, God?*

Okay. I'll think about it.

I want to be humble. I want to be teachable.

But in my heart, I was afraid I still wanted that best-seller list more.

8

We learned the next morning just how our household would run with Captain in charge. He stood guard over the dogs' bowls, daring them to come closer. Frenchie and Claire dashed back and forth, rending the air with frustrated yelps. Burton crawled under CeeCee's chair, slobbering and moaning.

With Stella running interference, CeeCee finally managed to get the cat out of the kitchen long enough to put the dogs and their bowls out on the porch.

I filled a bowl with milk, added some dry dog food—that was all we had—and placed it in a corner away from the door leading to the porch. Captain crouched over the bowl, growling in his throat as if he thought we might want to share.

Burton whuffled at the screen door, pushing his nose up against it and whimpering whenever CeeCee passed by.

Stella left for the Citgo earlier than usual, and CeeCee surprised me by going out for a walk. I decided the dogs were safe on the porch and retired to my office.

To my surprise, Captain followed me. I watched nervously as he inspected the room. Giving a mighty leap, he landed on top of my file cabinet, where he settled down for a nap.

Every time I stopped typing he opened those glimmering green eyes to a narrow slit, as if demanding to know why I wasn't working. I found myself looking at him as if asking permission to stop long enough to think.

Captain was the wrong name for that cat. It should be Simon, like in Legree.

That noon CeeCee was almost her old self. She said her walk had cleared her head, and when she returned she was in a good mood. "You should see the size of some of the cats in this town! They're jungle animals," she reported over lunch.

Captain yowled, and she hastened to add, "Not as big as ours, of course."

Ours? Since when? Had we decided to keep this tyrant? He turned to look at me, and I realized what we wanted didn't matter. Captain had decided to keep us.

It was so great to see my daughter excited about something, to see a splash of life in her eyes. I knew she was working at this, and I was pleased.

"And the Fergusons have those two huge German shepherds. They lunge at the fence, and I'm terrified it won't hold them. I don't want to be around if they ever get loose."

"Start carrying dog biscuits," Stella said around a mouth full of corn chips. "You'll have them standing in line waiting for you every morning."

"Good idea, Grandma. If I'm lucky enough to get the post office job I'll buy a bag right away."

"Better get a big one," I said. "We've got a lot of dogs around here."

CeeCee reached for the fruit salad. "I'm not sure about that postal uniform. I look wretched in shorts. I need to wear long pants to cover my fat knees."

I tried not to laugh. Cee was herself, if only for the moment. Coming here was a good idea, though I'm still not convinced the three of us . . . well, seven, counting three dogs and the cat, will ever be compatible. But sitting down to lunch together like this was nice. Laughter in place of tears was even better.

Thank You, God, for this moment.

* * *

After lunch I couldn't get Pastor Healy's remarks out of my mind. Pride. I didn't like his definition. It hit too close to home.

I had never thought of myself as being proud. I did the best I could with my work—surely I was allowed some measure of satisfaction without being made to feel guilty. But I couldn't deny he had stepped on my toes. I guess if I hadn't had them out where they could have been stomped, I wouldn't have felt it quite so much.

I let my mind wander to safer subjects and found myself thinking about the break-ins again. Why would anyone want to rearrange someone else's furniture? I didn't even want to rearrange my own! What did we have here? A Martha Stewart wanna-be?

Who was it said that nothing ever happened in Morning

Shade? Suddenly we had a real mystery—the mystery burglar—and I had a workable plot for my book.

"The whole town is talking about that woman who was here," Stella announced, bursting into my office, unasked as usual.

"What?" I turned from my computer. I wasn't getting anywhere with my story anyway. I'd worked all morning and into the afternoon and made no progress.

"She stopped to ask for directions, and everyone wonders who she is."

"You didn't tell anyone—"

"No, but speculation runs high, and it's not going to do a bit of good to avoid talking about it. The cat will be out of the bag before sundown."

Considering the type of cat we had, she was probably right. Trying to hide Captain would be like throwing a towel over a volcano and hoping no one would see the smoke. Captain had a way of making his presence known. But after all, he was just a cat. When people found out what the woman did, they would think it was funny—a joke. A joke on CeeCee. I didn't like that thought.

"As long as you don't loosen the string," I warned. "Cee has enough trouble."

"I wouldn't do that. It will probably die down soon anyway. Maybe we'll have another break-in. Nothing like more mystery in town to feed folks' imaginations." Stella wandered toward the kitchen. "Well, we're having bridge this afternoon. I'd better get the table set up. Do those wheat crackers taste funny to you?"

"Not at all. I ate some for lunch."

"Hmm. I think they have a little whang to them."

Stella seemed excited by her turn to play hostess again. Seemed to me her turn came around rather often. I suspected they preferred to meet here because it was private and they could gossip freely. And it also seemed like the weekly bridge game had become almost a daily event.

A sudden commotion brought me to my feet and running toward the kitchen.

"You get away from there, you sorry excuse for a cat!" Stella screeched.

I stepped up the pace. If Stella tangled with the cat, no telling what would happen. I slid to a stop at the kitchen door. Stella stood in front of the table, flyswatter in hand, guarding a plate of lemon bars.

Captain wove back and forth in front of her with the silent, crouching pace of a prowling lion, his eyes a glowing emerald green. One ear, newly slashed, hung at an awkward angle. He had slipped out of the house several times, returning hours later with a rakish, satisfied expression and several fresh wounds.

The neighborhood cats would soon learn to keep a wary eye out for our resident terrorist. The word was out among the feline crowd: new cat on the block.

Stella swung the flyswatter in his direction, and he squatted and hissed at her. I intervened before war broke out. After all, I had an interest in this. My kitchen had become their battleground.

Stella was so mad she did a little hissing and spitting

herself. "I caught that cat getting ready to jump on the table. If he touches those lemon bars I'll make roadkill out of him."

I tried to calm her down. "Roadkill is something that's been run over."

"That's what I'm aiming to do, run over him."

"Why don't you put the bars in a plastic container with a tight lid so he can't get at them?"

"Because I've got them arranged on a plate. They look nice that way, and I'm not going to change them. I'll teach that cat a lesson he won't forget."

I wondered how her blood pressure was holding up.

Captain's tail twitched from side to side. He growled low in his throat—a harsh, rumbling noise, warning of trouble to come. Hard to tell which one was the most stubborn.

The arrival of the bridge players sent Stella scurrying to the living room. I cocked an eye at Captain. "You leave those lemon bars alone."

He turned his head and stared at the wall.

"Go on, get out of the kitchen."

He padded toward the door while I stared at him, surprised. Somehow I hadn't expected him to obey an order.

The bridge players had no more than settled down to their game when the doorbell rang. My next-door neighbor, Victor Johnson, was there with his straw summer hat in hand.

"How do, Miz Diamond."

"Hello, Victor. Do you need something?"

Mr. Johnson is retired. His boys, Clyde and Pete, look after their father's basic needs, but Victor was always puttering around his house.

"Thought I might mow your lawn. I noticed it's getting a little ragged."

"Oh my, yes. Luke Matthews has ball practice this week, and he hasn't come around." The teenager couldn't be relied on, though he was a good kid. With all the commotion, I'd let the lawn go. "That's awfully kind of you. Are you sure you want to do that? It's hot."

Victor tried to peer around me, taking in the laughter bubbling in the background.

"I don't mind." He straightened. "I've been in your home on occasion, Miz Diamond. You got a right nice house. You sure wouldn't need your furniture changed at all. You've got good decorating sense."

I turned to look over my shoulder. I'd never thought of the living room being anything other than presentable most days. I invited Victor and his family in for cookies and tea during the holidays, but I never went to much fuss.

"Thanks."

Victor tipped his hat. "Gonna get at that lawn."

As I closed the door I thought about Victor's comment about the living room. Odd. Surely Victor wasn't the burglar. Was he? Hmm. How could I use that in my book?

I went back to work, keeping an ear cocked on the bridge players. The conversation fascinated me.

Pansy's voice penetrated the air. "Heard somebody was looking for CeeCee. An old friend? One no trump."

"More like a distant acquaintance," Stella hedged. "Sort of."

"Didn't seem to be CeeCee's type," Pansy said.

"Two spades. Must have come from a ways. Drove a

rental car," Simon added, which rather surprised me. He rarely commented on anything.

"I got a look at her. Skimpiest skirt I ever saw. She could get two like that out of a yard of material," Frances ventured after she passed.

"Did you now?" Stella said.

Frances went on, "The Cart Mart checker said she must have fallen in a vat of perfume; it was that strong."

This diverted my attention. Strange. I hadn't noticed the perfume. Were the dogs aggravating my allergies? Violet must have asked for directions at the grocery store. Not too many strangers or tourists passed through Morning Shade, so speculation would be rampant.

"I don't know how she could walk in those high-heeled boots," Pansy said. "Made my feet hurt just to look at them. What did she want with CeeCee?"

"She brought CeeCee a cat. Not that we particularly needed one. Seems like she knew Jake . . . pretty well. Gossip is real hurtful sometimes," Stella said. "My granddaughter can't help it that she married a Romeo. Don't know a man until you marry him, I always say. Then it's too late."

I mentally groaned, and I could distinctly hear three hands of cards simultaneously hit the table.

"You're not serious," Frances hissed. "That man fooled around with a woman like that? Poor CeeCee!"

Stella pruned. "Never said Jake was the most honest of men. He liked to play around. . . . Everyone knew that."

"My word!" Pansy exclaimed. "The cur."

I shut my eyes. Not exactly the word I would have used, but—

"What'd the lady want?"

"That's between her and CeeCee," Stella said. "Jake's gone, you know."

"Well, I know that!" Pansy shut up.

"Hum, bet CeeCee told her where to get off," Frances ventured.

Captain chose that moment to jump off the file cabinet in my office and stroll out to the bridge players. It got quiet—real quiet. I listened, bemused, as I pictured him strutting through the room, head high, tail twitching.

Trouble on the prowl.

"My word," Pansy said. "Did you say that woman gave CeeCee a cat? *That* cat?"

"*That* cat," Stella said. "His name's Captain."

"He looks like a captain, all right." Simon said. "I wouldn't want to cross him."

Stella changed the subject. "Anyone figured out who the mystery burglar is—anyone? Any new thought?"

"Not a word," Simon offered. "Not one word."

Her ploy worked. They were off, arguing about the identity of the burglar. I thanked my stars for Captain and for Stella's quick wit. Had to hand it to her—she was sharp.

The doorbell pealed and Stella yelled, "I'll get it, Maude. Don't stop working on account of interruptions."

I heard her shuffle to the door.

"Mercy—this is heavy! What's in it? Rocks?"

Then Frances's voice. "You shouldn't be carrying anything that heavy. You'll tear your back up!"

"It's research books I ordered," I called. "Just set them beside the doorway, Frances. I'll take care of them later."

The conversation had successfully been diverted away from Cee's newest quandary, and I was grateful. My daughter didn't need any extra pressure; she had more than she could manage right now.

* * *

CeeCee came in around four o'clock, dragging. "Hi, Mom."

"I was getting worried about you."

"Sorry. I should have called. I've been walking, trying to get some of this weight off. Got to fit in those postal shorts. Let me tell you, it's a lot easier putting it on than it is taking it off." She sank into a kitchen chair.

I stopped forming ground sirloin patties and brought her a glass of ice water. I shoved the patties under the broiler and lifted the lid on boiled new potatoes. "Dinner will be ready shortly. Why don't you go shower and change clothes?"

CeeCee untied her Reeboks and heeled them off. "My feet are killing me."

"You should live with my bunions," Stella said, ambling into the kitchen. "Then you'd have something to complain about." She poured herself a cup of tea and sat at the table. "Half the town has heard about Violet and the other half will by tomorrow. They want to know who she is."

CeeCee shrugged. "I just say she was a friend of Jake's."

"Boy, was she ever," Stella said. "I told my bridge club that same thing, didn't I, Maude?"

I nodded, a little embarrassed that Stel knew I had heard

everything the four of them discussed. The house is good-sized but not huge. "I think you used the term *acquaintance.*"

"Same thing."

"Go up and shower and change clothes," I urged Cee. "Supper is almost ready."

"I'm not hungry, Mom."

"Honey, you've got to eat. You can't starve trouble."

CeeCee climbed the stairs heavily.

As soon as she was upstairs, Stella looked at me. "What do you think?"

"About what?"

"You think any more of Jake's floozies will show up?"

I turned from the stove to stare at her. "Whatever put that in your head?"

She shrugged, defensive. "Well, it's possible. If they do, I hope they don't look like that Violet. And I hope we don't get any more cats."

Frenchie yipped, as if agreeing with her.

* * *

"Maude!"

"What?" The tone of Stella's voice alarmed me.

She poked her head inside my office, where I'd spent Friday morning slaving over the book. I was even making a little headway, mainly because every time my fingers stopped hitting the keys, Captain sort of growled in his throat. I'd asked for help—and I got Captain. The Lord must have a sense of humor.

"Pansy Conley was down at the fabric store this morning, and the clerk there called the police on her!"

"What?" I couldn't have heard right. "What for?" Pansy is straight as an arrow. With Hargus, her only son, representing the law in town, she wasn't about to do anything illegal.

"They said she threatened the clerk."

"Ridiculous. You must have heard wrong."

"No," she vowed. "I heard it right there in the Citgo, and several other people heard the same thing."

"Have you talked to Pansy yet?"

"No, but I talked to Frances and she'd heard it too."

"I can't imagine Pansy threatening anyone."

"Pansy told the clerk that she'd be good and sorry if she didn't give her a better price on the fabric she was cutting for her. Then she mentioned what happened to Lucille Stover."

I couldn't believe what I was hearing. Pansy Conley was the kindest soul on earth. The only reason everyone's put up with Hargus all these years is because they love Pansy. "There's something wrong with this picture."

"That's what I thought, but I heard right. You don't threaten anyone without them taking you seriously nowadays. I heard the airport has all those signs up that say you can't joke or laugh when you're going through security—"

I interrupted. "Where's Pansy now?"

"Somebody said she's so upset that she's locked herself in her room and won't come out."

Good grief! What was happening to Morning Shade? The whole town had lost its mind this summer, what with three unexplained break-ins, Simon's episode with the avocados, Captain, and now Pansy's being accused of threatening a fabric clerk.

What next?

9

I read an article once that said the typical symptoms of stress are eating too much, impulse buying, and driving too fast. Are they kidding? That's my idea of a perfect day—or it was before the roof caved in on me.

Now I had a daughter, a mother-in-law, three dogs, and a green-eyed monster living in my house.

Captain had been with us for a week and a half now. He'd taken to hiding and pouncing on unsuspecting victims. He wasn't particular who he pounced on. We'd all been hit, including Stella and the dogs. But when he took a flying leap at CeeCee's newly polished red toenails, I figured his days were numbered.

Problem was, I was getting used to him. I wouldn't go so far as to say I was *fond* of him, but his favorite spot on top of my file cabinet would be empty if we lost him—and I think I'd miss him. I've taken to talking out my story line with him. And I'm not sure, but I think he understands.

I was musing on Captain's role in my life when an ear-piercing whoop jerked me straight up in my chair. I leaped to my feet and ran into the living room, expecting to find that Captain and CeeCee had tangled again.

CeeCee was doing a happy dance in the middle of the living room, one arm straight up in the air. She looked like she had when she was a child and used to pretend to be an Indian princess.

"What's going on?"

"I got the job!"

My heart leaped. The postal job. "Congratulations!" I did my own little happy dance.

"I'll have the country route south of Morning Shade."

Stella shuffled in from the kitchen. "What's all the yelling about?"

CeeCee danced Grandma in a circle. "I got the job at the post office!"

Praise God and hallelujah. I'd almost forgotten how to react to good news; it had been so long since I'd had any. I hugged my daughter tightly. "This calls for a pizza celebration!"

CeeCee's eyes held unshed tears. "Double cheese and pepperoni. Oh, Mom, finally something good happened. Maybe—"

"Pizza!" Stella chirped, clapping her hands together. She frowned. "I can't chew crust."

"We'll order spaghetti for you," I said. "And soft breadsticks."

"Yeah!"

"I'll have a uniform," Cee went on, "so clothes won't be a problem. They'll provide a vehicle—one of those funny boxy-looking things. It couldn't be better! I've got to call Iva and thank her for her support." CeeCee winked. "It helps to have connections."

"Well, you know what they say."

"Who, Grandma?"

"Anyone with a lick of sense. He's God in the good times and still God in the bad times."

"Yeah—thanks for reminding me, Grandma."

"No. Thanks for reminding *me,* CeeCee."

I heard it and gave thanks. CeeCee was coming around. We'd get her back to church yet. I watched my daughter run to her room and joy filled me.

When I looked at Stella, I saw the same happiness in her face. "Wow. This is quite an event."

"I'll say," Stella agreed. "I thought she was going to turn into a potato chip, or start wearing blue fingernail polish and black lipstick."

I liked what this "investigation" had done for Stella. She was more alive than I'd seen her in years. She even forgot about her bunions sometimes, although she still left her teeth at various places. Early every morning she was up and out. Checking leads, she says. And that's fine with me. Whatever keeps her interested in living is good.

And now CeeCee finally has something to get her up in the morning.

I thought about that. Living. The joy of living. I'd lost that myself, for a while. But now that the new book was almost finished, I found myself gaining a new perspective on things. The whole process had given me a new lease on writing. Whether Stella solved the mystery of the phantom burglar or not, I had a good story—and that was a miracle in itself.

I returned to my office, my heart lighter.

"I'm going out, Maude."

"Okay, Stella."

"Me too, Mom."

"Okay."

Wow. An empty house. Quiet in which to work. Joy, indeed!

* * *

I was in my office as usual a couple of weeks later, supervised by Captain, also as usual. For some reason he had attached himself to me. It couldn't be that he liked me, or at least I hoped not. I'm not sure I want to be the type of person a terror like Captain would be attracted to. Like draws like. I'd heard that somewhere, but it didn't apply in this case. That cat and I had nothing in common.

It was early July and my newest published book, *Eyes of the Night*, was due to reach stores soon. If it hit the best-seller list, or even sold exceptionally well, my publisher would offer me another contract.

This is the time in an author's life when hope is renewed; I had another shot at the list.

A new contract would mean more money, and I certainly could use that. Before too many more months, I'd be facing winter with its heating bills, taxes, and insurance coming due. One thing—my manuscript was moving along . . . but it was beginning to sound a lot like Morning Shade.

I stopped typing. Was I doing the right thing, using the circumstances unfolding in our own lives and inserting them into the lives of the characters of my book? Right? Or wrong? I just didn't know. But with this new twist in the plot I had two mysteries developing and working out quite well. Yes, I had come up with a way to use Pansy's experience. I had even worked Violet in as a minor character. In fact, it was coming along better than I could ever have hoped.

Answered prayer?

Guilt nagged me. My characters were taking over, which is a writer's dream, but should I use my daughter's distress in a piece of fiction? air dirty linen in my quest for a best-seller? How far would I go to make the list? I needed to think about that. But my fingers kept returning to the keyboard, the characters coming to life on the screen.

I had to do something to keep the juices flowing. Something to get Stella more involved. I thought for a minute. I could "accidentally" lose the obituary page. That would upset her, but she probably wouldn't tie it to the burglar. Hmm. What if I hid her teeth? She was always leaving them lying around and forgetting where she left them. I could do that—not tell her where they were.

I stopped, appalled at the thoughts running through my mind. Had I stooped so low that I would consider hiding Stella's teeth? *Lord, forgive me. Don't let me ever do anything so thoughtless just to sell a book.* I was ashamed of myself, and God was probably ashamed of me too. I looked up to find Captain staring at me.

Even the cat was ashamed.

* * *

Thursday afternoon the weekly bridge players gathered in the living room. I kept the door wide open, telling myself it was for cross ventilation, but I knew otherwise. I was nosy. I stared at my computer screen, but truthfully I was dozing with my eyes open.

Captain napped on the file cabinet. I could hear the dogs in the kitchen, taking advantage of the tyrant's absence to gorge themselves while they could. Having Captain standing guard over their bowls, with tail twitching and that low rumbling growl deep in his throat, had thrown them off their feed. Even Burton might have lost an ounce or two. With him it was hard to tell.

When the bridge players started talking, I perked up. My brooding, green-eyed slave driver opened his eyes in my direction. Awake now, he stared in disapproval at my lack of activity. I made a face at him and settled into eavesdropping, hoping to hear something helpful.

"Wouldn't surprise me a bit if Midge Gainer wasn't the 'mystery' burglar's next victim," Frances said as she dealt the cards.

Pansy laughed. "Serve her right—she's needed a new kitchen table for years."

"Why should Midge be the next target?" Simon asked. "He—or she—hasn't hit in a few weeks. Maybe they've moved on."

Pansy frowned. "Everyone knows Midge has absolutely no decorating sense. She and Minnie could tie for most boring."

Frances folded her cards in her hands. "Her house isn't eye-appealing, maybe even a little cold."

I smiled. Pot calling the kettle black.

"There's no excuse for an uninspired house," Simon said. "It doesn't take a Martha Stewart to add a little color, to see that surfaces aren't littered with bric-a-brac that can be easily broken. I don't know why some people feel the need to keep absolutely every picture their children or grandchildren ever had made out for public view. Just keep the newest one, I say."

The three women weren't saying a word now. I imagined them staring at Simon. He'd made a comment here and there before, but he had never been as adamant about decorating miscues as he was today.

"One heart," Stella ventured.

"And color," Simon continued. "Hasn't anyone ever heard of a color wheel? Or bought a *House Beautiful, Victorian Home,* or *Home and Country* magazine? Any number of publications are available. Why, they've even got magazines with color schemes and such at the Home Depot or at Wal-Mart over in Ash Flat. It's not a difficult thing," he contended, his cheeks flushed.

Pansy spoke up. "Why, Simon, I never knew you were such a wellspring of decorating information."

"I watch *House and Garden,*" he said. "Pass."

Simon was really stirred up if he passed at this point. Quite obviously he didn't like the women's assessment of him.

"What do you think about this room?" Stella asked.

I held my breath. I'd said I would enjoy having our mystery bandit come into my home and lend his decorating expertise, but I wasn't sure I would want a full-blown critique from the bridge club.

"Nice," Simon commented. I could see him clearly in my mind's eye, his discerning gaze moving slowly about the room. "Could stand a bit more, well, 'splash.' I read where every room should have a touch of red. Maybe in a pillow, though in this room that might not work. Perhaps in a picture. Just a touch. Nothing jarring."

I considered what Simon said. He could be right. The room with its muted greens and mauves could stand a bit more color. Red might clash, but a bit in a picture would probably work. Maybe in a Thomas Kinkade print or something. Hmm. Good advice.

Stella changed the subject. "Been arrested lately, Pansy?"

"Stop that." I could imagine Pansy's cheeks pink with embarrassment. "I *wasn't* arrested."

"Hargus showed up."

There was a moment's silence before Pansy spoke again. "I am never going to live down that silly misunderstanding." The poor woman had been enduring her fellow bridge players' good-natured razzing for nearly a month now.

"Tell us again how you threatened the store clerk."

"Joyce was a little . . . nervous. She misunderstood me."

"I heard you told her she'd be sorry if the material wasn't on sale—"

"I did *not!* I told you, Joyce had only worked at the fabric store two days. She was at the bank in Ash Flat before then, you know. Well, I found this calico but no one was sure about the price, and the manager was out of the store. What I said was, 'If this calico isn't on sale, I'll be sorry.' Joyce thought I said, 'If the calico isn't on sale, *you'll* be sorry.' Then I made the mistake of mentioning Lucille's and Minnie's problems and before I knew it, Hargus walked in."

"I still don't understand why Joyce would think you were threatening her," Frances said. "She must be paranoid."

"Don't you remember? Joyce was working as a teller at the bank when it was robbed. The robber said almost those same words—'you'll be sorry'—and it just scared the dickens out of her. That's why she quit the bank. She's as nervous as a spider on a griddle." Pansy paused, then said firmly, "Subject closed."

"Remember what Hargus said when he got there and found out his mother was the culprit?"

"Gave me a talking to, he did," Pansy admitted, "though I don't know why. I didn't do anything. It was Joyce's mistake. . . . Well, it was a big stink over nothing, and I don't appreciate being the object of ridicule all these weeks, let me tell you."

I had to smile at that. She didn't mind holding other people up for ridicule, but when the shoe was on her foot, it pinched. The bridge club was a veritable hotbed of gossip. And I was using their speculation in my book. So what did that make me? I squelched the sudden spurt of concern. Nothing to be ashamed of. I was just listening.

"CeeCee have any more visitors?" Pansy asked.

"None I've seen. Anyone for tea?" Stella responded.

Thank you, Stella, for changing the subject. Like Pansy, I didn't enjoy having our personal affairs hung out for everyone to see.

The four settled down to play a serious hand of bridge, and I returned to my work, keeping one ear turned to the door in case one of them had further comment about either the most recent robbery or a possible future one.

The meeting broke up a bit later in a spate of good-byes.

"Hey, Maude?" Stella called.

I carefully saved my work. "Yes?"

"Simon and I are going out for ice cream. Want to come along?"

"No, I'm going to work until dinner. You two have an extra dip for me."

"Mint chocolate chip," Simon tempted.

"You wicked man. You know my weakness, but I really have to work. Deadline looming, you know."

Stella got her purse and rummaged around a few minutes in a side pocket, then handed me a wad of cash. I stared at the bills blankly.

"What's this?"

"I want to help with my expenses."

I protested and tried to give the money back, but her features firmed. "Take it, Maude. Don't be proud."

"Stella, you barely have enough to live on each month. I'll get another check as soon as I turn in this new manuscript." I was suddenly reminded of the widow's mite. What an unselfish act Stella had just performed.

"I want to help," she said. "I live here too, you know."

I knew, and suddenly I was ashamed of the way I had resented her. Stella had livened up my life considerably, and maybe that was a good thing.

* * *

The Fourth of July passed uneventfully. A few days later, Stella came in as usual, letting the front door slam behind her. "Hey, Maude!"

"What?" I finished typing a paragraph.

Stella sat down in the chair by the door and untied her black oxford shoes, sighing when her feet left their imprisonment. "Leroy and Genevieve are due home tomorrow. I'm going to fix that tuna casserole James liked so well."

"That sounds good."

I turned around and settled back to hear the newest information on the Prescott break-in, still the talk of the town.

"I talked to Hargus. What a fount of information he was," she complained. "Wouldn't tell me a thing. Sat back, crossed his arms, and asked me, 'So what?' That's all he'd say. 'So what?' Doesn't mean a thing. Every time I come up with a possible suspect, he just stares at me and says 'So what?' and I want to slap him."

Not surprising.

"But I talked to Koletta at the Kut 'n' Kurl, and to George at the Cart Mart. They think it's someone who knows us all, just like we thought."

"How could it not be? Everyone in town knows everyone else."

"Well, everyone thought the Gainer house would be next. No one thought about the Prescotts' cottage. Didn't think Leroy's awful paintings would be enough challenge for the Neat Nick Burglar. But—" she grinned—"you have to admit, the grapevine on the wall was quite a touch."

"Quite," I agreed. I had taken to leaving my front door unlocked on the rare chance the burglar would pick my house, but it seemed to me the culprit was sort of rubbing Leroy's nose in his lack of talent.

"So, I got to thinking . . . could the burglar be someone who heard speculation about whose house might be next?" Stella mused.

"That could be anyone who overheard you and others at the Citgo."

Stella agreed. "But how about someone at Shady Acres?"

I frowned. "You think that's possible?"

"We play bridge there every other week. We've played in the rec room mostly. Someone could have overheard us."

"I guess that's possible, but it's just as likely one of you might be the culprit." At this point I'd believe anything was possible.

"Ha!" Stella huffed. "Pansy might be ornery enough, but she couldn't move furniture. Frances is strong enough to move a mountain, but you know she wouldn't have a clue how to decorate a room. And Simon . . . well, he's so neat and picky he's just prissy. And too quiet. A quiet man is usually up to something sneaky, but I can't see Simon making the effort to break in to anyone's house."

Her observations were interesting. I'd have to make a note of them before my next brain backfire.

Stella stood with her shoes in one hand. "I still think the Gainers' house is a good bet. If the burglar strikes again, that's where he'll hit."

"He hasn't been consistent," I ventured.

"What do you mean?"

"I mean there isn't a pattern. We don't know when he might strike again, if he does. After all, he might run out of places to sabotage."

"I'd lay money on the Gainers'. I'll tell Hargus to stake out the place."

"You know you're not going to 'tell' Hargus anything."

"Then I might have to do it myself," she threatened, limping out of my office.

"Don't you dare, Stella," I called after her. "If you get arrested, I'm not bailing you out!"

"My friends are being frightened," she called over her shoulder. "It's not right, and Hargus isn't doing a thing to stop it."

Surely she wouldn't stake out the Gainers' house, would she? I never knew what she might do next.

* * *

"Mom!" CeeCee called out a few hours later.

"In here."

Cee appeared at my office door. "Were there any phone calls?"

"No. Sorry."

She sat in the chair Stella had vacated earlier. "I've been thinking about the way I've been such a drip, crying all the time. Thanks for putting up with me."

"That's okay. You put up with people you love. It's part of being a family."

"I don't know what I thought I was doing, carrying on like that. It didn't help anything."

"Oh, I don't know. The sale of chips and dips boosted a profit at Cart Mart."

She laughed. "They made quite a bit off Ding Dongs too." She sobered. "You know, Mom, it wasn't that I was grieving all that much for Jake. I think it was the loss of security. I'd never worked, I had all those bills, and I just didn't know where to turn. Even the perks of being the wife of Jake Tamaris—the clothes, the nice house, the car—weren't really mine. They weren't even paid for. I think that was what hit me so hard. I had no security.

"I've been away from the Christian lifestyle for a long time, Mom. I've been exposed to too much that was contrary to the way I was raised. I know you and Grandma have something I don't have, and I'll come around to your way of thinking someday, but I'm not ready yet. Give me time."

"All right, Cee. I'll give you time, but I'll be praying."

She smiled that sweet, loving smile I hadn't seen for so long. "Thanks, Mom."

"And if that doesn't work, I'll get Stella to pray too."

CeeCee laughed with me. "Then I'm done for. She is one stubborn lady."

That she was, like a one-hundred-pound bulldog. Problem was, half the time she couldn't find her teeth.

As if on cue, Stella stuck her head in the door. "Maude, have you seen my teeth?"

"Your teeth? No. Did you look on the coffee table?"

"I've looked everywhere. I don't think it's nice to play tricks on someone my age."

"Play tricks? Are you accusing me of hiding your teeth?"

I could feel my blood pressure coming to a slow boil. After all I'd done for her, to be accused of stealing her nasty teeth.

"Someone took them, and we're having fried chicken for supper. How am I expected to eat chicken with no teeth? I guess that's one way to save on groceries. Hide my teeth so I can't eat. Well, I'm not long for this world anyway, and I don't suppose it matters how I go. Might as well be from starvation as not."

"No one took your teeth, Grandma," CeeCee said. "Why would anyone want them? Mom and I both have our teeth. Why would we need yours?"

Stella paused, hand clasped to her heart. "My word! The burglar! *We've* had a break-in."

"Ridiculous." I couldn't help the shiver that ran up my spine. I had trifled with the idea of hiding Stella's teeth and pretending it was the burglar. Now that her teeth were missing, she had jumped to that exact conclusion, and no one knew I'd had that idea.

No one but a green-eyed tomcat.

I stared at Captain. He blinked.

"For goodness sake, Stella, I don't care how much you eat. You've put your teeth down somewhere and forgotten them."

"Now you're accusing me of losing my mind. Next you'll be saying I'm as dumb as Hargus."

Better than thinking a cat could read my mind and make things happen. Stella was really in a snit, her eyes flashing. If I hadn't been so angry, it would have been funny, her standing there fairly quivering with outrage, her upper lip sucked in, so mad she sputtered.

CeeCee coaxed Stella out of my office to look for her teeth.

Half an hour later they were back, and Stella had a full upper plate.

"Where did you find them?"

"Under the couch." CeeCee grinned. "Burton had them."

Stella made a face. "I scrubbed them with Ajax. Made them taste funny, but at least I know they're clean."

I shook my head. And there for a while I thought . . . well, I wasn't sure what I thought.

Captain was just a cat.

He delivered a swift slap to Frenchie's nose. Frenchie yelped and retreated under CeeCee's chair.

A cat you didn't cross.

* * *

Tuesday night, a week later, Stella picked up her purse after supper. "I think I want some ice cream."

"We've got some here," I reminded her.

"I want blackberry ripple."

"I'll drive you."

"No, I want to walk. It's a nice evening."

I couldn't understand why she wanted to walk downtown again. She'd complained about her bunions earlier. She should be putting her feet up on a footstool. But I wasn't going to argue with her. At least she had her teeth in instead of leaving them on the coffee table.

I sat on the front porch for a while, looking down the street, wondering for the thousandth time what was going on in our town. Why would someone in Morning Shade, a town where nothing important ever happened, go into people's homes and move things around? It didn't make sense. But then, why should I complain? The mystery had made a good story line for me. I'd meet my deadline.

I wondered if Jack Hamel had found a ghostwriter. Guilt nagged me. There was plenty of that around.

While I sat in peaceful solitude, dusk turned to full darkness. Lights came on up and down the street. I could hear CeeCee letting the dogs out for their nightly run, hear her cooing to them like they really were her children. Finally I entered the house and went to the kitchen, glancing at the clock as I picked up a glass for a drink of water.

Ten o'clock? "Cee, what time is it?"

"The clock's right behind you."

"I thought it might be wrong."

She glanced at her watch. "No, it's right. It's ten o'clock."

"Stella's not home."

CeeCee blinked in surprise. "Grandma isn't home?"

"No. She said she was going for ice cream earlier. I expected her back shortly."

"Are you worried about her?"

"Well, she is eighty-seven years old. Anything could happen to her. Come on. We've got to go look for her." I rummaged in the junk drawer and found two flashlights with fairly good beams. "She could have fallen or had a stroke—I'll never forgive myself if anything has happened to her."

CeeCee called the dogs in and took one of the flashlights. "You take the right side of Culver; I'll take the left. Go all the way to Citgo and ask in there if anyone has seen her. She might have wanted a latte."

"Latte?" CeeCee's eyebrows lifted. "Really?"

"She's become quite fond of her morning latte. She might have wanted one tonight."

We searched for an hour, checking all the alleys, asking anyone we saw whether they'd seen Stella. Everyone knew her. Several people stopped their cars to ask if we had a problem. None of them had seen Stel. We compared notes back at the house, sitting on the porch steps.

"I'm getting really worried."

"Maybe we should call Hargus," CeeCee suggested.

Stella would hate that, but by now I didn't care. "Okay." I went inside and dialed the number for Hargus's office. "No answer."

"Call his house."

I did that. "No answer."

"Call Pansy. Maybe she knows where he is."

I dialed Pansy's number. When I asked where Hargus might be, she asked why I wanted him. Trying not to alarm her, I simply said I needed to ask him a question about police procedure.

"Hargus went to a special stock-car race."

"Hargus is at the stock-car races," I repeated and hung up. "So he'll be no help. I think we need to spread out our search. We'll take the next street over. Make sure you check behind every bush, every alley—"

CeeCee hugged me and I just wanted to hold her. I was really worried about Stella. It was nearing midnight and no one had seen her. What could have happened to her? Could she have asked the wrong question of the wrong person? Could the mystery bandit have gotten tired of Stella poking her nose into the investigation? Had she guessed who the bandit was? My heart pumped like a steam engine.

"Shall we take the dogs?" CeeCee asked.

"And have them do their business in the neighbors' yards? We have enough trouble. Be back in forty-five minutes."

CeeCee took off through Victor Johnson's yard, and I cut down beside our yard to investigate adjacent streets. If anything had happened to Stella I wouldn't be able to live with myself.

I shined my flashlight behind every bush, behind every house. I'd probably be reported to the highway patrol because of someone thinking I was the mystery burglar. But it didn't matter. I had to find Stella.

Thirty minutes later I heard voices coming from the Stantons' front porch. I shone my flashlight on my watch: 12:43 A.M. What were the Stantons doing up this late?

I rounded the corner of the porch, ready to offer an explanation for my late-night meandering, when I saw Stella—sitting primly on the white wicker bench, chatting with Verna Stanton as if it was the middle of the afternoon.

"Stella!" I blurted out. "*What* are you doing here?"

Stella peered over the railing at me. "Hey, Maude. I'm talking to Verna. We played some dominoes, then had some ice cream—what are you doing here?"

I mounted the porch steps. "Do you know what *time* it is?"

She blinked in surprise at my tone. "What time is it?"

"Twelve forty-three! I thought you'd been knocked in the head or, at the very least, had a stroke!"

"Goodness me, I had no idea it was that late. We were just . . . talking." Stella's bottom lip firmed. "I'm a grown woman. I can stay out as late as I want."

I bit back an unkind remark. Just who did she think she was, taking that tone with me? I was old too—I needed my sleep. "We'll talk about this tomorrow! I'm beat. I know Cee is—"

"You've got Cee out at this time of night?"

"Looking for you!" I clarified. "We were both out of our minds with worry!"

Stella stood up with a patient sigh. "Verna, it's been nice chatting with you. Sorry to wear out my welcome."

"Nonsense. I've enjoyed the visit. It must be nice to have a daughter-in-law to look after you."

Verna's own daughter-in-law, Renee, had always been a pain in the neck, and still was apparently, though she'd moved to Springfield some years earlier. But Verna shouldn't have implied that Renee didn't care about her mother-in-law. Never wash family linen in public was my motto.

"Let's go home, Stella. Maybe we'll meet Cee on the way."

Stella waved at Verna as we left the Stanton yard. I slowed my steps so she could keep up with me, and we trekked slowly down the street to the corner. I avoided crossing any yards at this point. Now that Stel was found safe, I couldn't risk her stepping in a hole and breaking a bone at this time of night.

"I'm old enough to stay out as long as I want," Stella grumbled. "I'm not a child."

"Next time let someone know where you are."

"I don't have to."

"No, but it would be nice just the same."

CeeCee was coming down the street on her side when we turned the corner. "Grandma! You're all right!" She bent and hugged Stella.

"I don't know why you'd think I wasn't," Stella muttered, though I felt her fingers grip my arm. I bent my elbow to allow her to hold on as we made the last few yards to the porch.

"It's so late, Grandma. We thought something happened. Where were you?"

"I'm not a teenager."

No, you're eighty-seven—but I said that only to myself. No sense getting her riled up any more.

"No, you're not. That's the point, Grandma."

CeeCee glanced at me over Stella's head. I shook my head, indicating I'd explain later where Stella had been.

We all went to bed, exhausted, aware that morning would come far too soon. Still, this might be something I could use in my book. Maybe.

Probably.

Maude, you're scrum.

10

Stella returned from the Citgo, and I could see from the look on her face she had news.

"What?" I asked before she was fully settled.

"There's been . . . another burglary," she wheezed.

She must have run all the way home. I waited, giving her time to catch her breath, although I wanted to prod her into talking. This was unbelievable. Finally I could stand it no longer. "Who?"

"Shirley Shupbach. We were just talking about her the other day."

I frowned, trying to remember her.

"Tall, skinny, blonde. Picky clean. Got a personal vendetta against dust."

I remembered now. One of those women who always sent the silverware back at a restaurant. I wouldn't be surprised to see her whip out a portable squirt bottle and disinfect the table before ordering. "What did the burglar do this time?"

Stella grinned. "You'd never guess. Removed all the plastic covers on the furniture, took up the plastic runners, and left one of those glass vases with marbles and a fish in the bottom and a peace lily growing out the top."

I'd seen those at Hobby Lobby in Little Rock and thought about buying one—until I remembered Captain. It would only take him about three seconds to shred the lily and help himself to his private sushi bar. "How did Shirley take it?"

"Hard. Claims if she finds out who's guilty, she'll make him pay for getting her furniture dirty. But get this. Sam likes the change. He said those plastic covers were hot. Pansy said he gathered them all up and burned them. Said he wasn't going to live in the plastic palace any longer."

"Well, I never." You had to say one thing—our burglar was creative. Shirley's house would look better without the plastic covers, and the fish was a nice touch too.

"Shirley had Hargus come over, said he looked around but didn't say much. I'll bet. Didn't think much either, if I know him. That boy is as useless as wooden teeth. He couldn't find his socks on a cold morning."

I had to admit Stella had a point. Hargus was in over his head. I'm sure he knew it too. That's probably why he just sat in his office drinking coffee and eating donuts. If he waited long enough, maybe Stella would solve the mystery for him.

"Speaking of Hargus, I think I'll go over and rile him up a little. Get him out of that office and investigating these break-ins."

"Be nice, Stella. He still is what passes for the law in Morning Shade. You've already had one run-in with him."

"I'm not afraid of Hargus. If he gives me any trouble, I'll sic Pansy on him."

She left my office like a bloodhound hot on the trail. I stared at my computer screen. Now, how could I use this? There had to be a way. Just give me a minute and I'd find it.

* * *

After the fourth burglary another week passed—a week of perfectly ordinary life. I'd forgotten what that was like, and I appreciated the normalcy.

Over breakfast one morning CeeCee chattered like a magpie about her job. Six weeks, and she was still loving it. "I get my route mail, make sure it's sorted by name, bundle it, and stack it in my car so I can reach it easily. Then off I go. I usually finish about four—it's not a difficult route. And then back to the office to finish up. Home by five most days."

She was so enthusiastic it almost hurt. I was so thrilled for her.

"I'm off to Citgo," Stella announced. "Maybe something's happened overnight I don't know about. Blast that Hargus. He told me yesterday I should go home and crochet a doily. *Crochet*. I've never crocheted in my life. He thinks I'm old—I *am* old," she groused, talking to herself. "But being old doesn't mean I can't still think."

She shuffled out of the kitchen, still mumbling under her breath. Something about Joshua being nearly a hundred years old and God still using him. CeeCee and I grinned at each other. Evidently Hargus could do a little riling too.

"I'm off to work, Mom." Cee stopped at the doorway. "Boy, it feels good to say that."

"Yes, it does. Have a good day." I waved her out of the house.

Stella left not long after.

I'd worked for a couple of hours when I heard a strange noise coming from the back of the house. I ignored it for a moment, but then it began to bother me and I went to investigate.

The three dogs were on the enclosed back porch. We propped the back door open so they could run in and out at will during the day, and we locked them in at night for their own safety. At least they're not underfoot in the house all the time.

Right now Frenchie and Claire were yipping and pacing around Burton, who—

"Oh! Oh!"

Burton lay on his side, gasping for breath. I bent beside him. His watery eyes looked up at me, begging. I had no idea what to do for him. Obviously something was seriously wrong.

Leaving him for a moment I sprinted to the phone and dialed the vet's office. I'd once had a real cat—a nice, friendly, cuddly cat, not a monster like Captain, and had never taken Dr. Phillips's number off the list by the phone.

I explained what was happening, and Dr. Phillips advised me to bring the dog to his office as quickly as possible. Not knowing what to do, I grabbed a towel from the downstairs bathroom and gently gathered the miserable pooch into my arms.

I held his head on my lap as I drove to the vet's office. "It's okay," I soothed. "We're getting help."

At the vet's, Dr. Phillips grabbed Burton out of my arms and headed for a back room. I paced the floor in the waiting room, praying. Yes, I was praying for a dog. He had to get well. CeeCee would be beside herself if anything happened to one of her babies.

An hour later I had to make a difficult decision. Burton's condition was terminal. There was nothing Dr. Phillips could do for him.

"I'm sorry, Maude. He's suffering, and—"

"There's nothing you can do? Cee—"

"Maude, I know this is a sedentary dog, but somehow . . . he must have gotten into some foreign substance. Something toxic. I'm sorry, but there's nothing that can be done for him."

At least we couldn't blame Captain for this. He'd spent his time sitting on top of the file cabinet glaring at me.

I swallowed the lump in my throat. I couldn't get in touch with CeeCee right now, and it wasn't right to make Burton suffer. "Do what you have to do."

I drove home with a heavy heart. How was I going to tell Cee about Burton? So quick . . . so swift. Like life.

I tried to work until CeeCee came home but I accomplished nothing. As soon as my daughter arrived, I shut down the computer and went out to meet her.

Frenchie and Claire danced around her. Captain condescended to wind around my feet, meowing.

"Hi, babies—Mom? Where's Burton?"

I guess my expression gave me away. I didn't want to tell

her, but I had to. She followed me inside, the poodles jumping up on her as if wanting to be comforted. Even Captain seemed upset.

I went into the kitchen. "Come here," I invited. "I've got something to tell you."

She eyed me curiously. "What's happened to Burton?"

We sat down at the table. I took her hand and held it. "I found him this afternoon on the porch. He was so sick, honey. . . . I did everything I could."

"Oh," she breathed. Tears surfaced as my words took root.

"I rushed him to Dr. Phillips, but Burton was in pain, and there was nothing the vet could do to make it better." I felt my explanation was horribly inadequate, but there was little else I could think to say.

"Oh."

"Cee—"

"Not now, Mom." She left the room and ran up the stairs.

The evening was stressful, with CeeCee crying and holding Frenchie and Claire, who seemed to grieve as well. Stella just shook her head, not understanding Cee's grief over the loss of an animal. My own heart was heavy, having had to make a decision like that without CeeCee's help. While it may not make sense to Stella, or perhaps not even to me, for CeeCee, this was just one more in a whole string of devastating blows.

* * *

The following Monday I'd finished a very late lunch, a tuna sandwich at the computer, when the phone rang. I'd almost forgotten I was the only one home, and it rang several times before I picked up.

"Miz Diamond?"

"Yes?"

"This is Hargus. Is Stella home?"

"No. I think she's at the Citgo. Did you check there?"

"Yeah. She hasn't been in all afternoon."

She hadn't? That was news to me. Where could she be? It was hot out there. Had she had heatstroke? I'd never forgive myself if anything happened to her. "What . . . what happened?" I asked.

"There's been another break-in. I want to talk to her about it."

I started breathing again. "Oh, I thought something had happened to her."

"I ain't worried about something happening to her. I want to know what she's been doing."

I blinked at the menace in his voice. It sounded like he thought Stella was involved. He had to be kidding. "Hargus, you can't be hinting you think Stella had anything to do with this break-in. You must be out of your mind."

"No, Miz Diamond. There's nothing the matter with my mind. She's had her nose in this investigation from the get-go. I ain't been able to keep her out, and I warned her. Now I want to know where's she's been and what she's been up to. She's got some explaining to do."

"Hargus, you leave Stella alone and get out there and find out who is breaking into houses. Don't you dare blame her for these incidents!" How on earth had Pansy ended up with a son like Hargus? He must have been switched at the hospital. If he had a brain, he'd be dangerous. I was starting to get steamed. "I'm going out to look for Stella, and when I find her, you're going to apologize for these accusations."

I slammed down the phone and grabbed my car keys. As I rushed out the front door, a yellow streak dashed past, almost tripping me. Captain! I caught sight of him disappearing around the corner of the house.

Well, I couldn't worry about him right now.

I drove around looking for Stella. If she wasn't at the Citgo, I had no idea where to find her. I traveled every street in town, getting more frantic by the minute. Where was she? How could she do this to me?

I had about given up when I saw her sitting on a bench in the park. I slammed on the brakes, almost giving myself whiplash. She was going to hear from me. Not that she'd pay any attention, but letting off steam would do wonders for my blood pressure. I parked the car, got out, and strode toward her. "Where have you been?"

She looked as innocent as a Christmas angel. "You looking for me?"

"No, I've been driving all over town wasting gas just for the fun of it. Hargus is looking for you."

"What's he want?"

"There's been another break-in."

That got her attention.

"No! Where?"

"I have no idea. I was so upset I forgot to ask. Hargus thinks *you* did it."

Her expression shut down like someone had closed a shade. She didn't say anything.

That scared me. "Stella! Talk to me. What have you done?"

"I haven't been breaking into anyone's house," she flared. "Is that what you think of me?"

"No, never. But you're hiding something. I can tell." And I was going to wring it out of her in a minute. I was too old for this kind of stress.

She looked stubborn, her lower lip set in a mulish pout.

"Stella! Talk."

"I was doing a stakeout."

It took a minute for that to sink in. "You were what? What did you stake out?"

"Midge Gainer's house. I was sure it would be next." Stella looked thoughtful. "Now, how could I have been wrong?"

I ran my hands through my hair in frustration. "You'll be the death of me yet."

"Nonsense. You've got a lot of life left in you. Now me, I'm not long for this world. Let's go."

"Go? Go where?"

"To the Citgo. I want to find out who was hit this time."

She beat me to the car.

She was right about one thing: that part about not being long for this world. Pull another stunt like this one, and I'd wring her neck.

The Citgo was almost empty when we got there, but Frances, Simon, and Pansy had a corner table. They waved as we came in. Stella stopped for a latte, probably needing sustenance. I got plain coffee and paid for both of us. By the time

I reached the table they were chattering like a flock of birds. Cuckoo birds.

"So whose house got it this time?" I asked.

"It was way over on the other side of town," Pansy said, making it sound like Morning Shade had doubled in size overnight.

"Helen Loften's house," Frances added.

I nodded. I'd forgotten Helen. She should have been my number-one choice. Helen was Morning Shade's scarlet woman. Or as close as we came to one. She'd played a bit part in a movie once and it had gone to her head.

Her house was something else again. It was decorated in her version of a movie set. Mirrors, pink lights, huge porcelain urns full of dusty silk flowers. And she burned incense.

No one in Morning Shade burned incense.

Helen dressed different too. Like one of those old-time screen stars. Romantic satin and lace, and high heels. Actually, she was sort of fun in an offbeat way. She looked like a peacock in a hen yard, and she didn't care.

I liked her.

"So what was changed at Helen's?" I asked.

"You know those angels holding flowerpots in the foyer? They're gone," Simon said.

"And the lace curtains replaced with nice drapes and the incense burner put in the closet along with the big porcelain urns and half of the little pillows." Frances shook her head. "Cleaned it out like a dose of salts."

"And there's a nice picture of a bowl of roses in place of that simpering cherub sitting beside a pool," Pansy said.

"What did Helen say?" I asked, wishing I had brought my notebook.

"Oh, she just laughed. Said the place needed clearing out; she'd meant to do it herself but she hadn't got around to it yet." Frances took a sip of latte. "She liked it."

"Obviously a woman of taste." Simon grinned, picking up his change. "Well, time to go. Bridge at Shady Acres this week."

"If Stella isn't in jail," I said. "Hargus suspects her of breaking into Helen's house."

"Oh, don't worry about Hargus. I'll take care of him," Pansy said.

I realized I was tired. "You ready to go home?" I asked Stella.

"No, you go on. I'm going to sit here for a while."

I eyed her uncertainly. "What are you plotting now?"

"You've got a suspicious mind. You know that? I'm just going to sit here and visit. I'm not a baby. I don't need to be watched."

"Actually, you could use a keeper." I left, but I wasn't happy.

* * *

"Mom!" CeeCee burst in through the back door, letting the dogs out for a run at the same time.

"Oh, honey, I'm glad you're home—"

"I had one terrific day!"

She didn't look terrific. Her hair was falling from the ponytail she'd pulled atop her head, her uniform was wrinkled and soiled with a suspicious stripe of mud on one hip, and both knees were skinned.

"You did? Well, good, sweetie—"

CeeCee laughed. "Old Mrs. Barnes's Norwegian elkhound decided he didn't like the look of my vehicle—or me—today. I dropped a piece of mail and had to get out of the car to pick it up, and Max—that's his name—sprang across the yard and knocked me flat. Fortunately he'd lick me to death before he'd really hurt me." She held up one hand. "*Un*fortunately, my hands and knees suffered from his exuberance."

"At least you're not hurt. I'm not so sure about that uniform."

"I'll drop it off at the dry cleaners' as soon as I change." She dropped down in a chair and leaned her elbows on the table. "Mom, I got a call about the house. The real estate agent thinks she might have a nibble."

"That's great news, Cee. Will you realize anything from the sale?"

"Not a lot. By the time I pay the sales commission, what's left over will go toward Jake's bills. But it will help get some of them off my back." She leaned back. "It doesn't seem to matter as much as it did. I've got a job, I'm making friends, and for the first time in years, I know they're my friends because they like *me*, not because I'm Jake's wife."

She looked more confident than she had since she'd arrived. I was proud of her. She still had a long way to go to regain what Jake had taken from her, but bless her heart, she was working on it.

The phone rang. CeeCee ran up the stairs to her room to change. I got up to answer, and Captain almost tripped me.

The familiar voice of my agent greeted me. "Just checking in, Maude. How's the book going?"

"It's going." Not as well as I would like, though. If I could chain Stella to the bedpost, it might go better. How could I be expected to write when I had to drive all over town looking for her? I was still ticked over that one.

"I wonder, have you given any more thought to Jack Hamel's book?"

Man, Jean was getting as annoying as the Holy Spirit! "No, I can't say I have. I thought I had already made myself clear. I don't want to write the book."

"It's a lot of money, Maude."

It was at that, and I needed money. But I wasn't ready to sell out, and that's the way I saw it. God gave me this talent. He expected me to use it to write the stories He sent my way.

But is that what I was doing? I wasn't really writing my own story. I was using what was happing in Morning Shade to write my book. I pushed the thought away.

"Tell you what, Jean. Give me a few days and let me see if I can work it into my schedule." I could always find some excuse not to.

"Okay, Maude, but don't complain if he gets someone else. You had your chance."

She was probably miffed, but I didn't care. I just didn't want to write that book. I didn't want to look too closely at my reasons. I had faced the problem squarely that day at the church, and I knew it shouldn't matter whose name was on the cover. At the time I thought I had gotten over my reluctance, but like creeping fog, my pride in my work had slipped back.

Money was nice, but so was recognition. I told myself it was really a business decision. How could I reach my goal of making the best-seller list if I spent my time writing books no one would know I wrote?

A terrible thought hit me. What if I did write Jack's book and it ended up on the list? It would—sure as dawn. With a big name like Jack Hamel, it couldn't miss. Could I handle making the best-seller list after all these years and no one but me would know? That could be a very bitter pill. Money aside, I now had another reason not to want to write the thing.

* * *

Saturday morning was bright and clear. I didn't feel like sitting in front of a computer. I was burned out, didn't care if I never wrote again.

Oh, I would, of course. All I needed was a break from routine. I was getting stale. I needed to get out and experience life so I would have something to write about.

Stella was sitting at the kitchen table reading the obituary column. "Jake Harzfeld died. Did you know him?"

"No. Did you?"

"Can't say that I did. Might have seen him sometime. He lived here in Morning Shade."

"Well, I don't know everyone in town." I fixed my bowl of cereal and dropped a slice of bread in the toaster, hoping not to get a burnt offering in return. Stella fiddled with the controls on the toaster like some people played the radio dial. Since she came to live here, I had learned to take my toast any way I could get it, because I usually forgot to check the setting.

Today I was in luck. A little darker than I liked, but it would do.

"Mabelle Hanks. Only seventy-three. Not all that old." She peered at me over her glasses. "You're in the wrong business, Maude. Should have been an undertaker. You'd never run out of customers. Course, you can't count on any repeat business."

I drank my coffee, remembering that there had been a time when I could eat my breakfast without listening to a play-by-play recital of the obits.

Stella folded the paper and pushed it aside. "Eight this morning. Must be something in the water. They're dropping like flies."

"Stella! That's gross."

"Death isn't gross. Just a fact of life. Comes to everyone. I know my time's coming. I won't be around to bother you much longer."

She had a spring in her step these days, a glint in her eye. And if she kept on like she was going, she'd probably outlive *me*. In fact, if she kept on like she was going, she would probably drive me to an early grave.

CeeCee entered the kitchen like a thundercloud popping over the horizon. "Look at what that cat's done." She held out a sandal holding one very fat, very dead mouse.

"Yuck." Stella wrinkled her nose. "Wonder where he got that?"

I didn't even want to think about it. I was just glad he hadn't deposited the thing on my keyboard. CeeCee dumped the mouse in the trash, prompting an unearthly howl from Captain. He prowled around the trash can, tail twitching, literally spitting with rage that his offering had been rejected.

The poodles split for the back porch, toenails scrabbling against the floor. I wouldn't have thought it possible, but I missed Burton.

Captain left off trying to reclaim his mouse to pace back and forth in front of the door to the porch, terrorizing the dogs even more. Claire threw a yipping fit, while Frenchie cowered against the far wall, giving pitiful moans.

CeeCee bit into her toast so hard her teeth clicked together. "That cat has to go."

Well, you don't mess with CeeCee's babies. Captain had gone too far this time. Although if he hadn't given her that mouse, it might have gone better for him.

Stella looked up from reading the paper. "Go? Go where?"

"Anywhere except here. Where is it written I have to take care of someone else's cat?"

"Now you're talking," Stella agreed. "I'll bet we could palm him off on Shady Acres. I read somewhere that it's good for older people to be around animals."

I snorted. "I don't think the person who wrote that had ever met an animal like Captain."

"Probably not," Stella said. "Don't know that I've ever met anything like him before, either. Someone must have broke the mold after they made him. Good thing too."

"He's one of a kind, all right," CeeCee said. "But his days in this house are numbered."

I decided to change the subject. "I don't feel like working today. Why don't we go on a picnic?"

"Good idea, Mom." CeeCee sprang to her feet. "Why don't I run up to Cart Mart and get us something to take?"

"Better yet—" I fished in my purse for my MasterCard—"why don't you go to the Citgo and get something hot from the deli?"

"Sure, that sounds even better."

I washed the dishes while CeeCee was gone. Stella retired to her room to get ready. I changed to jeans and a blue cotton shirt, rolling up the sleeves. This would be fun. I hadn't been on a picnic in a long time. I needed to stay in touch with the beauty of God's creation.

No wonder I was having trouble writing. I had stifled inspiration by staying indoors too long. I paused in the act of tying my sneakers. Seemed like I could come up with lots of reasons why I couldn't write. Or were they just excuses?

Did I really want to write anymore? I was tired of living on deadlines. Always pushing to write whether I felt like it or not. Dealing with the pressure of rewrites. Who needed it?

Well, to be honest, I did. Writing didn't bring in a lot of money, but it kept me in groceries and gas. It was better than running a register at Cart Mart, although at the store I would at least meet people.

I believed God had given me a message that I expressed through my writing. But what if I was wrong? What if God was trying to get through to me? What if He really wanted me to write Jack Hamel's book?

My shoelace snapped.

Sighing, I reached for another pair of shoes. If only I could fix my life that easily.

I swiped a brush through my hair and went downstairs.

CeeCee was back from the store with two sacks of stuff.

I smelled chicken and something tangy, a salad of some kind. I spotted a bag of salt-and-vinegar potato chips peeking out the top of one bag. Well, she was trying, and I was proud of her.

She had bought a plastic red-checked tablecloth to take with us. Stella was at the refrigerator removing cans of soda to be placed in the cooler Cee was filling with ice.

"Anything I can do?"

"It's done." CeeCee pressed a paper towel to her hand, blotting a bloody scratch.

"What happened?" Had Cee tangled with Captain? I thought she had more sense.

"Captain didn't like being put in the carrier, but like it or not, he's in." She looked so satisfied I laughed.

"I wonder how Violet dealt with him?"

"I don't know, but I hope he scratched her too." CeeCee tossed the paper towel in the trash and finished filling the cooler. "There. All ready."

I was confused. "We're taking Captain on the picnic with us?"

"Right." CeeCee nodded. "But we're not bringing him back."

My heart sank. I didn't like dumping animals. Even one as cantankerous as Captain. But he was Cee's cat. I guess she could do as she pleased.

We loaded the car. Captain seemed resigned to his carrier. In fact, he looked like he had gone to sleep, but I doubted it. Under lowered lids, those green eyes would be alert, looking for a way to get even.

I drove out of town, heading for the countryside. "Where are we going?"

"What about the nature center?" CeeCee asked. "There are tables so we can eat in comfort, and if we want to walk, they have nature trails."

"And rest rooms," Stella added. "In case nature calls."

At the nature center, Stella headed for the freebie rack, picking out brochures and maps. She came back with a handful. I wondered what she planned to do with them. She fanned them out like playing cards. "Look at these. They're free."

"What do you want with them?"

"I don't know, but I'll think of something. Not much in this world is free. Be a shame to pass up something that is."

Well, that was one way to look at it, I guess. We drove to the picnic area and found a table. CeeCee spread her red-checked cloth, and I set out lunch.

I opened the paper plates, the kind that don't bend under food, and divvied up chicken strips and some kind of hot vegetable, then opened the plastic container of pickles and the one with potato salad. I handed Stella a Coke, then took it back to open it for her.

I reached for Stella's and CeeCee's hands, and I prayed out loud for wisdom and strength. I figured we needed all we could get. So far we had managed to get along without coming to blows, but we still had time.

CeeCee opened the cat carrier and Captain emerged, blinking in the sunlight. Stella tossed him a crust of bread, but he looked at it in disdain, refusing to accept it. He watched me, and I thought I could read an accusation in those obtrusive eyes. Surely he didn't know we intended to leave him. Or did he? Sometimes I thought that cat was part human. Other times I thought he had a touch of Satan in him.

CeeCee put the carrier back in the car. A light breeze riffled the treetops. A sparrow hopped through the grass, careful not to come too close. Captain came from an assumed doze to full flight. The sparrow lost a couple of feathers, but he got away.

We ate in silence, enjoying the beauty of the park. We had the picnic area to ourselves. Captain minced across the grass, stepping high. He wandered close to the table and I slipped him a chicken strip.

I still felt guilty about CeeCee's plan to leave him behind. Probably he would be all right, but I didn't feel right about it.

After lunch Stella decided to nap in the car. Captain disappeared in the underbrush. Cee and I sat in companionable silence.

Finally she sighed. "What am I going to do, Mom?"

I shoved the leftover food back into the picnic basket. "About what?"

"I can't live in your house forever. Somehow I have to make my own way."

"You can stay as long as you want, Cee. As for what you will do, that's something only you can decide."

"But it's not just me. It's you and Grandma. You had enough to put up with, without me dumping my problems on you."

"Well," I laughed, trying to lighten the enormity of the moment, "Stella would say, 'Don't worry about me. I won't be around much longer.' " I made CeeCee look at me—straight at me. "Jake didn't consider the ramifications of his actions. I'm sorry about that. I'm sorry all of this has landed in your lap."

She drew a deep breath. "It never stops. I get one bill paid and another pops up. I solve one problem and another comes along."

"No, problems don't stop. The degree of difficulty just changes."

"I want to do what's right, Mom. I just don't know what that is."

If my daughter was anything like me, she both feared and accepted new challenges, scary as the consequences might be. I didn't look forward to more change either, but life happens.

"Cee, you weren't a bad wife. You were a good wife. It's Jake who wasn't a good husband."

My daughter simply nodded her head very slowly, as if wanting to believe but not quite able to accept the truth.

"I'm serious, Cee. You did your best, but it takes two to make a marriage. Jake wasn't husband material. That wasn't your fault. Don't blame yourself for his shortcomings. God doesn't hold us responsible for someone else's sins."

"I know that, Mom, but I feel like such a failure."

I sighed. How I wished I could spare my daughter from the inevitable pain of growing up. "We all fail sometimes, honey. It doesn't help to blame ourselves for things that are not our fault. I know God has a plan for your life. In His time and in His own way, He'll open a door for you. You just wait and see."

Her lips quivered. "I hope you're right."

Stella woke up and came over to join us. "About time to be going. I've got things to do."

Like what? I wondered, but I didn't ask. Sometimes it's better not to know. I placed the leftover chicken strips on a rock where Captain could find them. I looked up to find CeeCee watching, but she didn't say anything.

We were quiet leaving the nature center. CeeCee was driving and I couldn't resist watching my side mirror for a glimpse of Captain. About a mile down the road CeeCee pulled into a driveway and turned around.

"Where you going?" Stella demanded. "Forget something?"

"Yes," CeeCee replied. "My principles." She looked over at me. "I know he's a pest, but I can't abandon an animal, even one like Captain. It just isn't right."

I agreed, but how were we going to get that cantankerous cat back inside the carrier?

We spent the better part of an hour calling that cat, but he never came. Finally we gave up and drove home.

"Well, at least we tried," CeeCee said as we pulled into our driveway. "I don't feel quite so guilty since we went back to look for him."

"You don't have to feel guilty at all." I pointed at the front porch. There on the top step, with a satisfied smirk on his face, sat Captain.

He had beaten us home.

Stella had the last word, as usual. "You know what they say—trouble always comes home to roost, and that cat is pure-dee trouble."

11

The next Saturday morning found us all in the kitchen at the crack of dawn, even CeeCee. Stella, of course, always gets up before the sun. The rest of us prefer to sleep in. I heard her open the front door on her way out to collect the paper.

Today promised to be a nice mid-August day. Puffy little clouds, tinged with rose from the morning rays, floated overhead. There was a flurry of activity around the bird feeders, and a rabbit hopped across the lawn, throwing Frenchie into a yipping fit.

Captain spat and Frenchie cut off the sound in midbark, producing something like a gurgle. When Captain crouched in the classic pose of a lion about to spring, the poodle yelped and dashed for safety, colliding with Stella as she entered with the paper.

CeeCee got them untangled and handed Stella the paper, which she had dropped in the commotion. Frenchie cowered under a chair, peering at Captain, who ignored him. Actually, he ignored the rest of us too. He only noticed us on his terms. No doubt about it, he ran this ship.

Stella sniffed. "Can't even bring in the paper without falling over a dog. Don't know why you can't keep them outside. Dogs don't belong in the house."

"These dogs do." CeeCee's voice held a hint of steel. Evidently she could speak up when someone complained about her dogs.

"Humph!" Stella shoved her coffee cup out of the way to make room for her reading material. "Never allowed dogs in my home. 'Course, when you live in someone else's house you have to make allowances, I guess. Well, no one can say I don't try to get along."

I gritted my teeth and kept quiet, blotting out the sight of Claire in the middle of the kitchen floor, proving once again that she was *not* housebroken. "Cee . . . "

"I'll get it; don't worry. Claire, sweetie, we don't do that."

Claire wiggled her little rear end, apparently believing that CeeCee had just handed her a compliment.

I forced myself to keep quiet. I would have let my daughter come home, even if she had brought an entire zoo with her. Sometimes it seemed like she had. I had told CeeCee she could have the dogs here, so I couldn't complain . . . but what had I been thinking?

We planned to leave for Ash Flat right after breakfast. Stella was already dressed and ready to go. CeeCee was barefoot and wearing her nightshirt. And they were both a bit huffy over the dog incident.

I poured cereal into my bowl and added milk. Coffee.

I needed coffee. About a quart. Whatever had ever possessed me to initiate this trip? Stella hated shopping, so I wondered why she wanted to go. Probably figured it would be a good way to irritate someone.

She opened the paper to the obituary column. "Mary Oswald died. She lived over in Evening Shade. I knew her when I worked at the power company. She wasn't old—seventy-nine. Just in her prime." She rattled the paper. "Did you know her, Maude? Short and dumpy. Lived on Big Macs and fries. I'll bet her cholesterol was higher than a weather balloon."

"I think I know who she was. Didn't she used to work at the Cart Mart?"

"Yeah, she was a checker. Always had the front register. Looked kind of sour most of the time. Guess she wasn't into smiling."

Into? Stella's vocabulary was getting downright contemporary. Must be the influence of the crowd at the Citgo. I dropped a piece of bread in the toaster and checked the setting. Sure enough, she had slid the indicator over to *dark*.

"John Dickerson, eighty-three. Did you know him?"

"Never heard of him."

CeeCee rolled her eyes, showing lack of appreciation for the morning parade of the newly deceased.

Stella ignored her. "Says he died after a short illness. That's going to happen to me one of these days. I'll get sick, and boom, I'll be sitting in heaven playing a harp."

"I didn't know you could play a harp, Grandma." CeeCee's eyes sparkled with mischief.

"I can't. Maybe they'll give me a tambourine." Stella grinned and went back to her reading. "George Pickering, sixty-five. That's young. Wonder what the problem was. Doesn't say. Looks like they'd give a body more information."

I spread butter and cherry preserves over my toast, feeling the need of nourishment to get me through this day.

CeeCee fixed toast and spread it with apple butter. "Can't you find something more cheerful to read?"

Stella peered over the paper. "I like reading the obituaries. Reminds me that I'm still alive. I don't expect to see another Christmas, but the good Lord gave me one more day, and I guess that's something to rejoice about."

"Okay, Grandma." CeeCee finished the last of the toast and rose from the table. "If it makes you happy to read the obituaries, you have my blessing."

"Well, that makes my day." Stella went back to reading the paper, and I left to get dressed.

Captain was waiting at the door of my office when I came downstairs. He yowled when he saw me. Evidently, my taking a day off didn't meet with his approval. I ignored him and called up the stairs to Cee.

"You ready?"

"Coming."

Stella poked her head out of the kitchen. "You are leaving those two helpless dogs in the house with that cat? They'll be nervous wrecks by the time we get home."

"No, I'd better put them on the porch." CeeCee hurried to the kitchen and I sat down to wait. Stella took her teeth out, looked at them, and put them back in. I could hear CeeCee filling the dogs' bowls with food and water.

"Better put out food for Captain too," I called. It might prevent his tearing through the screen door to get at the dogs' dishes. I'd learned not to trust that cat.

CeeCee finally emerged from the kitchen, and I got everyone into the car. As we pulled out of the drive, Stella pointed. "There goes Hargus. Probably hot on the trail of a clue."

"You think so?"

"No, I'm just giving him the benefit of the doubt. I've given up on him catching the burglar. He's too slow to catch a cold."

I laughed. She had a point there.

The drive to Ash Flat was pleasant enough. A good rain had revived the pastures and guaranteed a colorful fall. A red-tailed hawk watched from a fence post as we drove past. Summer flower beds were starting to wind down, but one display of red and yellow gaillardia and deep blue sage caught my eye. I might try that combination next year. Or then, remembering the poodles, I might not.

The parking lot at Wal-Mart was almost full, but I managed to find a place close enough to the door so that Stella wouldn't have to walk far. Although she would have thrown a fit if I said so. She might claim to have one foot in heaven, but she resented any attempt to make allowances for her age.

Inside the store we separated. I headed to office supplies to get a new printer cartridge and stock up on paper. CeeCee looked through the CDs, and Stella was in Pharmacy hunting for denture cream. She went through that cream almost as fast as Cee went through chips.

I checked out the book rack. Only two copies of my books, none of the latest one. I hunted up the store manager and complained, and he promised to do something about it, but I knew he wouldn't. No wonder I couldn't make the best-seller list. I couldn't even get local stores to stock enough books to make a difference.

When we met at the checkout, I noticed Stella had a bottle of pale pink lotion called Rain Garden. I wondered what it smelled like. Something light and flowery, I hoped. My allergies wouldn't tolerate anything too exotic.

CeeCee had three CDs, four bags of chips, and a new sleep shirt. Her arms were full of assorted items. I sighed. There went her paycheck, but she had earned it, so I guess she got to spend it.

The next stop was the Pilgrimage Bookstore. I wandered to the back of the store, looking for my titles. I found six copies, which wasn't too bad, but I had hoped for better. The best-seller rack was at the front of the store; my books were at the back. It wasn't fair.

I wandered around reading titles and fighting my resentment. Why couldn't my books be up front? After all, I was a local author. I'd even done book signings here. You'd think they would show some appreciation. Who would find my books way off at the back of the store?

CeeCee and Stella left, wandering on down the street. I shot a quick look around. The clerk was busy with another customer. No one else was in the store.

I let my hands wander over the best-seller display, carefully rearranging the volumes. Then, after making sure no one was watching, I slipped to the back, pulled my books off the shelf, and carried them to the front of the store. A furtive shove and my books were where they belonged, on the best-seller rack where they could be seen.

They looked good there.

As soon as I left the store, I got hit with a guilt trip. I should be ashamed of myself, and I was. Just not ashamed enough to go back and risk getting caught switching them back. After all, I hadn't taken space from anyone else. There was plenty of room for my books on the rack. It wasn't like I had taken some other writer's books and put them at the back of the store. I wouldn't do something like that.

Well, I could think of a couple of writers I might do that to. But then again, the Bible says, "Do for others as you would like them to do for you." So I guess that would be a no-no.

Being a Christian sure put a crimp in my behavior sometimes.

Maybe not often enough.

We decided to lunch at Miss Molly's Tearoom. I'd been there before and liked it. CeeCee chose a salad, and I settled for a grilled-chicken sandwich.

Stella read through the menu three times before deciding on a bowl of cheesy potato soup. "I can't eat that crunchy stuff," she complained. "My teeth are bothering me."

I hoped she wouldn't take them out. The world wasn't ready for the sight of Stella waving her teeth around in public.

After lunch we strolled down the street, window-shopping. Stella stopped in front of a store window. The Handy-Dandy Discount Furniture Store. Must be a new store—I hadn't noticed it before.

"My stars, look at that." She slapped her hand to her chest, looking stunned.

I looked, but I couldn't see anything to throw her into a heart attack. "What?"

"Those lamps! They're just like the ones the Neat Nick Burglar left at Lucille's. And that vase—" she pointed to a piece of lead crystal—"that's a twin to the one he put on Minnie's mantel."

"Are you sure?"

"Of course I'm sure. This must be the place where he bought that stuff!"

Well, what do you know? She just might be right. Ash Flat is close enough to Morning Shade that our burglar could shop for items as needed. That answered one question—*how*. Now we needed to discover *who*.

CeeCee held the door open and we hotfooted it inside. Stella led us through the aisles on a "surveillance run," as she called it. I had stopped to look at some place mats when she struck a pose like Sacagawea pointing the way west.

"There!"

A nice selection of curtains filled one corner. Stella pounced on a pair of rose pink, lined drapes. "Exactly like the ones he hung at Helen's. This is the place, all right! Who'd have thought we'd stumble on an important clue like this?"

I couldn't see that it helped all that much. Sure, the burglar from Morning Shade could have whipped over to Ash Flat and picked up what he needed—or what *she* needed, I amended. I was still leaning toward a woman. A man wouldn't have noticed the details the burglar seemed to see. But we still were a long way from having a name for Stella's Neat Nick.

Stella led the way out of the store, with CeeCee and me following like baby ducks all in a row. Once outside, she glanced back at the window. "Hargus would never find this place in a month of Sundays."

"Are you going to tell him?" CeeCee asked.

Stella clicked her teeth. "Tell him? He won't tell *me* anything. Besides, if I told him I'd found this place, he'd just say, 'So what?' like he always does. 'So what?' He makes me tired."

I decided she had a point. Anyway, my money was on Stella. When it came to smarts, she had Hargus beat, hands down.

CeeCee wanted to look in the Classy Review Boutique. Stella swore she needed a latte to get her brain cells perking, and I wanted to go back to the discount store and take another look at those place mats. We agreed to meet back at the car in an hour.

Inside the store, I sorted through the place mats, unable to decide between two patterns, the ones with fruit or the birdhouses. I was leaning toward the birdhouses, when a familiar figure caught my eye. Vinnie Trueblood from Morning Shade. He lived three streets over from us and passed our house every day on his morning constitutional.

Vinnie was our perennial bachelor. Practically every town has one. Always available to fill in as a dinner guest or provide an escort, but allergic to the call of matrimony.

He was a dapper dresser, with white hair and a mustache, gleaming dark eyes, and a courtly manner. Most of the single women in Morning Shade had tried to catch him, but Vinnie didn't play favorites.

He flitted around the store, picking up a porcelain figurine and putting it down, pausing at a pile of jungle-print cushions, fingering a tapestry throw. He stopped by a display of glassware, hefting a blue pitcher shaped like a cannonball. A matching set of glasses caught his eye, and he ran his finger around the rim of one before moving on.

I hid behind a cabinet of brass flowerpots, peering around the wooden sides while trying to stay out of sight, making like a TV sleuth.

What was Vinnie Trueblood doing in the Handy-Dandy Discount Furniture Store, where Stella had discovered items like those left behind by the burglar? Could Vinnie . . . ? I started to shake my head in denial, but stopped. Stranger things had certainly happened.

Now he stood in front of a collection of vases. One made of frosted pink glass with a fluted rim seemed to be his favorite. He compared it to one with pink roses painted on the side, but the frosted pink won the day. I watched as he carried the vase to the sales counter, one hand scrabbling inside my purse for the notebook I always carried with me.

My word! This could be Stella's Neat Nick Burglar in person, and no one else knew about it. This definitely was one for the book.

"May I help you?"

I yelped, hitting the same high frantic note Frenchie

achieved when attacked by a mean-eyed cat. I whirled, heart pounding.

Behind me stood a clerk who was the spitting image of my fifth-grade teacher: gold-rimmed glasses, dark hair worn in a bun, disapproving look, and all. The suspicious gleam in her eyes rattled me even more.

"Uh . . . place mats," I babbled. "I need place mats."

A quick look behind me revealed Vinnie paying for his vase. He'd be leaving soon, but I couldn't follow him because old Gimlet Eye was in my way. She probably thought I had been peering around that cabinet to make sure no one was watching before I lifted a set of mats. I was sure I looked guilty enough to warrant that suspicion.

I grabbed the birdhouse mats and bared my teeth in an embarrassed smile. "I'll take these."

She nodded, unsmiling. "Right this way."

I followed her, relieved when she stopped at the counter to ring up my purchases instead of taking me to a back room and calling the police. I paid my tab in silence and crept out of the store, no doubt looking like a thwarted thief.

I almost bumped into Vinnie, who was standing on the sidewalk in front of the store.

"How do, Miz Diamond?" He didn't lift his hat because he wasn't wearing one, but the effect was the same.

"Uh, hello, Vinnie." My voice squeaked and I swallowed and tried again. I indicated the Handy-Dandy Discount Furniture. "Nice store."

"Sure is. Got a lot of nice things." He shifted the plastic bag he carried to the other hand, avoiding my eyes.

"Do you come here often?"

He considered. "Not often, no, but it's a nice place."

"A lot of furnishings, like . . . lamps . . . and crystal vases . . . and drapes." I almost whispered the words, leaning close so he could hear.

He looked startled and backed up. "You feeling all right, Miz Diamond?"

I sighed. "I'm feeling fine, Vinnie." Didn't the man understand what I was getting at? I was onto him. The way he had wandered around the store looking at things proved—to me, anyway—that he had a reason for buying just the right item.

He stepped around me, looking cautious. "Well, I'd better be going. You take care, now."

I watched him walk down the street. If I was right, there would be another break-in soon, and some lucky woman would own a frosted pink glass vase with a fluted rim.

I wouldn't tell Stella what I'd seen. I'd just wait until it happened, and then casually mention that Vinnie Trueblood was our burglar.

I couldn't wait to get home to my computer. This had really given me fresh inspiration for my book. I just might make that deadline.

* * *

After supper Stella settled down in front of the TV, tired from her day in Ash Flat. CeeCee walked over to Iva's, leaving me alone. I could have gone to my office and worked, but I wasn't in the mood. I sat on the front porch for a while, swinging gently and thinking about Vinnie

Trueblood and the pink vase, and wondering whose house would be next.

Finally I got up and wandered down the sidewalk, enjoying the quiet. Trees in the yards I passed threw inky black shadows over the walk. From somewhere to my right I heard the sounds of a catfight—Captain, showing the world who was boss.

From the houses I passed came the homely sounds of daily living. Behind each of those doors was a family like ours—people who lived, loved, laughed, and argued together, and who would stand together against all odds.

I hadn't wanted Stella and CeeCee to move in with me, but now I couldn't imagine life without them. I still longed for solitude sometimes, but I needed it in smaller doses now. Cee was finding her way, settling into her job, and making friends. Trying to solve the mystery had given Stella a new interest, and she was the better for it. As for me, my book was coming along, thanks to our phantom burglar.

Morning Shade was a good place to live. Even a quiet, backwater place wasn't immune to crime, I supposed, but it was still hard to picture someone deliberately breaking into his neighbor's house and rearranging things. As if he knew better than they did what was best for them.

Though I had to admit, some of his victims had liked the new arrangement. I tended to agree with Frances, though: if I had to have change, I wanted some control over it.

A shadow of movement at the corner of the Duponts' house caught my eye. Someone was lurking there, half hidden by the branches of a forsythia bush. I stopped under the lowering limbs of an elm and waited.

After a long moment, while I held my breath, a dimly seen form inched toward the Duponts' side door. I moved stealthily forward, ready to pounce. If Vinnie Trueblood was making a raid on this house, I would catch him in the act. I wasn't afraid of Vinnie. He was too polite to hurt anyone.

I heard the creak of the Duponts' door. I moved faster, intent on getting closer, my shoes silent on the grass. I'd wait until he got inside, and then I'd—

Wham!

Something metallic whacked me on the shin. I tumbled forward, hitting the ground with a mighty thump, losing my breath in a loud swoosh. I fumbled around in the dark, trying to discover what had tripped me. My flailing hand hit a metal handle. I had fallen over Walter Dupont's wheelbarrow. That man! He never put anything where it belonged.

I could hear the burglar making tracks for the backyard. I'd missed my chance!

I pulled myself upright, checking for broken bones, but it seemed the only thing damaged was my dignity. I limped home, wishing I could get my hands on Walter. When I got through with him, he'd be glad to put his tools away. I slipped in the back way to avoid having to answer questions from Stella and went upstairs to my room.

This being a detective was a lot harder than I had anticipated.

12

We are the Three Caballeros. Stella came up with that idea. Has something to do with a farcical movie she liked, starring Steve Martin, Martin Short, and somebody else . . . Chevy Chase, I think. I thought *Musketeers* was more appropriate, but the point is, we've bonded, which I never expected.

All my worries about how three women with different personalities and needs could live together under one roof were fading. We get irritated with each other occasionally, but nothing we can't handle. I think we have learned from each other. The age difference has given each of us a new perspective, broadened the way we look at things. It has been a time of growth for all of us.

Early this morning I'd been awakened by a rumble of thunder, followed by a heavy downpour. Welcome rain. I had rushed around closing windows and mopping up water.

I still felt distant from my story line and characters, even though the writing moved along. Usually by the time I got this far into a book I would be excited, involved in the lives of my characters. I felt none of that this time. I carefully arranged my index cards, rechecking the sequences of events like prize ducks in a row. The story moved. It had life. Why didn't I like it?

A solution. That's what I needed. If Hargus—or Stella—could solve the break-ins, I could wrap up the book.

Jean would love it. My publisher would drool. Granted, I'm using CeeCee's problems and the town's woes as a large part of the book, but no one would guess that the story is autobiographical. Only a few people in Morning Shade will make the connection. The fact that I'd made the police chief a bumbling idiot built like a fireplug, and the young woman a chubby mail carrier could be considered pure coincidence. CeeCee will notice the similarities, but she won't care. It won't be a problem.

The front door slammed.

"Maude?"

"In here."

Stella shook out her umbrella. "It's finally stopped raining." I pictured her standing the umbrella in the corner beside the front door to drip on the inlaid floor.

"That's nice."

She appeared in my office doorway. "This furniture-swapping thing has me stumped. It doesn't make sense. It's not even a good burglary."

I shook my head. Not good news. I needed an ending. A conclusion. A *point* to the story.

She shifted her purse from one arm to the other. "It's hot in here."

"Uh-huh."

I heard her start toward the stairs, then a clicking sound that barely registered before I heard the whir of the attic fan. Before I could move, a blast of cool air was sucked through the window and over my desk, whipping papers into the air like Hurricane Andrew, plastering them against the opposite wall.

Captain leaped to his feet, back arched, yowling like a banshee. His tail stood on end, and his hair bushed out to twice his size, like he'd made a sudden contact with a light socket. My hair jacked straight up. The two of us surely looked like some cartoon drawing. Captain came down off the file cabinet as if jet propelled, making a mad dash for safety under my desk.

"Stella!" I screeched, lunging out of my chair to salvage three-by-five cards gyrating across the office floor. *"Stella!"*

I gave up trying to catch debris and ran for the stairs, scrabbling for the switch to the attic fan.

A moment later Stella appeared at the top of the landing. "Why did you turn that off? It's stuffy in here. All the windows are closed." She blinked down at me. "What happened to you?"

"I shut all the windows this morning because it was raining." I leaned against the wall. "My office window was the only one open. When you turned on the attic fan, all of the air came in through a two-by-two space."

"Oh."

When I'd had the attic fan installed above the top of the stairs a couple of years earlier, the installer had assured me it was top-of-the-line and would cool down the house in under thirty minutes. He hadn't exaggerated. The way my house was laid out, opening a couple of windows in a bedroom upstairs and turning on the fan would create a gale-force wind, which worked fine when the bedroom windows were open. But try it with only a small window in one room open, and you've got a disaster.

"Want me to open some windows?"

"Yes! Please!"

I tramped to the downstairs bathroom to peer into the mirror. The bride of Frankenstein stared back at me. Humidity and wind had sent my coarse, gray, feather cut standing on end and poking straight up from my scalp. Another thirty seconds and I would have had an automatic face-lift. Come to think of it, that wouldn't be such a bad thing. What with all the emotional ups and downs this summer, I felt like I'd aged ten years.

I peered closer at my drawn reflection. I needed rest. A really good rest. Perhaps a vacation . . . now that the book was almost finished. Or would be finished, as soon as I could think up an ending or Stella solved this case, whichever came first.

I racked my brain. How could all this burglary business be resolved? Hargus was useless, and Stella, after all, was only able to do so much. I might have to take a hand myself, although my success as a detective had been limited so far. However, I did have an angle—the pink vase that hadn't turned up yet. I expected it to any day now.

And that wasn't all I had to think about. Though I'd tried

to convince myself all writers based their stories on everyday occurrences, I didn't want to hurt my family. Was it right to be writing about them in my book? I'd lost hours of sleep over the question and was no nearer an answer than before.

But if it was all right to use the Morning Shade burglaries, would I feel this uneasy? Was my conscience trying to tell me something I didn't want to hear? I didn't want to answer that.

And then there was Jack Hamel's invitation. I still hadn't resolved that in my mind. Could I complete the project, as easy as it sounded, then walk away from my work and pretend I had nothing to do with it? Was God going to bug me till I conceded? Probably so.

I put a lot of myself into my books. They were a part of me. Part of my life. It would be like walking away from my family. I frowned. Well, that was rather dramatic, but still, how could a writer who cared about her work deny it was hers? Should I just grab the money and run?

I didn't write for money; I wrote for the Lord.

However, there was another way to look at it. This book would not be my creation. The material belonged to Jack. The information provided was his. All I would do is transcribe the story, putting it in order, organizing, typing. Jack would suggest changes, revisions, corrections, and I'd polish. No more than a secretary would do for her employer if he had a paper to present at an annual meeting.

I could do that, couldn't I? Was I so shallow I'd miss an opportunity to serve God because of professional pride? Another question I didn't want to answer.

I was certainly learning about myself this summer. Some

of the things I was learning, I didn't really want to know. I guess it's always jarring to be brought face-to-face with what we're really like, with the entire facade swept away. It's humiliating to realize that God already knows those things about us. But it's reassuring to know He loves us anyway.

I went to the kitchen to get a cup of coffee, toying with the idea of eating a cookie or two. Stella was standing in front of the refrigerator with a jar of mayonnaise in her hand.

"What are you doing?"

She glanced up in surprise. "Well, as much as I hate to admit it, I can't remember whether I need to put this away or make a sandwich."

I chuckled. "It's almost eleven-thirty."

Stella sighed. "Then I must have been thinking about fixing lunch."

"I'll get the lunch meat. Remind me if *I* zone out."

"*Zone out?* What kind of a term is that?"

"The young folks say it—or used to," I explained. "Their catch phrases change so fast I can't keep up. Anyway, that one seems to fit. I do zone out sometimes, especially when I'm working."

"Hmm. I think Hargus has a terminal case of 'zone out.' "

I laughed. Sometimes Stella was a charming roommate.

She laid the newspaper aside to make room for the sandwich fixings. She'd folded it to the obit page this morning, *tsk-tsk*ing over the number of deaths in the community. "They say this is a nice small town, but it seems to me there are a lot of people dying to get out. My name will be there some morning, but I won't be around to read it."

"Why do you obsess on death?" I asked her for the millionth time. "You're perfectly healthy. Enjoy your blessings." I slathered mayonnaise on slices of white bread.

"I thought sure I was dead this morning. I woke up and nothing hurt." She shook her head. "But then I got up."

"Your name isn't going to be in the obit columns for a long time, Stel."

"I don't know—I'm eighty-seven, and that's gettin' up there."

"You're a *vital* eighty-seven. After all, you've practically run the burglary investigation. Hargus hasn't been much help."

Stella slumped into a kitchen chair. Her small frame looked rather tired this morning, and I thought maybe I should insist she stay home today and rest. But she'd probably get her back up and hoof it over to the Citgo or stage another stakeout just to prove she could. Bullheaded to the end.

I'd rather she was like that, though, than sitting around waiting to die. This one would meet death head-on, fighting all the way. The words *bail out* were not in her vocabulary.

"Haven't found out who's been getting into folks' houses, though." She looked defeated.

"No gut instincts?"

"Nothing to get Hargus excited about."

"Hargus doesn't get excited about much."

"Except my 'intruding' into his case, as if he was doing anything but sitting in that office. I'm set to do some more stakeouts."

"Stakeouts? Where? You can't watch every house in town." I didn't want her doing this again. Would she ever learn to mind her own business? Probably not. Would I like her as much if she did? Probably not. Her curiosity was an important part of Stella. I was learning to accept her as she was. Now, if I could do the same for myself.

"No, but I'd still bet the Gainers' house is going to be hit next."

"What makes you think that?"

"Gut instinct."

I put the sandwiches on two plates and poured iced tea. "You can't do this yourself, Stel. It's not safe."

"Humph. Who's going to help me? Hargus? He says I'm in the way."

"I don't want you doing stakeouts. What if the culprit is dangerous?" This wasn't the first time I'd considered that possibility.

"What's he going to do? Hit me with a bag of hard candy?"

Stella used to think she was terminal; now she was ready to take on criminals. Her eyes sparkled with determination. The burglaries had not only breathed life into Morning Shade; they'd revived my mother-in-law. At least I could be thankful for that.

Where our relationship had always been somewhat adversarial in nature, now I genuinely cared about her. Had she changed, or had I? I supposed it didn't matter. At least we weren't rubbing each other's fur the wrong way.

Speaking of fur, Frenchie and Claire had been subdued since Burton's death. I was a bit restrained myself. Every time

I thought about having to approve the vet's putting Burton to sleep I felt this sadness inside—for CeeCee, for me, for the other two animals that seemed to be mourning their friend. Even Captain had mellowed. He still made life miserable for the poodles, though.

I checked the back porch and found the two dogs lying by the back door, faces in their paws, looking forlorn. And lonely. I knew the feeling. I opened the door and actually picked up Claire and put her out on the grass. The dogs did their business before lying down in the shade. I left them there. There wasn't a cool spot to be found in this humidity. I'd keep checking on them and making sure they had plenty of water. CeeCee would baby them when she got home.

No one had to baby Captain. He stalked through the kitchen, still affronted by the attic-fan episode. He had groomed himself for thirty minutes, those green eyes glaring. I figured we were lucky he couldn't talk. He'd probably have blistered our ears.

The poodles aside, Captain hadn't been such a terror lately. Maybe the walk home from the park had done him good. He still ran a tight ship, but he was nicer to the crew—as long as we didn't forget who was boss.

I never admitted it to CeeCee and Stella, but I had been glad to see Captain sitting on the doorstep when we returned home. He was an ornery, high-tempered feline with a superior air. He fit right in with this bunch of nonconformists.

"I'm going to talk to Hargus," Stella announced.

She knew my feelings about bothering Hargus, but I knew my need to finish the book. "Don't do anything foolish."

Stella's mouth quirked up on one side. I wasn't sure if the

effect was caused by ill-fitting dentures, or if it was a half smile. "A thought just struck me, but I don't want to say anything about it until I've got a bit more to go on. Let's just say the culprit—or culprits—are getting a little sloppy. A good eye for color, but careless. I think we're dealing with rookies."

Okay, another thing to worry about. When Stella got that gleam in her eye, trouble was just around the corner.

* * *

I worked all afternoon, polishing and rewriting. I wanted the story ready for the finish . . . whenever I had a finish. I hoped Stella was behaving herself and not going off half-cocked. I hoped Hargus wouldn't let her get into trouble—though the idea of Hargus protecting anyone was a scary thought. The man freaked out repairing flat tires, for heaven's sake!

"Mom?"

CeeCee's voice drew me back to the present. I'd been immersed in my work all afternoon and had lost track of time. "In here."

CeeCee was still dressed in her mail-carrier uniform when she appeared in my doorway.

"How did your day go?"

"Any day I'm not attacked by dogs, have a deer leap in front of my car, or meet some farmer driving down the middle of the road on his tractor, it's a good day. I saw Grandma in town talking to Hargus. What's she up to?"

"She's working on the break-ins—hoping to convince Hargus to set up a stakeout."

CeeCee laughed. "Laurel and Hardy."

I smiled, thinking of the comical duo popular in the . . . fifties? My, how time flies! Although Stella would have been incensed, I could see the resemblance.

Cee stepped into my office and collapsed into a chair. "Whew, it's hot out there. Mom, I've been thinking. When I get a little bit ahead, I'll try to find something to rent. I can't expect you to keep me here indefinitely. You raised me once. It's not your responsibility to do it again."

"This will always be your home, honey."

She kicked off her shoes and wiggled her toes. "I know I'm welcome here. You'd never turn me out, but there are the dogs and Captain. It might all get to be a bit much."

"I'll let you know when it does. In the meantime, don't worry about it. I'm actually getting fond of Captain. He sort of grows on you."

CeeCee nodded. "Like poison ivy grows on a tree. I can't say I've noticed any redeeming qualities."

"He has very few," I admitted, "but I think I would miss him if he left."

"Like missing a toothache that stops hurting."

"Hmm. He's a pepper, all right. Treed the Reeds' bulldog yesterday. Sent him into the house with his tail tucked and yelping like a baby. The bigger they are, the quicker they turn tail. The Reeds were not happy. I had to apologize."

CeeCee laughed. "Well, other people have watchdogs. We have a watchcat, and I guess that makes us the winner."

Captain gave her a smug look, as if he understood every word. Some days I was sure he did.

"Mom?"

"What?"

"Iva was telling me about the Labor Day Picnic. They have craft booths and music."

"And they make apple butter in great big copper kettles. You can smell it cooking all over town."

"It sounds like fun."

"It is. We'll have to go this year." I had forgotten about the Labor Day Picnic. I had always gone with Herb. Now for the second year, he wouldn't be here to go with me. The thought saddened me, and I realized I hadn't been thinking about him much lately. Too many other things, like his mother, to worry about.

CeeCee stood up, tugging at her waistband. "Look, it's getting looser."

"Amazing! How did you do it?"

"Well, for one thing, I stopped eating so many potato chips."

"That must have been a blow to the Cart Mart. Probably caused their profits to nosedive."

"And there's my job. It gets me off the couch and moving."

"Well, it's working. I had noticed the postal shorts were more becoming than they were at first."

"No more chubby knees. Or at least not as chubby as they were."

Thank You, Lord, that I have my daughter back again. That weepy female full of self-pity wasn't the way I wanted her. The old Cee was making a comeback, and I was glad.

Stella popped in. "You won't believe this, but there's been another break-in!"

"You're kidding!" I saved my work and swiveled around to face her. "Who this time?"

"Wilson Parker. You know him. Lives alone over on Forest Avenue. Big, old, two-story house he inherited from his mother."

I remembered, yellow with white trim and a wraparound porch. Wilson kept it in exquisite condition.

"What did the burglar do this time?" CeeCee asked, showing more interest than usual.

Good. She was waking up to the fact that there was more to life than her personal problems.

"Well, it's a strange one."

I waited, ready to spring my little surprise. I could see Vinnie fumbling through the glassware at the Handy-Dandy Discount Furniture Store and finally choosing that frosted pink glass vase with the fluted rim. Although why he would waste a delicate piece of glassware on Wilson was beyond me. I remembered the way Wilson kept house and reconsidered. Maybe it was a perfect match.

"You'll never guess." Stella tried to drag it out as much as possible.

I started to prod her, then thought better of it. This was her story—let her tell it.

CeeCee was more impatient. "Come on, Grandma. Talk. Tell all."

Stella grinned and sat down, enjoying her moment in the limelight. "You know how it is, a man living alone and all. Wilson keeps his house clean; I'll say that for him. Not a lot of things sitting around like a woman would have. For a man he does well, but some things are apt to get a little disorganized. Well . . . " She paused again.

"Stella!" I'd had enough of this game-playing. I wanted the details. My computer was waiting. This could give my story another boost. If this worked out the way I expected, I would have my ending.

Stella shrugged. "Oh, all right. The burglar ignored the downstairs, but he went through the upstairs like a high wind."

CeeCee's eyes were wide with anticipation. "What did he do?"

"He went through Wilson's closets, every one of them. Do you know that house has seven closets? What would a man want with seven closets? Seems sort of immoral to have that much space."

"Wish I had seven closets and the money to fill them," CeeCee said. "I'd go on a shopping spree that would make Ivana Trump look like a piker."

"What would you do with all those clothes?" Stella changed to her soapbox expression.

I tried to head her off before we got a lecture on frugality. "Stick to the subject. What happened at Wilson's?"

Stella shook her head at CeeCee. "Clothes don't make the body."

"No, but they sure dress it up."

I butted into this discussion. If I didn't get some facts on this burglary, I would pop. "Come on, Stella; out with it. What happened?"

Thankfully, that got her back on track. "Well, Mr. Neat

Nick Burglar outdone himself this time. He rearranged those closets—all seven of them."

I stared at her blankly. That wasn't what I had expected to hear. "He rearranged the closets? Are you serious?"

"Yep, he rearranged them. Put the suits together. Color-coordinated the clothes. Hung the blue shirts together, white ones together." She leaned closer. "Wilson has a pink shirt." She pursed her lips. "A pink shirt hanging right there in his closet, as big as life. What do you make of that?"

"What's wrong with a pink shirt?" CeeCee asked.

Stella sniffed. "It's not manly. My James wouldn't have been caught dead in pink."

I tried to picture my father-in-law in pink and almost choked at the idea. No, big James hadn't been the type to wear pink.

CeeCee sighed. "Grandma, that is so old-fashioned. Men are free to dress as they please. Women too."

"Humph. Judging from the skimpy clothes women wear anymore, it's *undress* as you please these days. You won't catch me running around showing my belly in public. Some of them even have little gold rings in their navel. You telling me that's all right?"

I had a mental picture of Stella in a midriff top standing by James in his pink shirt and shuddered. The mind could only handle so much. That image threatened to blow my circuits. "The break-in," I nudged. "Go on."

Stella pulled herself together. "He not only separated the clothes by color, he spit-shined the shoes."

"He did that?"

I tapped my pencil on the desk, thinking. Shined the shoes? Arranged closets? We were talking a lot of work here. And it would have taken time. "How could he be sure Wilson wouldn't come home and catch him?"

Stella nodded. "I thought of that, but it seems Wilson was gone to Little Rock for the plumbers' convention and there wasn't any need to hurry. The burglar threw away the mismatched hangers, too, and vacuumed the closets. Really cleaned them good."

I didn't understand. Closets? That wasn't what I had in mind. "No pink vase?"

Stella stared at me. "A pink vase? In a clothes closet? What are you talking about?"

"The break-in. The burglar didn't leave a frosted pink vase with a fluted rim?"

"Why would he leave a pink vase?" Stella demanded. "To go with that pink shirt?"

I closed my mouth, not about to ask any more, but I still wondered what Vinnie had done with the vase. Maybe he planned to use it in another break-in. That's what he meant to do, of course. The next break-in would involve a pink vase. Count on it.

"You know what I think?" Stella asked.

"What?" I didn't even know what I thought. I was too confused to have a thought.

"I think this burglar enjoys playing tricks on people, but they're not mean tricks."

I thought about that, realizing she had a point. There hadn't been anything malicious in any of the break-ins. Oh, maybe a jab or two, like the watercolors and the candy at Minnie's, but nothing too out of line. Evidently our burglar was a kindly soul. Kind but weird. Definitely weird.

Stella pushed herself up to a standing position. "Well, I've got some things to think about. I think I'll go to my room and lie down."

I blinked. "Lie down? Are you feeling all right?"

"Feeling fine. Just thought the old brain cells might kick in better if the body was resting. Call me for supper."

After Stella left, CeeCee lingered, although I was impatient to get back to my manuscript. Ideas were forming in my mind. I could use this. It would add depth to my book. A kindly burglar who wasn't afraid of work should rate a full chapter.

CeeCee didn't show any signs of leaving. "I've been doing some thinking. Driving that mail route gives me time to think about a lot of things. And—" she smiled—"I need to apologize to you."

"For what?"

"For being such a wimp about everything. I know how I acted, how I moped around here feeling sorry for myself. I apologize. You didn't need me on top of everything else."

"You were grieving."

"Yes, that was part of it, but I think mostly I was mad at Jake."

Well, I'd been there. I had spent the first months after Herb died alternately grieving for him and being angry at him for leaving me alone. Maybe it was part of the healing process. But CeeCee had more to be angry about than I had.

Whatever his shortcomings, Herb had been faithful to me. "You were grieving for more than Jake's death, even though that would have been enough. You were grieving about lost dreams, for disappointment—"

"I was disappointed in myself as well as in him. Does that make sense?"

"Sure, it does. I've been there, though coming from a different place. When your father took that sales job and had to travel so much, I thought things were never going to be right again. I had this picture of what I thought my marriage was going to be. Even at that point in our lives, after we'd been married quite a while, I still had this 'perfect' picture of our marriage. Having your father on the road all the time didn't fit into the picture frame. But it worked out. We made it work.

"You wanted your marriage to work, but quite obviously Jake didn't. That was his fault, not yours. Still, there's a grieving process—you're entitled to that. It's only natural, honey."

"I guess so. However, I'm not grieving all that much anymore. I'm seeing Jake a lot clearer now than I did when I was married to him. I should have listened when you warned me about the importance of marrying someone who shared my Christian faith."

At least the advice hadn't gone in one ear and out the other.

She stood, grinning. "I guess I have to learn everything the hard way."

"Well, we remember those lessons better."

"Anyway, I just wanted to say thanks. You and Grandma had a lot to do with snapping me out of feeling sorry for myself. I don't know what's in my future, but I'm not afraid of it like I used to be."

"Praise the Lord for that."

"If you and Grandma can face tomorrow without falling apart, I guess I can too."

CeeCee was coming around, becoming the person I remembered so well. It felt good to see her making decisions again. I just prayed they would be the right ones, made for the right reasons.

My daughter skipped upstairs to shower and change. I took myself to the kitchen to think about what to fix for dinner and to wonder why Stella felt her brainpower worked better when she was flat on her back. I snickered. We were all individuals here.

Stella came in as I was lifting browned fish filets out of the skillet. Captain walked the floor, excited to a fever pitch by the intoxicating smell of fried fish. We even had an individual cat.

Stella was unusually quiet during dinner and I didn't ask about her day. Figured the PI was worn out, even if she wouldn't admit it.

After dinner Stella walked down to the Citgo, her steps slower than usual, I noticed. She had been pushing too hard. I needed to make her slow down. *Sure, Maude*. I would have as much luck trying to stop the sun from coming up in the morning.

CeeCee went for a walk, and I took my Alpha Smart to the porch swing to catch a little fresh air. It would be cooler in the house, but I had a need for outside stimulation. Captain padded around the yard pouncing on bugs. He wandered through the yard, tail twitching, green eyes glowing. The lion was on the prowl.

I still felt uneasy about my manuscript, not sure that I should use the Morning Shade burglaries, as I had taken to calling them. CeeCee wouldn't care, I was sure. Or would she? Hargus might, but did I care about how Hargus felt? Of course I did. I was ashamed of myself. Hargus was a pain, but that was no reason for me to deliberately embarrass him.

I pushed against the floor, gently swaying the porch swing back and forth, thinking. If I only didn't need the money so much I'd forget the book. But then I was beginning to think God wanted me to write Jack Hamel's book. And if I was obedient, I would write it. Obedience. Success in God's eyes.

I'd talked to Jean yesterday. Jack was still holding out for me to do the book. Anyone that stubborn must know something I didn't. Maybe he had gotten a message from God: "M.K. Diamond has to write this book." I doubted that, but I was sort of proud that Jack thought I could do a good job. I still didn't like the idea of not getting recognition for my work. It didn't seem right. But I could live with it if I had to.

The breeze rustled the leaves of the elm trees bordering the walk. The founding fathers had planted those trees back when Morning Shade was a young town. Now the town was old, the founding fathers were gone, but the trees remained.

The thought depressed me. My work was temporal. What difference did it make whose name was on the cover? I didn't know the answer. I only knew that no matter how much I tried to explain it away, it did matter to me.

13

Saturday again, and I had the house to myself. CeeCee and Iva had gone to Ash Flat, and Stella had walked down to the Citgo for her daily dose of latte. It seemed everyone had something to do except me. Good time to finish the book, but I wasn't in the mood to write. September was right around the corner, and it was still as hot as the sweatband in a fireman's helmet, and I was on the verge of a major pity party. I needed to head it off.

I couldn't find any reason for my gloomy outlook. Everything had been going well. CeeCee was a lot more cheerful since her house had sold, bringing in almost enough to pay off Jake's bills. The real estate agent had jacked up the price because the house had belonged to Jake "Touchdown" Tamaris, and some sports nut had paid the full asking price without even trying to bargain. CeeCee was ecstatic.

I should have gone to the Citgo with Stella and had biscuits with sausage and gravy, something she had developed a craving for. Instead, I had stayed home and had my cereal and coffee. I was in a rut.

Someone once said the only difference between a rut and a grave was the depth. Cheerful thought.

The dogs were on the porch again, but I had no idea what we would do with them when the weather turned cold. They couldn't stay outside, and Captain refused to let them stay inside.

I turned on the computer and waited for it to boot up. Captain had abandoned his place on my file cabinet this morning to perch in the window, where he could keep watch over the yard. He rumbled in disapproval when birds or a stray cat trespassed on his property.

I started typing, not expecting much, but suddenly the words started flowing. I had actually written three pages when I heard the front door slam, then open and close again more softly. Stella. At least she was consistent. If she opened the door a dozen times a day, she did it the same way every time.

"Maude?"

"I'm in here, Stella." *Where I am every day at this hour.*

"You working?"

"I *was.*" Now, why did I say it like that? Stella's interruptions don't bother me nearly as much as they used to. I guess like they say, it's possible to get used to anything.

"You'll never guess what's happened now."

I saved my work and leaned back in my chair, ready to listen. Seemed like I was a lot quicker to listen to gossip than I used to be. Not exactly an improvement in my character—

or the Lord would probably look at it that way. At least I didn't repeat what I heard. Except in my book.

"What?" I wasn't in the mood for guessing games.

"Frances almost got herself arrested."

"Frances?" *Miss Prim and Proper?* "You mean she's the burglar?" *Say it isn't so.* I would never believe Frances could be our burglar. Too many years of regarding her as the conscience of our local school had ingrained in me the notion that Frances never had an improper thought, let alone performed an improper deed. I might have said she could be a suspect, but deep down I never believed it.

Stella gave me a blank look. "No. Whatever put that in your head?"

"*You* did. What else could she get arrested for in Morning Shade? We don't have anything else going on."

"Well, she's not a criminal. You can forget that. Hargus thought so, but if he'd had any sense he'd have known Frances never broke a law in her life. She won't even jaywalk."

"Hargus really believed she'd break into people's houses?"

"Yeah, isn't that a hoot? Except Frances is not amused. Claims it has damaged her reputation. She's scratching mad. I guess she's got a reason for feeling that way. She did try to pave the way for all those kids she taught. They wouldn't go wrong following her example. Be bored, maybe, but not wrong."

"Stella! That wasn't nice." I knew what she meant, but Frances lived what she believed. Pansy walked the line because of Hargus. Frances walked it out of conviction. That's why I couldn't comprehend why she could be in trouble with the law.

Stella was right, though—saints could be boring. It's the flaws that give us character—or turn us *into* characters. We have a lot of characters in Morning Shade. One of them was sitting in my office.

"Why did Hargus think Frances was the burglar?"

"Well, she got caught rearranging the statues in Connie Fortis's yard. You remember we talked about her house as a possible place for the burglar to strike."

"She did what? Frances? I can't believe it."

Stella untied her shoes and kicked them off. "My bunions are acting up today."

"I noticed you limping when you came in. Are you all right?"

"Just my hip hurting. Slept wrong last night, I guess. Gave me a hitch in my get-along. I'm all right except for a little trouble with those *-itis* boys. You know—*sinusitis, arthritis,* and *bursitis*. Today it's *arth*. I'll recover."

"I should hope so." At least she wasn't complaining about not being long for this world. "You're not just kidding me about Frances? Some of those statues are heavy. She could hurt herself lifting them. Why would she want to rearrange them, anyway?"

"Seems like Connie bought a new statue of a woman with a water jug on her shoulder. Wasn't wearing much in the way of clothes, and Frances thought it was disgraceful."

I wasn't following this conversation. Frances just went into Connie's yard and changed things because she didn't like it? What were we coming to in Morning Shade? Whatever happened to live and let live?

"Well, it wasn't what an upstanding member of the Presbyterian church would be expected to put on display. I'm sort of surprised at Connie myself."

"But still, you can't just rearrange your neighbor's yard art. It isn't done."

"Well, Frances did it. She said those draperies the statue is wearing don't leave much to the imagination. Not that Frances ever had much imagination. But I guess what she has, got a shock."

I shook my head. "Frances, of all people." She'd always been one to mind her own business—not like Stella, who thought everyone's business was her business. For Frances to be in Connie's yard rearranging the statues was enough to blow my mind. The little I had left, anyway.

Stella yawned. "I'm missing sleep thinking about these break-ins. The surprising thing about all this is that Frances never seemed the type to be an activist. Never joined a protest; never gets excited about anything. Dull as dishwater. I love her dearly, but she's never changed her hairstyle or the way she dresses—or anything else—since I've met her."

"Well, she doesn't like change."

"So why was she changing Connie's yard?"

Beats me. But then I'd not have thought Stella would go on a stakeout, or Simon would get blamed for stealing avocados, or Pansy would be accused of threatening a store clerk. And now Frances. They would have to change the name of their bridge club to The Four Felons.

"How did Hargus find out about it?" I asked.

"Connie saw Frances hiding that heavy statue behind a tree and got scared. You know, Maude, we've got a lot of women in this town who are a pack of cowards. I guess the women's movement passed them by. They don't know they've been liberated to take care of themselves. Now me, I'd have marched out there and asked Frances what she thought she was doing."

Yes, she would have. Had to hand it to her. For her size, Stella was as spunky as they come. She'd even taken on Captain, with a flyswatter, no less.

"Did Hargus take her in?"

"He tried, but you know Frances used to be his schoolteacher. She just looked down her nose at him and told him to get back to his office and behave."

I laughed. "I'd like to have seen that."

Stella grinned. "He said, 'Yes, ma'am,' and turned tail and ran. I think he was afraid she'd make him stand in the corner."

I had to snicker, picturing it. Frances could turn on that schoolmarm attitude at the drop of an eraser. She had ruled her schoolroom with an iron hand. I had reason to know—she had been CeeCee's teacher too. Evidently she hadn't lost her touch.

Stella stood up, holding her shoes. "We going to the Labor Day Picnic next week?"

"Cee wants to go, and I'll probably go over for a while. What about you?"

"Oh, I'm going. At my age, I don't have many years left to

celebrate. Man's days are hard and few in number, and I've about run out of numbers. I may not be around next year."

"You're livelier now than you were when you came here. This mystery has been good for you."

"Maybe so, but I think living here with you and Cee and that wild menagerie has helped liven me up. Taken years off my life—maybe even stretched it out a few more months."

"I enjoy having you here, Stella." I was surprised at how much I meant it. At first I had been depressed, not sure how we would survive, but now I had no desire to go back to being alone.

Stella sat down again. "You know, Maude, I never wanted to live with you. Probably you didn't want me either, but I feel right at home here."

"I'm glad." And I was touched. She looked so earnest sitting there. I thought of all the times I had resented her or had been irritated, and realized now that she had probably felt the same way about me. But we were working our way through to a better relationship.

"You're a good woman, Maude." She stood up and started for the door. "One thing, I've never known you to lie. If you said it was raining, I wouldn't bother to look outside. I'd just grab my umbrella."

She left and I sat openmouthed, staring at the door. Stella had just paid me a compliment. That was a first.

I sat in front of my computer, staring at the words I had written. My story. No, Morning Shade's story. What would Stella think of me when she read it?

CeeCee came in while I was fixing supper. I was trying out

a new recipe for potatoes, mashing them with cream cheese and sour cream and baking them with lots of cheddar on top. A hundred calories in every bite. Just what I needed. All that sitting in front of a computer screen had broadened more than my outlook. I needed to get out and move. Even Stella got more exercise than I did, with her daily walk to the Citgo.

When Captain wound around my feet, I reached down and ran my hand along his back. He purred. My mouth fell open so far my teeth almost fell out, and they weren't the removable kind. This was a first. Captain had a large vocabulary, including spitting, hissing, and cursing. Purring wasn't a part of it. Evidently you *can* teach an old cat a new trick. I was willing to bet the sensation was new to him too.

* * *

Labor Day was cool and partly cloudy, but Stella predicted sunshine before noon. I figured she would probably hit it since her bones were more reliable than the TV weatherman.

I could hear Stella and CeeCee downstairs and breathed a sigh of relief that Cee didn't stay in bed until noon anymore. She hadn't bought a bag of chips for weeks. With walking and watching her eating, she had lost at least ten pounds and on her it looked good.

I hurried through my shower, dressing in black slacks and a black-and-white top. Dressier than my usual jeans but wouldn't show dirt. I intended to enjoy myself today. It still didn't seem right, Herb not being here to go with me, but I'd had to face a lot of things without him by now. This would just be one more.

CeeCee had fixed breakfast, a casserole recipe she had gotten from Iva. Bacon, sausage, cheese, and eggs, poured over slices of bread and allowed to sit overnight, then baked. The scent wafted up the stairs to meet me. Wonderful. We'd have salads tomorrow to make up for all the rich food we'd eat today. But Stella claimed she couldn't eat salads. Made her teeth hurt. So probably we'd be back on our regular menu. Oh, well, who cared. Something would get us anyway. We might as well go fat and happy.

CeeCee dished out her casserole, and Stella poured the orange juice. I noticed we were using a set of cut-glass juice glasses I'd had for years and never used because they were too nice for everyday. I raised my eyebrows.

Stella looked at me over her eyeglasses. "Might as well get the good of them as to leave them for someone else. They're just things, after all."

I thought about it and decided she was right. What good were a lot of pretty possessions if you kept them shut away in a cabinet where no one could enjoy them?

CeeCee smiled. "I'm the only one both of you have to leave anything to, and I'd rather use them while you are here to enjoy them with me."

I nodded. "Sounds good to me."

Stella put the butter on the table. "We ready to eat?"

"I am." CeeCee's casserole smelled too good to resist.

Cee reached out to take our hands. "I'm saying the blessing this morning."

I blinked back tears. This day was already blessed.

After breakfast we put out food for the dogs and the cat

and left for the park to enjoy the picnic. CeeCee and I could have walked, but Stella needed to ride and I wanted the car there so she would have a place to rest if she got tired. I didn't say that, of course, because if she thought I *wanted* her to rest she would go until she dropped.

She planned to meet her bridge club at the park, and I had put some lawn chairs in the trunk in case they wanted them. One of the fun things to do at the picnic was sit and watch people go by. Better than a movie.

We didn't have a cute name for our Labor Day festivities like a lot of the other towns did; we just called it the Labor Day Picnic. There were craft booths scattered up the midway. Local businesses had booths, and the 4-H tent sounded like Old McDonald's farm with all the mooing and squealing of members' pets.

Stella had entered her prized peach pickles—something she couldn't have done if she had still been at Shady Acres. She claimed she wouldn't be disappointed if she didn't win a ribbon, but I suspected she would be. CeeCee had assured her that even if she didn't win, she *should*. I had to agree. Stel made a mean peach pickle.

CeeCee and Iva planned to meet at the needlework booth. Iva's invalid mother usually won a ribbon for her quilts. Since she couldn't do much of anything else, she quilted. Her work was beautiful, and it helped bring in money to supplement Iva's salary.

Being friends with Iva had been good for Cee. Not just because Iva had helped her get a job, but because it had given Cee a chance to notice that other people had problems too.

I wandered down to the bandstand and found a seat off to the side where I could watch without getting in the way. There was a lot of local color here I could use in my book. I wanted to jot down notes, but didn't want to offend anyone.

Arnold Frisk and the Windy Mountain Boys were tuning up. Arnold was a fixture at the picnic, and he wasn't a bad singer—or he wouldn't be, if he could overcome the lamentable habit of singing through his nose. He thought he sounded like Willie Nelson. I thought Willie had grounds to sue.

Stella and her buddies toddled past. She was eating a chili dog with onions and cheese. She'd be in heartburn heaven tonight. Bring on the Maalox.

CeeCee and Iva wandered by, laughing and talking. I eased my notebook out of my purse and started taking notes. I could use the picnic in my book. Maybe make a full chapter of it.

Arnold started singing "Achy Breaky Heart." I shuddered. Billy Ray Cyrus, he's not. Except, maybe, in his dreams.

I watched the people milling around or sitting down to rest their feet and listen to the band. Was the burglar at the picnic, looking for a fresh victim? It was hard to picture anyone I had known all my life as someone who got his kicks out of going into a neighbor's house and rearranging their possessions. I sighed. Seemed like I couldn't leave my work at home, even when I wanted to.

Thinking about the burglar, I decided it could be almost scary. Here in this body of people was one who had no respect for the privacy of others. He didn't do any damage. I kept coming back to that. A burglar who *helped* his victims? In this day and age?

Two people I never expected to see together wandered through the crowd, holding hands. Vinnie Trueblood and Helen Loften? I blinked.

They looked like they had stepped out of a vintage movie set. Vinnie wore a gray pin-striped suit and a white shirt. An ascot? Surely not. I couldn't see his feet, but I wouldn't have been surprised to see spats. Helen was resplendent in lavender satin and lace. She minced along in matching lavender satin slippers, holding a stuffed monkey. Vinnie had apparently been successful at throwing balls at the tenpins in the Jaycees' tent.

I shook my head. Helen and Vinnie holding hands? She laughed and talked, and he looked besotted. Had the scarlet woman snagged the dedicated bachelor? I thought of all the broken hearts Vinnie had left behind and wondered how Helen had managed it. They chose seats not far from me, and Vinnie buzzed around her like a bumblebee intent on a particularly fragrant blossom. He caught my eye and blushed.

I smiled and waved.

Vinnie looked as uncertain as he had that day in front of the Handy-Dandy Discount Furniture Store in Ash Flat.

Ah-ha! I could scratch Vinnie off my list of suspects. That frosted pink glass vase with the fluted rim was no doubt sitting on the mantel in Helen's pink living room.

So where did that leave me?

Still looking for an ending.

A young couple with a little girl who reminded me of CeeCee at that age walked past, the child clutching a cone of cotton candy and making a royal mess. The mother left her alone, which I thought was good. Too much worrying about messes can spoil childhood. Let them make a mess now. When they're grown, they have to clean up their messes.

Watching them, I realized I missed Herb more than I had expected. I didn't think about him as much as I used to. More to the point, I had stopped resenting him. It wasn't Herb's fault I was alone. He hadn't planned to die. Who knows? If he had lived longer, he might still have bought that life insurance policy.

I sighed.

Okay, that's it. Time to stop feeling sorry for myself.

I'm going to stop being so proud and write Jack's book—as soon as I finish my manuscript. The money I will make from that one book will ease my financial problems and give me a cushion to fall back on if I need it.

The thought brought a smile to my face. A genuine smile. Who ever thought obedience could feel this good?

* * *

I met Lucille Stover in the cereal aisle of the Cart Mart the next day. She brightened at the sight of me. "Maude! Haven't seen you for ages. I've been waiting for your next book to come out. Made the best-seller list yet?"

I would have been upset, except that she really was interested. I reflected sourly that nonwriters hadn't a clue. They all thought you wrote a book and sold it, wrote another and sold that, got rich on the proceeds, hobnobbed with celebrities, and lived high on the literary hog.

Little did she know I'd been chasing that list all the years

I'd been writing, only to have it dangling in front of me, just out of reach, like a carrot in front of a donkey. It kept me going. That's about all I could say.

"Found out anything about who broke into your house?" I asked, changing the subject.

She looked smug but sober. "You know, I was upset at first, but Harold likes the change so much, and I've gotten used to it. I'd have to say he did us a favor."

"But don't you want to catch him? Maybe you could put everything back like it was and use it as bait to entice him back."

Lucille shrugged. "No, I don't want to catch him. I didn't like the idea of someone being in the house, but now . . . it doesn't bother me anymore."

"Well, I guess you can get used to anything." Even Lucille. I decided Stella was right: she had no sense of humor at all. Sure, it was a lousy joke, but she could have smiled.

I took my loaded cart through the checkout line and went home.

Stella was in the living room, the television blaring as she watched her favorite talk show. I carried the groceries to the kitchen and started putting them away. She turned off the TV and followed me, pouring a glass of apple juice and dribbling it over the floor as usual.

"You know, Maude, I've been thinking about that Neat Nick Burglar. You think there's some reason why he picked those houses to burgle?"

I stopped what I was doing and thought, staring at the can of tuna I held. "It seems to me he had to have some reason for his choices."

"And so he had to have been in those houses sometime before."

"Probably so. You might have something there, Stella. Maybe you should tell Hargus."

"Hargus." She sniffed. "A lot of good that would do. He'd just help himself to another donut and say, 'So what?' That's his battle cry now. Try to get him to listen and he just glares and spouts, 'So what?' I don't know how Pansy ever got stuck with that boy. Must take after his father."

"I think he's in over his head." I wished someone would find out *something*. My deadline was only a month away, and I needed to end my book. I'd tried various endings, but nothing seemed to click. I was stuck. I'd try to solve the case myself, but my previous forays into detecting had left me feeling foolish.

I cringed at the memory of hiding behind that cabinet in the Handy-Dandy Discount Furniture Store, spying on Vinnie while he bought the pink vase for his new love. What had that clerk thought? Probably that I was a jealous wife checking on a cheating husband.

My face burned.

14

Only two weeks left in the month. Two weeks away from deadline, and the mysteries remained unsolved. I wanted to prod Stella with a gentle nudge, but she was already doing everything she could to identify the culprit. By now nearly everyone in town was suspect.

I had scratched Vinnie Trueblood from my list since he and Helen had become an item. They planned a Christmas wedding and I wished them well. I might even buy them a wedding gift—but not from the Handy-Dandy Discount Furniture Store. I never planned to go in there again. A pity, because that blue cannonball pitcher would go nicely with my new birdhouse place mats.

I was in the kitchen fixing lunch when Stella came home from the Citgo. She sat down at the table and untied her shoes. "My feet hurt."

I added mayonnaise to the tuna salad and stirred. Stella's teeth were bothering her too, so I was trying to fix something she could eat.

"Guess what, Maude?"

"What?" The tone of her voice alerted me. "You don't mean—"

"Yep! Another burglary! Nancy Pickett's house. Gave it a good cleaning."

"Cleaning? You mean the burglar cleaned her house?" I glanced around my kitchen. I used to keep my house spotless, but what with pushing a deadline, having the place overrun by two dogs and a cat, CeeCee scattering newspapers, and Stella abandoning her teeth in unexpected places, the house was ready to be condemned. If I ever found out who the burglar was, I'd bribe him to hit here.

Stella nodded. "Vacuumed, dusted, mopped—even cleaned the bathrooms."

"Well, I declare." Yep, I'd pay him to come to my house. The bathrooms? I couldn't believe it. "Did he leave anything?"

"That's the funny part. Nancy had that old aquarium—nothing in it; the fish died a long time ago—but she kept the tank because she was used to it. Well . . . " Stella paused dramatically.

"Don't quit now. Get on with it."

She grinned. "It is sort of interesting, isn't it?"

"Very interesting. So, talk."

"You know something, Maude? You're kind of short on patience."

"And getting shorter all the time!"

Stella grinned again. "Well . . . "

"You said that."

"The burglar cleaned the tank, put in fresh water, and added fish."

"What kind of fish?"

"Guppies, I think. Anyway, Nancy is real pleased because she's got something to watch now. She says it's better than television."

"Considering what passes for entertainment on TV these days, she might have a point." I spread the tuna mixture between slices of bread, my mind racing. What kind of a burglar broke in to clean a house? Clean *bathrooms* at that. If that didn't take the cake.

Stella poured herself a glass of iced tea. "And that's not all. The bathroom towel rack was loose. He tightened it, and he replaced the burned-out bulbs in the light bar. You know how moldy grout can get? He cleaned that too."

"He didn't! Well, forevermore." I hated cleaning grout. No matter how hard I tried, I couldn't get it to look decent.

Stella nodded. "That house shines like a new dollar. Nancy says she'd like to meet up with the burglar and shake his hand. She wants to know what he used on that grout. She's never been able to get it that clean."

"What does Hargus think?"

"Hargus?" Stella positively snorted. "He wouldn't know what to do with a thought if he had one. He's sitting over in his office drinking Chocolate Cow and reading those race-car magazines. He's not even trying to solve the cases." Her shoulders slumped. "I'm not sure I can solve them either. Every time I think I've got an idea, I find out I'm wrong. I'm old. What do I know about anything?"

"You know a lot, Stella. Don't give up now. Whoever is doing this is bound to make a mistake somewhere. He can't go on forever without getting caught."

She took a bite of her sandwich. "I know you're right, but sometimes I get discouraged. Pansy and Frances don't have any ideas either. Simon doesn't seem interested anymore. Seems like we're just butting our heads against a wall and getting nowhere."

"You'll get a break somewhere. Wait and see." I didn't like seeing her so down. Stella was a funny, smart lady. Until she came to live here, I had never realized how much she had going for her. We'd always gotten along, but we hadn't been close. Living in the same house had changed that.

She finished her sandwich and stood up. "Maybe you're right, Maude. I need to do some thinking. If I really set my mind to it, I might come up with an idea. I think I'll do some thinking now."

I heard her going upstairs, probably to take a nap. I needed to do some thinking myself. Maybe I could give Stella a hand. Hargus was in over his head, no doubt about it, and since no damage had been done in the break-ins and half of the victims were delighted with the results, the sheriff wouldn't worry about it. He had more serious crimes to work on. Hargus needed help, all right. It was time I lent a hand.

I wouldn't jump to conclusions this time. The memory of my run-in with the clerk in Ash Flat still made me wince.

I had something else to worry about too. I wasn't sure I could submit my book as I'd written it. I have infringed on my daughter's privacy and Morning Shade's eccentricities.

The way I've used these events in my book oversteps a writer's liberties.

I've prayed about this, lost sleep over it, agonized over it . . . and yet, I can't seem to walk away from it. For once I wish God would give me an answer in a booming voice straight from the throne.

I spent the afternoon in my office staring at the screen, reading what I had written and becoming more and more uncomfortable. My characters were likeable. I felt like I really knew them. As a matter of fact, I did know them. I met them every day on the streets of my hometown. And if I recognized them on the pages of my book, you could bet they would see the resemblance too.

Probably they wouldn't be happy.

CeeCee was still excited about her job. She'd met people on her route who remembered her from her childhood—from school plays, band performances, and other school activities—and she'd been amused at their exclamations over "how big" she'd grown. They evidently had forgotten that she was over thirty now. She entertained us each night with her experiences.

I didn't know why I was so happy. My home was in a state of uproar, with Stella's slippers and teeth indiscriminately abandoned, Captain waging war on the dogs, and CeeCee dashing in and out. I didn't have my book finished, and I wasn't sure I should finish it.

Every day brought new challenges. But I was meeting them with the Lord's help. If I had known what this year would bring, I would not have greeted it with hope and anticipation. But now, knowing what we've experienced,

I found myself filled with gratitude that we'd made it this far.

I wasn't sure I would ever be comfortable with the book, but I had to say that, lack of enthusiasm aside, it had become a good one. It might even put me on the best-seller list. Wouldn't that be an irony? The book I didn't like might turn out to be the best one I'd written so far.

* * *

Monday morning I couldn't work. I finished my cup of coffee and stared out the window at a pair of blue jays squabbling over the sunflower seeds. Out there a world was going on without me.

September had finally cooled the air somewhat. Chicory and Queen Anne's lace had disappeared from the roadsides to be replaced with wild sunflower and goldenrod. I hadn't heard the whippoorwill for some time now, but quail sounded in the fencerows when I drove out of town.

I had to mail the manuscript next week or call and ask for an extension. Neither choice appealed to me. Maybe I should flip a coin.

I couldn't stay in my office another minute. I decided to play, put work away for a while and go for a drive. I needed to go to the Cart Mart. And maybe the fresh air would help me make a decision I had put off too long.

Chance took me down Poplar, past Minnie's house. As my Buick approached her pink stucco bungalow, I saw a familiar figure dart around the corner. I slowed the car. What was Simon doing at Minnie's house?

I rummaged in my purse for my cell phone and quickly dialed home.

"Diamond's Morgue. You stab 'em, we slab 'em."

"Stella, haven't I asked you to please answer the phone properly? It could be my publisher calling."

"But it's not. What do you want?"

"I'm on Poplar, near Minnie's house." I slowed almost to a stop, then pulled over to the curb. "I think I saw Simon going around the corner."

"At Minnie's house?"

"Yes. A man darted around the corner of the house as I approached. It looked like Simon."

"That's strange. Minnie had a dental appointment this morning. Do you still see him?"

I rolled down the window and peered out. Minnie's front yard was empty. "I don't see him now."

"Minnie has a privacy fence in the backyard. No gate out the back. I helped her plant irises back there last year." I could hear Stel clicking her teeth, a sign she was busy thinking.

I tried to help her along. "What would Simon be doing there? Clearly Minnie isn't home. Her car isn't in the drive."

"Maybe he needed to borrow a cup of sugar or flour. He could come here. You've got plenty. Or he could have just decided to drop by unexpectedly to visit—but he knew Minnie had the dentist appointment. We talked about it yesterday. She's getting a molar capped. What would he be doing at Minnie's, anyway? They've not been the kind of friends who would feel comfortable dropping in on each other." Stella hesitated. "I'm going to call Hargus."

"Oh, I don't think you need—"

I heard a click on the line, and I punched the Off button. I sat in the car, wondering what to do. I couldn't get out and explore. How would that look? A sixty-year-old woman sneaking around Minnie's house. If Hargus showed up, he'd probably arrest me. Oh, yes. That would look good on the front page of the newspaper. Definitely not the kind of publicity I needed.

I could have been wrong. What if it wasn't Simon? What if a real burglary was going on? My pulse throbbed. I started to get out of the car, but changed my mind. Better go slow. This might not be anything I needed to get involved in. Stella was calling Hargus. He'd check this out. I didn't need to be here if there was trouble. My best bet was to leave and let Hargus handle the situation.

Starting the car again, I drove to the Cart Mart, where I did my shopping. I was so nervous I had to bite my tongue to keep from telling the checker that another burglary was going on. What was wrong with me? I'd put two bags of salt-and-vinegar chips in my cart by mistake and had to take them out again. By the time I got home I was tired and more than willing to put my feet up for a while.

I carried in the groceries. The house was empty, which worried me. Where had that woman disappeared to now? I found a note on the kitchen table from Stella saying she'd "gone to work."

The morning marched on with no sign of Stella, no word from her. I tried to work but made no progress. How could I think when I was worried about Stella and Simon? With

Hargus on the loose, he could have them both in jail by now. I glanced at the calendar, then back at the blinking cursor. Even Captain seemed restless. He couldn't seem to get comfortable in his spot on the file cabinet. Finally he jumped down and strode toward the kitchen. I could hear him crunching his food.

Finally I turned the computer off and pretended to get some things done around the house—cleaning off the desk, making files . . . that sort of mundane chore that has to be done on occasion and that I had put off as long as possible.

Still no sign of Stella. I started to get worried. I didn't like it when she was out of the house for long periods without my knowing where she was, knowing she was all right. She was eighty-seven, after all. She could have been considerate enough to call.

When the morning waned to midafternoon I couldn't stand the suspense any longer.

Once again I drove downtown. I wanted to go by Minnie's house, but prudence convinced me that if anything had happened I'd be in the way. This was just another way of saying I didn't want to get involved.

Hargus's truck wasn't in front of his office as it usually was. That seemed strange. I stopped at Citgo to get a latte and possibly hear some gossip.

"We don't know where she is," Penny said, a frown creasing her brow. "We were just discussing whether to give you a call to see if she was sick."

I suddenly felt clammy, and I had a really uncomfortable feeling that Stella and Hargus were up to something. A stakeout? What was Hargus thinking, allowing himself to be talked into this bit of TV policing? "You mean she hasn't been here at all this afternoon? That's strange. She always comes here."

"I saw her over at Hargus's office yesterday afternoon," Maury Peacock offered. He was buying a pack of Snickers bars. "She was there quite a while."

I didn't think it was wise to mention the Simon incident—not in front of Maury. "She'll show up after a while," I said.

I was trying to convince myself. She hadn't come home for lunch. I could imagine all sorts of scenarios, and I didn't like any of them. Why hadn't Stella checked in? Of all the frustrating, irritating women, she took the cake. Probably she was all right, or at least I tried to believe she was, but I couldn't help worrying.

I sat down in a booth, sipping the hot latte while I tried to decide what to do next. Though I'd assured Stella's compadres that she was fine, I was more than a little disturbed about her whereabouts. I had been against the stakeout idea, but Stella was Stella. Even though I had warned her never to do it again, I had no assurance she would listen.

And now there was this thing at Minnie's house. I never should have called her. All it did was give her a reason to get involved. Not that she needed a reason. She'd poked her nose into this mystery from the get-go.

Of course, it wasn't all Stella's fault. I had encouraged her to get involved. Just to provide fodder for my book. Was this the way I took care of Herb's mother?

I was in my car, waiting to turn onto the highway, when Hargus's truck came roaring around the corner and skidded to a halt in front of his office. No one could miss his entrance. Everyone on the street turned to watch, and several people stepped out of stores to see what was happening.

Stella and Simon slid out of the passenger-side door, and I froze. So, Stella *had* been with Hargus all this time! Then my mouth dropped open when all three tramped into Hargus's office and slammed the door. Concerned about Stella, I gunned the Buick across the intersection and parked behind Hargus's big vehicle.

When I stepped into the office, Simon was sitting next to Hargus's desk and Stella was making coffee. She turned when she saw me come in. "Hey, Maude. Want some java?"

"Stella Diamond, I've been worried half to death about you!" My gaze swept the office, looking for criminals and finding nothing out of the ordinary.

"She's here because of me," Simon said. I noticed he looked a little guilty when he said it.

"You? You were at Minnie's house? I thought I saw you there."

Stella walked over to Simon, her hand resting on his slumped shoulder. "Simon is the burglar."

"What?" I was dumbstruck. That nice, harmless-looking, little old man?

Stella nodded. "Doesn't that beat all you've ever seen?"

"I didn't mean any harm," Simon said.

It took a moment for me to find my voice. "Why would you play such a hoax on the town?"

Simon shuffled his feet restlessly. "Everyone always claims nothing exciting ever happens in Morning Shade, and, well, I thought it would be fun to prove otherwise." He looked the picture of innocence. "I pulled it off real well, don't you think?"

Hargus grabbed his belt and yanked up his pants. "Simon, I'm ashamed of you!"

Simon shook his head. "I didn't commit any crime. We all agreed to have a little fun—Lucille, Minnie, the Prescotts—"

"The victims were in on this?" I exclaimed. Grown adults would actually *consent* to this prank?

I sank onto the wooden chair closest to Simon and wanted to laugh at the absurdness of this situation. I lived in a town that had to *invent* crime. I was suddenly more proud of Morning Shade than I'd ever been in my life.

"Hargus, you're not going to charge me with anything, are you?" Simon looked hopeful. "Actually, we all had a ball—and we didn't touch anybody's things except our own."

Hargus pinched the tip of his nose with his fingers, looking real businesslike. "Well, I suppose since you've been breaking into each other's houses, no one will want to press charges."

Simon's shoulders slumped in relief.

Hargus narrowed his eyes. "You do plan on stopping this nonsense, don't you?"

Simon nodded, looking apprehensive.

I mentally groaned when I realized that I couldn't end my book on this note. No one would believe it.

Hargus looked stern, but I figured Stella and Pansy could straighten him out. There didn't seem to be anything I could do, so I went home, leaving Simon's fate in someone else's hands.

One thing you could say for Stella. Eighty-seven still wasn't too old to crack a case.

Life's a hoot, huh?

* * *

September waned. Autumn had started to paint the hills with the first signs of red, gold, and russet. The air was crisper now, with cool nights. It wouldn't be long until the cries of wild geese moving south would sing a haunting melody from the sky. To me, fall was a lonely time—beautiful but holding a reminder of winter winds and cold-locked earth.

Friday morning I sat staring at the computer screen, prepared to fish or cut bait. The story had no shootout, no lightbulb-overhead confessions.

In short, no big-boom ending.

Could I even write the end of this manuscript? I didn't know. I scrolled through the chapters, time after time fighting my conscience. My daughter, Stella, my friends and neighbors. Would they see themselves in this caricature of small-town living? Why, Simon had proved that Morning Shade couldn't produce a single, worthwhile mystery. I still had to question whether I had the right to use the story. I had worked hard on it, and even without an ending, it was good. Something bothered me, but I didn't know what.

Suddenly I saw the answer in front of me, plain as the nose on my face. *I* wasn't in the story. Everyone else was, but not Maude Diamond. Had I so separated myself from reality that I hadn't included my own eccentricities? What did that say about me?

The story had funny moments, but would anyone else see them as humorous? Or would they feel mocked, be wounded by my words? Was it humor, or was it exploitation?

I had not written fiction; I had merely transcribed my own town's and family's problems. God could not be pleased with me. My story would hurt too many hearts.

My finger hesitated over the Delete key. Could I do it? What if this book was my ticket to the best-seller list? I felt in my bones it could be. It could.

I stared at the blinking cursor. Weeks, months of sweat and toil.

I shut my eyes and hit Delete. Then I took my backup disk and erased it.

Done.

Gone.

All my work. Gone.

I laid my head on my workstation and felt hot tears roll down my cheeks.

Then the truth hit me like a bad smell. I was basing my self-worth on a silly list of titles. This month, twenty authors would be overjoyed. Ten thousand more would be disappointed. They, like me, had worked as hard at producing a best-seller as anyone else, and also like me, they would feel like a failure.

But now I knew the truth. I wasn't a failure. God measures success by obedience—nothing more.

"Surely Your goodness and unfailing love will pursue me all the days of my life. . . ." The Twenty-third Psalm surfaced in my mind. God's goodness and unfailing love . . . did He promise me all goodness?

I know He didn't. I will always have both good and bad in my life. But He did promise His unfailing love, and I'm relying on that.

"We know that God causes everything to work together for the good of those who love God and are called according to His purpose for them."

I heard a knock on my door. I quickly wiped my eyes with the heels of my hands. "Yes?"

"Mom?" CeeCee opened the door a crack.

"Yes, sweetie?"

"The new list is out."

"The best-seller list?" Like I didn't know. Or care.

She nodded. "You're not on there this month, but, Mom, I want you to know I think you're a great writer and I'm proud of you."

"Thanks, Cee." I smiled.

"I mean it, Mom." Her eyes glistened. "You're the best."

Epilogue

Now October has something to crow about. It's my favorite month in the year. The air is crisp; a hint of woodsmoke curls from chimneys. CeeCee, Stella, and I can still sit on the front porch, though the beverage of choice has changed from iced tea to hot coffee.

Spring and fall are my favorite seasons. New beginnings: a time to regroup. In this house we all need time to refocus, to let go, to think about new starts. Stella has started a new life living in her daughter-in-law's house. CeeCee is starting over without Jake. And I'm learning to get by without Herb. It has been a time of transition, but I think we're through the worst of it.

My daughter looks and acts more like the old Cee. Kicking back in her lawn chair, she sighed. "Life is good, isn't it, Mom?"

I had to laugh. I'd had the same thought myself. Life had done a one-eighty turn, and once more my life had purpose.

"It is good," Stella agreed. "I think Simon learned a valuable lesson."

"What's that, Stel?"

"How do I know? But surely there *is* a lesson to be learned here. If nothing else, stay out of other people's houses."

"Sound advice for anyone." I grinned.

I would have hated to see any serious repercussions from Simon's lack of judgment. I felt a little let down that I hadn't thought of him sooner. All the clues were there: he watched *House and Garden;* he knew quite a bit about decorating; he knew what was wrong with the houses he broke into. I just had trouble seeing someone as nice as Simon as a burglar.

I leaned back, gazing at the stars, thinking of God and His wondrous ways. He sprinkled in good with the bad. All in all, it's a pretty fair system.

CeeCee sipped her coffee, her legs stretched out in front of her. What a change a few months had made in her life. She'd come to us beaten, depressed, feeling her life was over. Now she had friends and a job she loved; people on her route would meet her at the mailbox to pass a moment or two, bring her cookies or a piece of freshly baked coffee cake.

"Yes, life is good," CeeCee concurred, more to herself than to me or Stella.

"It is, indeed," Stella murmured. "I'm thinking about buying bananas tomorrow—haven't had any in a while."

CeeCee glanced at me. "What about you, Mom? You deleted your book. I don't know why, but you seem okay with the decision."

"I am," I admitted. "The book stank."

"Not a best-seller, huh?"

I hugged the thought to my heart. I'd never know, would I?

"I may never be on the best-seller list, but that's okay." I grinned at CeeCee. "I'm 'best' with my family, and that's more important. I may never have great wealth, but I've been given something better."

I had CeeCee's and Stella's attention. I'd thought a long time about what I'd gained in the painful process I'd just been through. "I've got life's greatest treasure. God's wisdom for my life."

I didn't understand the change, not fully, but I knew I had it, and that's better than any best-seller list.

CeeCee turned to look at me. "What are you going to do for money, Mom?"

"That's the best part. I'm going to help Jack Hamel write his book."

"Ghostwrite?" CeeCee exclaimed. "But, Mom—"

"I'm helping a brother," I interjected.

And that's exactly how I felt. I'm helping my brother—not to mention obeying God—and I'd like anyone to find fault with that. Jean had been surprised when I'd called her this afternoon to ask if Jack had found anyone.

"He's still praying you will be the one," she had said.

"Tell him his prayers have just been answered."

Jean hesitated. "Are you sure, Maude? You said you felt it would be a professional insult—"

"Well, I was wrong. I consider it a privilege. Tell Jack I'm looking forward to working with him on the book."

And I hung up, at complete peace with my decision.

I've come a long way in my Christian growth the last few

months. I've learned that pride is a sin in God's eyes. A sin I've stumbled over more than once. Jack's story will reach millions; M.K. Diamond's will not.

I struggle over many things that take away God's peace, I confess, but I have learned that I don't need the recognition of my peers to be useful and valuable. All I need is God's approval. That's enough. More than enough.

What's more, I could feel my creative juices starting to well up. Maybe this was going to be just what I needed to get past my burnout.

I rested my head against the back of the padded swing and stared into the night. Here we sat, three women fighting personal battles with a mixture of emotions, pride, and self-will, but we were no longer in conflict with one another. We listened to the sounds of Morning Shade settling down for the night—the slam of a screen door, a dog barking. Nice sounds. Peaceful.

"This is good," Stella said softly.

"Yes," I echoed. "It's good. And now that the mysteries are solved, I guess everyone's happy."

"I wouldn't say that," Stella said. "Pansy and Frances are upset. So am I, a little. Simon knew what was going on, but we got left out. I don't like being left out, Maude."

I hadn't thought of it like that. "No one does, Stella."

"So you know what, Maude? I'm thinking. I'm thinking this might be just the beginning of mysteries in our town."

Oh, groan. What was she up to now?

"Like what?" When Stella started thinking, things happened.

"I'm not through thinking yet, but Morning Shade just might have another mystery one of these days." She chuckled—almost wickedly.

Why, the old fox.

"We'll see if Hargus can break this one."

About the Author

Lori Copeland has published more than seventy romance novels and has won numerous awards for her books. Publishing with HeartQuest allows her the freedom to write stories that express her love of God and her personal convictions.

Lori lives with her wonderful husband, Lance, in Springfield, Missouri. She has three incredibly handsome grown sons, three absolutely gorgeous daughters-in-law, and five exceptionally bright grandchildren—but then, she freely admits to being partial when it comes to her family. Lori enjoys reading biographies, attending book discussion groups, participating in morning water-aerobic exercises at the local YMCA, and she is presently trying very hard to learn to play bridge. She loves to travel and is always thrilled to meet her readers.

When asked what one thing Lori would like others to know about her, she readily says, "I'm not perfect—just forgiven by the grace of God." Christianity to Lori means peace, joy, and the knowledge that she has a Friend, a Savior, who never leaves her side. Through her books, she hopes to share this wondrous assurance with others.

Lori welcomes letters written to her in care of Tyndale House Author Relations, P.O. Box 80, Wheaton, IL 60189-0080.

BOOKS BY BEST-SELLING AUTHOR LORI COPELAND

Women's Fiction

A Case of Bad Taste (coming Summer 2003) ....ISBN 0-8423-7115-X
Child of Grace.........ISBN 0-8423-4260-5
Christmas Vows: $5.00 Extra ....ISBN 0-8423-5326-7

HeartQuest

Brides of the West Series

- *Faith* ....ISBN 0-8423-0267-0
- *June*.........ISBN 0-8423-0268-9
- *Hope* ....ISBN 0-8423-0269-7
- *Glory*.........ISBN 0-8423-3749-0
- *Ruth* ....ISBN 0-8423-1937-9
- *Patience* (coming Fall 2003) ....ISBN 0-8423-1938-7

Roses Will Bloom Again.........ISBN 0-8423-1936-0
With This Ring (anthology) ....ISBN 0-8423-7822-7

Visit www.heartquest.com and www.movingfiction.net

Watch for a new

Morning

Shade

Mystery

coming

spring 2004

ISBN 0-8423-7116-8
Tyndale House Publishers

Turn the page

for a preview

from Lori Copeland's next book

Patience

book #6 in the exciting

Brides of the West series

ISBN 0-8423-1938-7

Available fall 2003 from Tyndale House Publishers

Denver City, Colorado
1872

"The dress is so beautiful, Mary!" Patience preened before the mirror's reflection. Almost the same size as Lenore Hawthorn, Patience was trying on Lenore's wedding gown while Mary made the final alterations. "Lenore will be a gorgeous bride, but I don't know how she and Ben are going to carry this wedding off with their folks so dead set against it."

Mary pursed her lips, then said, "Lenore's folks won't even let her come to town to try on the dress. If you hadn't agreed to stand in for her, I don't know what I would do. The wedding is tomorrow night."

"New Year's Eve." Ruth clasped her hands and beamed. "Isn't that romantic?"

"Humph," Mary mumbled around the pins in her mouth. "I don't know how romantic it is—Lenore's grandmother is

paying to have the dress made or poor Lenore would have to get married in a regular gown."

Harper, Lily, and Ruth sat near a cheery fire, admiring Mary's handiwork. "It's so beautiful," Ruth praised. "Mary, you have such a talent."

Mary blushed as she sat at Patience's feet, fastening delicate Irish lace along the hem and train. "I've enjoyed designing the dress."

The women turned abruptly as the door of the small sewing shop suddenly burst open and a masked man entered, pointing a gun. He stood for a moment, his beady eyes studying the situation.

Ruth gasped, reaching for baby Rose playing at her feet.

"Nobody move, ladies. And not a sound!"

The women did as they were told. Mary coughed, and the man aimed the gun at her. "I said *quiet!*"

Patience stepped off the stool, wide-eyed. "What—what do you want?"

The outlaw motioned for her to step forward.

Patience's left hand flew to her chest. "Me?"

"You. Get over here."

When Patience obeyed, he hooked his arm around her waist and dragged her out the front door. Swiftly mounting a waiting horse with her still in his grasp, the outlaw spurred the animal and galloped out of town.

Stunned, Patience shivered in the late-afternoon air. What had just happened to her? Nothing in her life ever went right! *Getting rid of trouble is like sacking fog,* she thought. *You grasp, fumble, and block, but it still keeps coming.*

The man's hold tightened. "Stop squirming, Lenore!"

"I'm not Lenore!"

"Yeah, yeah. That's what they all say." He dug his spurs deeper into the mare.

"But I'm not Lenore!" Patience yelled.

"Shaddup!"

Patience swallowed back hysteria as the culprit gripped her even harder and galloped around a curve. How could anyone mistake her for Lenore Hawthorn? Lenore was blonde and blue-eyed. Patience had brunette hair and dark brown eyes. What did the miscreant want?

Hatred between the Hawthorns and Ben's family, the McLanes, ran as deep as still water. There was no telling what fate awaited her if this man thought she was Amos Hawthorn's daughter. The families' insane feud had been going on for decades.

Images of her friends' thunderstruck looks when the culprit burst in shop and seized her flitted across her mind. If the situation wasn't so grave, she'd laugh, but right now all she could do was cling to her captor and pray she survived the wild ride.

The man was dirty, and his putrid breath repulsed her. Where was he taking her? How soon would he realize that she wasn't the intended bride? And what would happen then? Would he dispose of her before she could convince him that he'd made a mistake?

Relief suddenly flooded her. *Dylan.* Ruth's husband, a U.S. marshall, and Sheriff Jay Longer would come after her. She clung to hope as the horse's shod hooves pounded the frozen ground. They traveled a considerable distance. Wind stung her face, and cold seeped into her bones. She was without protection—no coat, only the lace sleeves of Lenore's wedding dress cosseting her from the icy elements.

Suddenly, as if the hand of God swooped down and smote the enemy, the horse stumbled and pitched forward, throwing Patience and her assailant over its head. Patience flew through the air to slam into the hard ground.

She lay unmoving for a moment, catching her breath. She was alive! Then, dazed, she sat up, trying to get her bearings.

The horse lay prostrate on top of the kidnapper.

She spied a man's boot sticking out from the carcass and wished she could feel compassion, an inclination to offer assistance to the poor unfortunate boot—man—scoundrel. The kidnapper must surely be dead or gravely injured, and she didn't have the strength to budge the horse.

But relief flooded her. She was free!

Getting slowly to her feet, she groaned when she saw her right hand; she must have broken her wrist in the fall. Testing her weight tentatively on one foot, she discovered she could walk . . . which she did as fast as her injury would allow, grasping the hem of the fragile gown, trying to protect the sheer material from the rough trail.

Moving steadily, Patience sucked in deep drafts, the icy

air stinging her lungs. Where was she? She had no idea; she wasn't familiar with the region. Since Jackson Montgomery and Dylan had brought the five mail-order brides to Denver City she hadn't ventured far from town. Her eyes searched the barren, snow-swept land. She hobbled faster, but she had no idea where she was going. Hysteria gripped her when she realized she would freeze to death if she didn't find shelter soon. Her teeth chattered, and her breath came in ragged gulps.

Run, Patience. Run as if your life depended on it.

MOVING FICTION

OTHER GREAT TYNDALE HOUSE FICTION

- *Safely Home,* Randy Alcorn
- *Jenny's Story,* Judy Baer
- *Libby's Story,* Judy Baer
- *Tia's Story,* Judy Baer
- *The Sister Circle,* Vonette Bright & Nancy Moser
- *Out of the Shadows,* Sigmund Brouwer
- *The Leper,* Sigmund Brouwer
- *Crown of Thorns,* Sigmund Brouwer
- *Looking for Cassandra Jane,* Melody Carlson
- *Child of Grace,* Lori Copeland
- *Into the Nevernight,* Anne de Graaf
- *They Shall See God,* Athol Dickson
- *Ribbon of Years,* Robin Lee Hatcher
- *Firstborn,* Robin Lee Hatcher
- *The Touch,* Patricia Hickman
- *Redemption,* Karen Kingsbury with Gary Smalley
- *Remember,* Karen Kingsbury with Gary Smalley
- *The Price,* Jim and Terri Kraus
- *The Treasure,* Jim and Terri Kraus
- *The Promise,* Jim and Terri Kraus
- *The Quest,* Jim and Terri Kraus
- The Left Behind Series, Tim LaHaye & Jerry B. Jenkins
- *Winter Passing,* Cindy McCormick Martinusen
- *Blue Night,* Cindy McCormick Martinusen
- *North of Tomorrow,* Cindy McCormick Martinusen
- *Embrace the Dawn,* Kathleen Morgan
- *Lullaby,* Jane Orcutt
- *Fatal Harvest,* Catherine Palmer
- *The Happy Room,* Catherine Palmer
- *A Dangerous Silence,* Catherine Palmer
- *Blind Sight,* James H. Pence
- *And the Shofar Blew,* Francine Rivers
- *Unveiled*, Francine Rivers
- *Unashamed*, Francine Rivers
- *Unshaken*, Francine Rivers
- *Unspoken,* Francine Rivers
- *Unafraid,* Francine Rivers
- *A Voice in the Wind,* Francine Rivers
- *An Echo in the Darkness,* Francine Rivers
- *As Sure As the Dawn,* Francine Rivers
- *Leota's Garden,* Francine Rivers
- *Firefly Blue,* Jake Thoene
- *Shaiton's Fire,* Jake Thoene